---- ★ ----

Pain seared through Roger's stomach. He clutched at the cloth of his tuxedo pants, wanting to rip it away. Oh, God, he had to eat something. He couldn't take this.

"Are you okay?" Scott asked.

The pain began to ease, slipping from excruciating to almost bearable. Roger forced himself to suck in air and relax. "I haven't eaten. I just need food."

"Yeah, well, then eat."

"I intend to," Roger said. He waited until the pain eased further, then picked up the three remaining hors d'oeuvres and put them in his mouth at one time.

"Take it easy," Scott said.

Roger almost swallowed them whole. "Scott. Go downstairs and bring me something. A sandwich if you can manage that."

Scott just looked at him, then said, "Sure, Roger," and left.

---- ★ ----

Barbara Burnett Smith

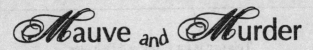

Mauve and Murder

WORLDWIDE.

TORONTO • NEW YORK • LONDON
AMSTERDAM • PARIS • SYDNEY • HAMBURG
STOCKHOLM • ATHENS • TOKYO • MILAN
MADRID • WARSAW • BUDAPEST • AUCKLAND

This one is for Bruce and Delphine,
because family is everything.

With lots of love.

MAUVE AND MURDER

A Worldwide Mystery/September 2006

First published by Five Star.

ISBN-13: 978-0-373-26576-3
ISBN-10:   0-373-26576-X

Acknowledgments

My thanks to Stan Roux, Professor, Section of Molecular Cell & Developmental Biology (formerly of the Botany Department) of the University of Texas. He gave me assistance with the department name, which has been changed completely. I didn't consult him on the plants I used in this book—for those I used *Deadly Doses,* by Serita Stevens with Anne Klarner and *Poisonous Plants,* a pamphlet from the Texas Department of Health.

Disclaimer

During my sixteen year career in the broadcast field I met many wonderful and talented people. I also met a few who weren't as wonderful, but I still learned from them all. Having acknowledged that, I wish to state up front that none of either kind is in this book! (Sorry, gang, but you are all thought of fondly.)

Barbara

ONE

CASSIE FERRIS SWORE under her breath, something she realized she was doing more and more often in the morning.

It's not my fault I'm late, Cassie thought as she hurried down the hall of Y-96 with its pea green industrial carpeting. *Technically I'm not even late,* she went on rationalizing. *But tell that to Roger Hell-on-Wheels-in-the-Morning.*

The voice of Johnny Mathis crooning "Chances Are" was coming over the monitor as she fumbled with her keys and unlocked the door of her office. Two short steps brought her to the front of her battered, gray metal desk. Without even pausing Cassie tossed her purse on the chair, spun around and headed out.

She did stop in the break room long enough to pour herself a cup of coffee and take a few quick swallows. It made her feel more casual to be carrying a cup of coffee when she greeted Roger. For a moment, she considered ignoring him until they were actually on the air, but she knew that would only make the four-hour morning show a battle. Not that she couldn't hold her own, she could, but the personal price was high.

She moved forward, turned the corner and saw Roger at his desk. His round head, with its thin black hair, was bent over neat stacks of clippings from the morning newspaper. Roger Weber had the lowest forehead Cassie had ever seen on a man and from this angle he looked like a hairy bowling ball with eyes.

She stopped in the doorway. "Good morning," she said, sounding almost nauseously cheerful. "Looks like you're hard at it."

Roger's office, twice the size of Cassie's, was brightly lit, freshly painted and newly furnished with a blond desk and credenza.

He looked up, his dark eyes glittering maliciously when he saw Cassie. His voice was laced with a sickly sweet venom. Like cyanide. "Well, if our dear Cass Woman hasn't decided to join us. Good afternoon."

The few sips of coffee in Cassie's stomach vibrated. She made her voice casual. "It's my car again. I guess I'm going to have to break down and get a new battery."

"But then you wouldn't have an excuse for showing up at noon. Whatever would you do?"

"I don't consider five-thirty in the morning the same as noon."

"No, it just doesn't leave you time to go through the newspaper. But don't bother," he said. "You've got good-hearted Roger to do all the show prep. Leave it to Roger. Just keep riding my coattails, Sweet Cassie."

Cassie could feel the hand holding her coffee cup twitch. *Some morning,* she thought, *I'm going to throw this*—but it wouldn't be this morning.

"I got some good material out of Texas Monthly and Time magazine, so relax, Roger. I do my share and you know it. If I didn't, you'd have me off the show in a flash."

Roger stared at her, perhaps flattered by the mention of his power. In the pause, the sound of the elevator reached them.

Bill Bankston, the station manager, rounded the corner. He was carrying two white paper sacks. Bill, with his thick dark hair, khakis and patterned golf shirt, looked like a successful computer nerd. The wire-framed glasses on his young face added to the image.

"Morning, Cassie," Bill said with a smile as he stepped past her into Roger's office. "Morning, Roger. Thought I'd bring some goodies for you."

"How nice of you, Bill," Cassie said, watching from the doorway as he opened the sacks and pulled out an assortment of pastries.

"You trying to butter me up, Bill?" Roger asked. "Or just make me fat?" Roger looked at Cassie. "And don't say 'fatter,' although I'm sure you'd love to."

"You two crack me up!" Bill said. "Always pretending to be at each other's throats. You're like a couple of kids."

Another of Bill's infamous dodges. The man could duck speeding bullets and flying insults with the agility of an eel.

Cassie decided to follow his example. She stepped forward to pick out a croissant with cinnamon and almonds. "These look great, Bill. Thanks."

"Yeah, thanks for the treats, Dad," Roger said. "And to think you got up early just for us."

"I hope this won't screw up the diet you're on, Roger," Bill said, perching carefully on a sidechair. "How's the gout by the way? Getting better?"

Roger looked down at his hands, which were even pudgier than usual. "Better. The pills and the diet seem to be helping. Although I don't suppose a break will hurt."

He reached for a sickly-sweet pastry lavishly coated with chocolate. A yellow cream filling oozed out of it.

"Maybe just a plain croissant would be better—" Cassie realized what she'd said and broke off. "Sorry, it's the mother in me coming out." Roger's angry expression didn't change, and Cassie went on. "Jenny gripes about it all the time. My mothering."

Roger stopped, the pastry halfway to his mouth. "What a kind thing to say—advice from Mama Cass."

"Maybe good advice," Bill said.

With great care Roger placed the pastry on the sack and selected another one without the cream or topping. "Then I'll follow Mama's advice."

It was Cassie's exit cue, and she took it like the pro she was. "Thanks, again, Bill," she said, hurrying out the door.

Roger: "Good morning! I'm Roger Weber, reminding you that it's six-o-two and time to rise and shine. We've got the best music from the 50s, 60s and 70s for you on the environmentally sound Y-96.

Cass: "We never pollute the airwaves."

Roger: "We don't even broadcast bad breath!"

Cass: "That was awful, Roger...in a pure and simple way, of course."

Roger: "I'm Roger Wonderful Weber, along with the multi-talented Cass Woman. Say something multi-talented, Cass."

Cass: "Good morning."

Roger: "Oh, now that was clever."

Cass: "But Roger, that's what you told me to say. In fact, you were going to write it down, but you didn't know how to spell—"

Roger: "It's now six-o-three on Y-96 and it's a wonderful day out there. Unfortunately, it's not so terrific in here..."

TWO

As SOON SHE WAS off the air, Cassie slipped into her office and closed the door. It wasn't much of an office, just a small windowless room. Everything in it except the blue and peach silk flower arrangement, looked like regulation Army issue. Still, it was an office, and she was the only jock besides Roger who rated one.

Years ago when she had started in radio as a traffic director, translating the sales staff's orders into neat commercial logs for the disk jockeys to follow, Cassie had been a nonentity, as colorless as a file clerk. Later, as a newsperson, she'd been thrust into the limelight, although the nature of radio news made it a pretty dim light. Now, as an air personality, people expected her to be eccentric. So far the only idiosyncrasy she'd been able to work up was the demand for absolute privacy from ten until ten-thirty. It was respected by the entire staff, which amazed her.

During her precious half-hour of solitude she did some show prep for the following day and attempted to boost her ego to somewhere near normal after the beating it had taken exchanging barbs with Roger Weber for four hours.

That Thursday morning at precisely 10:31 there was a knock at the door.

"Come in," Cassie called.

The door opened and Mandy McCormick, the sales manager, popped her head in. "Hi! Got a minute?"

"What's up?" Cassie asked, as she cleared things off the top of her desk.

Mandy entered, watching Cassie slide a can of Easy Cheese into her bottom drawer. "I see you're still on that healthy diet," she said.

"It's got proteins, minerals, and it doesn't have to be refrigerated or chewed," Cassie said. "What more could I ask for?"

Mandy shuddered. "Eggs Benedict."

"Yeah, well I could ask," Cassie said. "So, what have you come to con me into this time?"

Just over a year before, when Cassie had moved to Austin so that Jenny, her daughter, could attend the University of Texas, she'd run into Mandy. Mandy was an old friend from her own student days. It was Mandy who'd talked her into accepting her first position at Y-96.

"I'm not here to con you into anything," Mandy said, seating herself on a chair and running her manicured nails through her shoulder-length blond hair. "It's a business proposition, and I think you'll like this one." Mandy smiled. "Trust me."

"I always do," Cassie said. "I wonder why that is?"

"Because you should." Mandy became all business. "You know we're doing that special party tomorrow night with our new client, Happy Twosomes? And I—".

"The dating club? No, no, I'm not going."

"But, Cassie, it's absolutely crucial that you show up," Mandy said.

"I am not attending some video dating thing. Besides, you're going to have a full house as it is."

"The Cass Woman is always an extra draw," Mandy said.

"I'd be superfluous. You have the infamous Roger Weber as your star attraction."

"That's exactly why I need you!" Mandy put her hands on the desk and started to lean forward. When she saw the stains that had been there long enough to be called indelible, she removed her hands. "What if he gets drunk and does something horrible?"

"I can't corral him."

"You have a calming effect on him."

"What a lie! Besides, your Delirious Matchmakers will have a bouncer; if Roger gets drunk let them handle it." Cassie smiled wickedly. "With any luck they'll be over exuberant."

"The name of the client is Happy Twosomes," Mandy said. "It's a very chic place. They've got a health club and saunas and all that stuff. Their membership fee is outrageous, which means their clientele is the best."

"Rich," Cassie corrected. "And that doesn't mean nice."

"Okay, here's the bottom line—the client is really pushing to get you there. I just can't talk him out of it. I know I haven't given you very much notice, but you don't have any plans for tomorrow night, do you?"

"Flattery will get you nowhere."

Mandy leaned forward. "It's a party. For singles." She gave Cassie a meaningful look.

Mandy was the only ecstatically married woman Cassie had ever known, and as such saw it as her duty to marry off the rest of the world. Cassie, divorced for three years, was the perfect project.

"Listen, Mandy, I don't need any men in my life."

"Fine. But you do need money and the client is willing to pay double the usual talent fee." Mandy's eyes, the same color as her pale blue suit, watched Cassie closely for signs of wavering. When she saw none, she said, "You do need the money, don't you?"

Cassie looked away and her eyes came to rest on the framed photo of her two daughters, Jenny and Beth. The picture had been taken during Beth's last visit to Austin. It hurt Cassie's heart every time she looked at it.

She turned back to Mandy, her tone light. "Until Jenny gets out of school or Congress passes a bill to settle my accumulated debts, I need every dime I can get. And you know it. What would I have to do?"

"The usual. You know, mingle with the crowd. Just be the Cass Woman. Twice an hour do a call-in to the station. That's it."

Cassie stood up and rearranged the silk flowers. She didn't want to go. Because of Roger, because of the club, and a dozen other reasons, but the bottom line was that *her own personal bottom line* always needed cash.

She faced Mandy. "You know I hate it when you do this."

Mandy grinned. "Okay, the party is from five to seven, and we're supposed to be there early. You can ride with me."

"Never." That would leave her completely at Mandy's mercy. "I'll take my own car."

"Okay. But wear something wonderful. Dressy, but not too dressy, sleek, and I think a little sexy, but—"

"I'm changing my mind."

"I'm calling the client now to tell them you're coming." Mandy stood up, then swung back around to face Cassie. "And what do you think of having Jenny work the reception area during the party? It would only be for a couple of hours, but I'm desperate."

"I don't know…"

Jenny, Cassie's daughter, had started at the university the year before, when she was just seventeen. Cassie tried to keep her away from the limelight as much as possible, in part because that's the way Jenny preferred it.

"It would just be one night," Mandy said. "Why don't I call Jenny and let her decide?"

Cassie thought about protesting and changed her mind. As Mandy had said, it was just one night.

"Fine, call her. Only, Mandy," she said. "Don't sell her, okay?"

Mandy's eyes grew wide. "Me? Would I do a thing like that?"

TWO HOURS LATER Cassie had completed much of her show prep for the following morning and had checked the station's web site to pick up her e-mail fan letters. She even had most of them answered. She was congratulating herself when the phone rang.

"Hi, Mom." It was Jenny, home from her morning classes.

"Hi. How was your day?"

"Oh, good. You know." She was eating something and Cassie could hear the crunching.

"How's the botany class coming?"

"Fabulous." Jenny stopped eating, the better to enthuse. "We've got a field trip a week from Saturday. We have to identify all kinds of plants and it's a fourth of our grade! Can you believe that? Oh, and we got the results of last week's quiz. Guess who aced it?"

"My ace daughter, of course."

"It's not about you, Mom, it's about me. I got the A."

"Sorry," Cassie said. "There was something I was going to ask you…oh, I remember, did Mandy call you?"

"Uh, huh. Just a few minutes ago."

"And?"

"And, what?" Jenny asked.

"Are you going to work the promotion?"

"Yeah, I figure I could use the money."

"You don't have to, if you don't want to."

"I want to, okay?" She took a breath that Cassie could hear over the phone. "But, Mother, just so you know, you'd better make sure that Roger-Wonderful-dweeb stays away from me. I'm not going to put up with him."

"That's a great attitude."

Jenny snorted. "You know what I mean. Everybody at Y-96 acts like he's God, or something, and we all know he's an asshole."

"Jenny—"

"It's true! It's like the emperor's new clothes; you all pretend that he's not rude and obnoxious."

"We just do our jobs," Cassie said. Actually, they just coped as best they could. "Besides, he's Walter Kraley's pet. A Sacred Cow." Walter was the owner of Northland Broadcasting and Y-96. As such, his word was law, and anyone who questioned it found himself, or herself, looking for another job. Not an easy task if you'd really crossed Walter. He sat on the NAB Board and the Arbitron Advisory Council. His power and influence extended far beyond the stations owned by Northland.

"Walter adores Roger," Cassie went on. "He treats him like an adopted son, so it's a lot smarter to leave Roger alone."

"I will," Jenny said. "If he leaves me alone." There was a

pause, and she finished with, "Look, I'd better go. How about if I make spaghetti for dinner tonight?"

In reparation for spouting off? "Sounds wonderful. See you in a bit."

"'Bye."

Cassie shook her head. Jenny was only eighteen years old, and that age group had a tendency toward insolence or a distant idealism that they didn't follow through on. At least she hoped Jenny wouldn't follow through.

Cassie looked over at the picture of the girls, again. Jenny was the more vocal of the two, had always had the stronger personality, but that might be because she was the older sister. Beth was the quieter one, more sensitive. Sweeter. Especially when she'd been little, and even now at thirteen she was such a caring person. At least it seemed that way the little time that Cassie got to spend with her.

Cassie let out a sigh. It was a release of the always-present bit of pain that she tried to keep in the far reaches of her being.

Surely someday in the not-too-distant future she would have enough money to fight for custody of Beth.

During the divorce, Beth had been like a doll, prized and fought over. Brad, Cassie's ex-husband, had been relentless in his efforts—all of Cassie's transgressions, her less than wise reactions to the divorce, had come out at the custody hearing Brad had instigated. Thank God, Jenny had been old enough to choose her own living arrangements. Beth had just turned ten.

"It's going to be okay, Mommy," Beth had assured, putting her tanned little-girl arms around Cassie's waist. "I love you and they'll let me stay here."

"I know, Baby," Cassie had said, holding tight to her daughter.

The hearing had gone on for weeks and every day Cassie could see the judge being swayed toward Brad. And every day Cassie prayed for a miracle; that Brad would change his mind about wanting Beth; that the judge would see how much she loved her daughter and wanted her. But in the end the judge had announced that Brad would have custody of Beth. Cassie had been devastated, barely able to navigate the drive home. And then she'd had to break the news.

Her heart had swelled with unshed tears when she found Beth waiting in the living room. Beth had cooked macaroni and cheese and vacuumed the house, proud of herself for the accomplishments. She'd raced to Cassie, her pixie face with the upturned nose and wide, dark eye's expectant. "Is it over?"

"Yes, Honey. It's finally over."

Beth threw both arms around Cassie. "You see? I told you it would be okay. And I even made dinner!"

Cassie had just stood there, watching Beth, trying hard to be strong. "Honey, we need to talk a minute."

"But why? You said it was over."

And as Cassie watched, Beth's brown eyes turned liquid with huge tears. Then the tears began to spill down her cheeks and her beautiful, expectant expression crumpled. "Oh, no, Mommy. No!"

Cassie had scooped Beth up, holding her tightly. Jenny had come in and the three of them had clung together, crying, and promising each other that it would be all right.

"It's not forever," Cassie had said.

"I'll come back, soon," Beth had promised in a high, tight voice. "They can't make me stay away forever."

"That's right, Honey, they can't. I'll get you back somehow."

That had been three years before, and so far, Cassie hadn't found the money for another fight. But she would. Somehow she would.

Damn lawyers anyway, Cassie thought, wiping away a tear. *Damn all men. That's what you get for trusting them.*

She stacked the file folders one on top of each other. She was going home. Tomorrow was another day, and she was going to save her strength for it.

THREE

WAYNE ROOT RAN ALONG the hiking trail, his breathing coming in spurts, his lungs burning. His calves were hurting, too, and his head was pounding in rhythm with his steps.

His own fault really. You get older, you get lazy. Especially when you're married and you don't have to look good for anyone. So, he'd done the minimum exercise he could get away with to maintain his weight.

Now was a different story. Lucille was gone, taking with her his daughter, Angela. The thought brought an ache in his chest region that had nothing to do with the running.

He looked up. This was where the trail turned and wound up from the river. The easy slope felt like Mount Everest, but Root persevered until he reached First Street, where he would cross and head for the YMCA. The light was red, and Root bent over, sucking in air gratefully.

"Hey." At the word, he looked up to find a blue and white police car stopped at the light in front of him. The window was rolled down, and the heavyset cop riding shotgun said, "What do you think you're doing?"

"Breathing. What the hell does it look like I'm doing?"

The door opened and the patrolman stepped out. He opened the back door. "Get in. I can't stand to see a grown man suffer like that."

"I can make it," Root said.

"Like hell. You'll drop dead on the street, another casualty, and you won't even have the satisfaction of dying in the line of duty." He gestured to the door. "Get in. We've got some news for you. Might as well hear it from me first."

Root climbed inside, more grateful than he would ever admit. He slammed the door and they took off. Wilson, the uniformed patrolman who'd stopped Root, was already turned around in the seat. He was grinning.

"Guess who just gave it up?" he said.

Root groaned. "Not Elson. Tell me it wasn't Elson."

"Yeah, well I could tell you it wasn't, but it was."

"Shit." It was his big media case, an old Austin family with ties to the founding fathers, and he didn't even get to make the arrest. After all he'd suffered with those people, too. "Is Socorro there at least?" Socorro was his partner in homicide.

"Nope."

"So, what happened? Did Jacobs get some evidence? He didn't move in without us, did he?" Jacobs was the Senior Sergeant who oversaw their caseload. It would be very bad form for him to make an arrest on Root and Socorro's day off. But then, Jacobs was known for bad form.

Wilson was grinning, as was his partner, Grilkey, the driver. "Nobody got anything as far as I know. I was walking out to the garage—"

"We," Grilkey corrected.

"Right. We were walking out to the garage and there's Elson, parking in a 'police only' space. When I say something, he says, 'it doesn't matter anyway. I'm here to surrender. I'm Art Elson and I killed my brother.'"

"He surrendered to you? In the garage? Damn!"

"Hey, he surrendered to everyone, including the janitor." Wilson turned back around. "But, I figure if you show up now, you can probably be the one to sign the papers."

"No kidding?" Root was almost breathing normally. "Well, well, this must be my lucky day. Now, if they don't stick me with another high-profile case, I'll be one happy cop."

"Nobody gets that lucky."

QUIETLY, ALMOST STEALTHILY, Roger Weber slipped down the back stairs of Y-96. His heart pounded with triumph.

Radio was no better than high school with all its cliques: the rich ones, the pretty ones, the popular ones, the powerful ones. He was tired of being the outsider and the butt-end of all their jokes.

Knowledge was power, and he was acquiring both. He glanced at a sheaf of copies in his hand. As the saying went, he had his favorite by the balls.

He stepped into the hall and waited for some sound. There was only the distant music of the Supremes singing "You can't Hurry Love." As usual, he thought, Cassie was late.

A slow, malicious smirk slid across his shiny face. Maybe he could get her tossed out, too.

Once in his office he flipped open the top of his briefcase and eyed the papers in his hand.

Sweet victory.

"Good morning." Cassie Ferris stood in the doorway, her body, slender in her jeans and red sweater, was bent as if braced for a hard wind.

Roger slid the papers into the back pocket of his briefcase and snapped it shut. Then he locked it.

"My, my, we're almost on time this morning," he said.

"I'm almost always on time, Roger," Cassie said.

Roger slid the briefcase under his desk. "Meaning that half the time you're late."

Cassie's big, dark eyes were suspicious. "So, what have you been up to?" she asked. "I was here ten minutes ago, and I couldn't find you."

"Oh, really? Now I'm not even allowed to take a crap?"

She flinched. He'd scored another one against the pretty people.

"The newspaper hasn't come yet," she said. "Do you want me to run out and get a copy?"

"Don't bother yourself, Cassie," Roger said, his tone not quite hiding the smirk that lingered inside him. "My show isn't something you need to worry your pretty little head about."

"Our show," Cassie replied.

Roger smiled; he could afford to be generous now. "But, of course, our show."

Cassie took a tentative step forward. "Are you okay?"

"I'm fine. Wonderful."

Roger: "Wake up and smile! It's seven-oh-four, and, lucky you, you get to spend the next three hours with Roger Wonderful Weber!"

Cass: "And, I'll be along for the ride, too."

Roger: "How reassuring. Today is a big day. Besides being TGIF, tonight we have the party at Happy Twosomes."

Cass: "And, you're invited to come out and join the fun."

Roger: "There'll be live music by Chi-como, compli-
        mentary drinks for the first one hundred Y-96
        listeners, and a twenty percent discount on mem-
        berships."

Cass: "Plus you'll get to meet some of the Y-96 per-
        sonalities."

Roger: "Like me, Roger Weber."

Cass: "And me, the Cass Woman."

Roger: (pause) "I didn't realize you were going to be
        joining us, Cass. Need to meet a few men, huh?"

Cass: "Well, it's an opportunity for all of us to make
        new friends."

Roger: "If it works for you, I'll send my ex-wife."

His face was red, puffy, and his eyes rabid. "Why the fuck
doesn't anybody tell me anything?"

"Probably because they forgot, Roger." With rigid movements Cassie took off her headphones and placed them on the
console. She had to control herself not to step back. Roger
was working himself up and she wanted to calm him before
he reached the big bang stage. "I wasn't scheduled to go out
to Happy Twosomes until yesterday," she added.

"That's no excuse! This is the *communication* industry,
and nobody bothers to communicate!"

"Roger, it doesn't matter. You know now."

"Right!" His round face seemed to expand as it turned a
purplish color. "But I could have made a fool of myself on
the air, and does anybody give a shit? No!"

"But you didn't." Cassie felt rooted to her spot.

"Of course I didn't! I'm a professional. All I ask is a little professional courtesy from the rest of you. I should know better than to expect anything from a bunch of stinking, rank amateurs!"

Cassie's jaw was as rigid as locked steel. but she tried hard to sound nonchalant. "Roger, I'm sure Mandy just forgot."

"Yeah, well you knew." He leaned forward and poked his finger into her chest. "Why couldn't you tell me?"

Cassie felt her muscles constrict, felt her breathing shift. *Oh, God, I'm going to explode.* "I didn't think—"

"You damn well better start thinking! And you'd better start communicating!" He dismissed her and whirled away.

Cassie drew in air. "You prima donna!" She heard her words careening through the soundproof room before she realized she'd said them. "Did it ever occur to you that people are tired of your tantrums? Tired of you!"

"Oh, yeah," he said, whipping back to pin her with a venomous glare. His voice lowered to a dangerous purr. "You just don't worry your little brain about it."

Cassie swung around and stepped outside letting the door close behind her. She heard something slam into it. Roger had thrown his headphones.

She took two deep breaths. *I will not give in to his insanity.*

She leaned against the cool wall and forced her muscles to relax.

No matter how she felt, no matter what was said between them, she and Roger had a show to do. She was a professional broadcaster and a good one; she had to go back in the control room and finish the last hour.

Despite everything, she could do that—and she would.

As soon as she was off the air at ten, Cassie took the elevator upstairs and hurried along the hallway, then around the corner. Here were the salespeople's cubicles. The only one in evidence was Rachel Sankey who was on the phone. Her face was almost hidden by a sweep of red hair as she talked. Cassie went around the corner and continued moving down the ivory hallway with its plush gray carpet. Cassie had to warn Mandy.

She passed without seeing the displayed collection of old microphones and radios and stopped at Mandy's door. It was closed and the window was dark. Cassie breathed a sigh of relief. Mandy was out, and Roger might be cooled off by the time she got back.

Just then Roger himself came puffing furiously up the stairs, stopping in front of Irma Belton's desk. He planted his stubby legs firmly, and thrust his chest forward belligerently.

"So, where the is he?" Roger demanded.

"If you're referring to Bill, he's out." Irma, Bill Bankston's secretary, was a former school teacher, and she prided herself on remaining calm in the face of Roger's tantrums.

"Where out?"

"We've got ascertainments today and I don't expect him until sometime this afternoon." Ascertainments were when the community leaders met with broadcasters to inform them of the needs of the city. "He'll be back from the Driskill Hotel around five. Would you like to leave a message?" Irma asked.

"So, where's our over-paid Sales Manager?"

"Mandy is also at ascertainments," Irma said.

As the account executive for Happy Twosomes, Rachel

Sankey would be next on his list. Cassie moved backwards
down the hall to warn her.

"And I suppose Rachel Sankey is out, too?"

"Is this a quiz?" Irma asked, but the tiny quiver in her voice
betrayed her anger.

Cassie found Rachel with the phone still wedged between
her shoulder and her ear, but she was standing now, sweeping her purse and Mont Blanc fountain pen into her briefcase.

"Something's come up, Greg; I have to run," Rachel was
saying. "See you tonight." She put the phone down quickly.
Her normally pale skin was a sickly green.

"It might be good if you got out of here," Cassie said.
"Roger—"

"I heard!" Rachel snatched up the last of her things, and
the two women were out the door, scurrying for the elevator.

Roger's voice followed them. "Never mind, Irma, I
wouldn't want you to put yourself out!"

"I am doing my job—"

"Right. I'll find Rachel myself."

At the elevator Rachel punched the down button frantically, her gold bracelets clanging in punctuation. "Come on,
damn it!" The elevator whirred and then the doors swished
open. "Thank God!" They whipped inside, watching with relief as the doors closed silently in front of them.

"What's his problem this time?" Rachel asked, slumping
against the wall.

Cassie explained about the promo sheet that hadn't been
changed.

"I can't take this much longer," Rachel said.

"I know."

"I've got half a dozen clients I ought to be calling right

now, plus the big promotion tonight, and I can't even stay in my own office!"

Rachel had been with the station through seven years and two ownership changes. Her story was that she intended to remain until she could buy the place or married enough money to take her away in style.

"It's just so asinine!" Rachel went on. "A whole staff of supposedly rational professionals operates out of fear of that jerk! Instead of working we spend our time warning each other of his moods."

"I know."

"And Bill wouldn't even consider stepping on the toes of the Great-God-of-The-Morning," Rachel said. The elevator shuddered to a stop. She lifted her arm to look at the Gucci watch almost buried under the gold bangles. "This will throw my whole schedule off! Oh, hell, and I forgot I have ascertainments this afternoon. Damn Roger Weber, anyway!" Rachel said, as the elevator doors opened.

"And lucky us, we get to see him at the promotion tonight."

Rachel eyes formed angry slits, and her voice swelled with sarcasm as she said, "Lucky us."

FOUR

JENNY LEANED CLOSER to the mirror to apply one more coat of mascara, then stood back to study the effect. Not bad. Not that appearance counted for anything tonight. Everyone there would be a lot older than she was. Besides, she was on a mission.

Jenny saw the frown on her face and replaced it with a smile. She couldn't let her mom suspect that anything was up. Her mother would want her to look happy. To look nice. Actually, her mother would want her to *be* nice. And she would be—most of the time.

Her mom, on the other hand, was way too nice. She needed to get some backbone. Ever since her dad had gotten custody of Beth, her mom had changed and Jenny hated it.

For just a moment Jenny wondered if she might be making a mistake. Maybe she should just leave Roger alone.

Then again, maybe not.

HAPPY TWOSOMES WAS located in Northwest Austin, where money and good taste met. The facility took up an entire three-story brick office building. On the west side was a parking lot, dotted with live oak trees. On the right was a huge patio that resembled a modern day Eden or maybe some exotic candy confection. It was sprinkled with ornate stone tables topped with burgundy and mauve umbrellas. In carved stone boxes, and at the base of each tree, were flowering plants in full bloom.

As Cassie drove up to the building she caught a glimpse of the patio over the three-foot brick fence. The trees twinkled with miniature lights and the building was festooned with a mauve banner announcing the opening of Happy Twosomes.

"I guess they spent a dime or two on this place," Jenny said as they pulled into the almost-empty lot.

"And spent those dimes tastefully," Cassie added. "Did you notice the patio?"

They got out of the car and started toward the entrance. It was still light outside and the air was warm and muggy.

"Think they'd let us move in?"

"I don't know, but I'm all for asking."

Jenny looked Cassie over critically as they walked. "Do I pass?" her mother asked.

"Oh, it's not that. It's just, you know, there will be a lot of single men here. You might find a boyfriend, or whatever."

Cassie grimaced. "You sound just like Mandy. I'm not here to find a man."

"I didn't say you were, mother, but you are single. And you look nice. And kind of young. You could date."

Rather than take offense at Jenny's description of her, Cassie merely said, "No thank you. I'll leave youth, beauty and dating to the young."

"Okay. But, you know, you could get too old. You might be sorry." She opened the door and let Cassie enter ahead of her.

The interior lived up to the expectations created by the outside. The carpet was a soft burgundy; the fixtures were sleek black and chrome. On the walls hung Nagel prints. The couches were mauve, and the accent pillows were black and a pale mint green. In the background somewhere, Cassie could hear the sounds of a rock band tuning up.

She felt her stomach twitch at the thought of all the people who would be here tonight. Cassie was fine behind a microphone, relaxed in a way that most people never were. However, faced with a roomful of successful people in expensive suits and sleek haircuts, she always felt like the "before" picture in a magazine feature. Not that there was anything wrong with her—she simply wasn't slick.

"Oh great, you're here!" Mandy called. She was standing behind the long glass reception table. It was covered with name tags, and tiny bottles of bubble solution, the kind given out at weddings. On each bottle was a tag that read Happy Twosomes. The tags were in mauve. They added a festive touch to the elegance of the room.

On Mandy's left was a man Cassie had never seen before and on his right was Rachel Sankey. Rachel's red hair was pulled up in a style similar to Jenny's; she was wearing a deep green pantsuit with some very heavy gold jewelry that gleamed against her pale skin.

The only thing about Rachel that didn't look elegant and expensive was the tense expression on her face.

Before Cassie could ask about it, the man beside Rachel stepped forward and extended a hand. "Hi, I'm Greg Mayhew, the owner of Happy Twosomes."

He wasn't what Cassie had expected of a video dating club owner. He exuded boyish charm not quite in keeping with the dark brown hair that had a touch of gray at the temples. Premature gray, Cassie decided, and on him it looked good. His welcoming smile made his deep blue eyes, almost navy, crinkle.

Cassie smiled back at him as they shook hands. "Hi, Greg. I'm Cass Ferris, and this is my daughter, Jennifer."

"The Cass woman! Of course, I'd know that lovely voice anywhere."

"Thank you." Interesting, Cassie thought, his voice made her think of a professional speaker, too.

Then Greg turned his smile on Jenny. "Jennifer, it's nice to meet you." He looked from one to the other. "I can't believe you're mother and daughter. Sisters, maybe. And both so beautiful!"

Rachel grimaced. "I should have warned you, Cass; Greg is the most outrageous flirt in the world."

"That's merely charm," Greg said.

Cassie said, "Well, we work for Y-96, so we could use a little charm."

Greg laughed. "Thank you. Now, what can I do for you? Do you need equipment brought in?"

Somewhere in the background a phone chimed quietly. *If mauve had a sound,* Cassie thought, *that would be it.*

"No, we're doing it the easy way tonight," she said. "All I need is a telephone in a quiet place so I can call in your commercials."

"Certainly." He gestured toward a door to their right. "You can use the front office right over there."

"And we'll need a second phone for Roger. I'm assuming we'll do some two-voice commercials."

Greg thought for a moment. "Well, there's the lounge upstairs. Would you like me to show you?"

A young woman poked her head out of the nearby office door. "Greg? Sam is on the line. Says it will just take a second."

Greg nodded then said to Cassie, "My banker. I'll be right back."

As he moved off, Mandy said, "Okay, Jen. Let me show you what we need you to do."

"And while you're doing that, I'll look around," Cassie said, turning and entering the double doors behind them.

What she found was a room so large she could only think of it as a ballroom. The floor was polished parquet and there was a shiny black grand piano off to one side. Circular love-seats, in mauve of course, had been placed in small groups around low coffee tables at this side of the room. Huge ferns draped gracefully from chrome planters in one corner and a small bar stood in the other. To her right a temporary stage had been set up where band members and soundmen were making final adjustments to the equipment.

Through an open door on the far wall Cassie had a tanta-lizing glimpse of greenery. She crossed the room and discov-ered that up close the patio was just as charming as it had appeared from outside the building. Yellow flowers bloomed in all the planter boxes, lights twinkled, and a young man was setting up an additional bar near the entryway.

"Hi," he said. "Did you need something?"

"No, no. I was just looking around."

She returned to the front hall to find Jenny busily laying out blank name tags under the supervision of both Mandy and Rachel. Y-96 was playing softly on the sound system.

"Roger isn't here yet?" Cassie asked.

"No," Rachel said. "Our glorious morning man hasn't seen fit to grace us with his presence just yet. Ask me if I care."

"You care," Mandy said. "He's getting a talent fee, and people are expecting him."

"I'm still half hoping he doesn't show up."

She had good reason to feel that way. Immediately following his divorce Roger had made a big play for Rachel and she'd been flattered. He hadn't been at the station long, and he was still being touted as the god-of-the-morning who was going to boost the ratings and take the station to greater prominence. No one had seen much of Roger's dark side at that point. After two dates Rachel recognized that Roger in person didn't match his advance billing. She called it quits, and ever since, Roger had made her a special target.

Mandy put an arm around Rachel's shoulders. "Relax. Tonight he'll be worrying about his *public persona*, as he calls it. He'll be oozing so much good will you'll hardly recognize him. Besides, I primed the pump a little. I sent a limo for him and that always improves his mood."

"A limo!" Jenny said, looking up. "How come we never get a limo?"

Mandy pointed to Cassie. "Blame it on your mother. It's because she's too nice to bother bribing."

"But she can be bitchy when she wants!"

Everyone laughed, and Cassie said, "Remind me not to let you do my PR."

"Why not?" Greg asked, returning from his phone call.

"Long story," Cassie said. "So, Greg, would you mind if I looked around upstairs?"

"Not at all. Have you seen the downstairs?"

Cassie nodded. "It's spectacular, especially the patio. Or do you call those the gardens?"

"We used to call it the patio, but we just got the landscaping bill and now I call it outrageous."

"That's what comes of talking to bankers," Rachel said.

"And if you're going to do the big tour, you should hurry. It's almost time."

"Can I come along?" Jenny asked.

"Sure," Greg said. "Let's go this way."

This way was a circular staircase, in modern black steel that wound up to the second floor. Here the layout was much like the first floor except wooden panels divided the large room, so that one end was set up with seating areas and green plants. Three floor-to-ceiling bookcases filled with rows of video-tapes created the effect of a library and served as an additional wall.

"You already have this many members?" Cassie asked.

"An illusion," Greg said. "I brought in copies of all the videos from the Dallas club. As people sign up we'll replace the tapes." He held up large bound notebooks. "These have the pictures and biographies of all the members. Instead of names we use numbers. If you were looking for a date you'd go through this first and select a few people. Then you'd look at their videos."

"Amazing." It was all Cassie could think of to say.

They met two more staff people, and then Greg led them to the front of the building where there was a kitchen with a soda fountain and an old-fashioned popcorn machine, already filled with popcorn.

"Members can relax here," Greg went on. "Really feel at home; at least, that's the way we've planned it."

They moved behind the bookcases to the other end of the huge area where there were small cubicles, four on each side, all with VCRs and large monitors.

"For viewing," Greg explained. He took her across the hall. "This is where we make the videos."

The space wasn't large, only about ten by twelve, with woven tapestries on the walls and a camera set up in the corner.

"Nice."

"Oh, and here," he pulled open another door in the hallway. "It's the other video room, but tonight it's being used for staff and the Y-96 group. This is also the second phone for your call-in commercials." There was a portable bar and two trays of hors d'oeuvres. "Would you like something to drink while we're here?"

"Not me," Cassie said. "Jenny?"

"No thanks." She was looking around, taking it all in. "What are those?" she asked, pointing to the hors' d'oeuvres.

"I'm afraid you'll have to ask the caterer for specifics. Or eat a few and then you can tell us."

"No, thanks. But they do look good."

It was then that Cassie realized that Jenny was nervous about the evening ahead. She should have expected that. After all, as they say, like mother, like daughter. Beyond that, Jenny was the product of a small town, Abilene, and tonight she was an unofficial hostess for a very expensive party in Austin—a city Jenny still had a hard time calling home.

Cassie slid an arm around her daughter. "Looks like Greg has thought of everything."

"But there's more," he said. "Now, we go up one more flight and you'll see what sets us apart from other video clubs."

On the third floor they were shown a fully equipped gymnasium. This area could have been part of any expensive health club with its modern equipment and locker rooms. There was even a pool and the saunas that Mandy had mentioned.

"All this comes with membership to the club?" Cassie asked.

"That's right."

"You must be a genius."

"Yes, or an evil genie. My banker says he'll decide which when we see if it pays off," Greg said. "Which is why I brought in the best talent for tonight."

A LITTLE OVER an hour later Happy Twosomes was crowded with smiling, mingling singles. They danced on the parquet floor, thumbed through the biography books, marveled at the gym and flirted with each other in the garden. They blew bubbles, and laughed, as if they'd never seen such a thing before. Cassie spent her time doing call-ins, chatting with the guests and checking on Jenny. It seemed to her that both of them were beginning to settle in and relax.

She entered the small VIP lounge to do another commercial, alone since Roger still hadn't arrived, and found Mandy looking out a window.

"Anything interesting out there?" Cassie asked.

"Roger is finally here—thank, God. He's over an hour late."

"Can't wait to hear his excuse, since he's such a stickler for being on time." Cassie moved to the window and looked down. A steady stream of cars turned into the parking lot and a long white limousine was parked at the front doors. Roger, dressed in a tuxedo, was just stepping out. He glanced up at the window, and like a child caught spying, Cassie backed up. "Maybe he just wanted to make a grand entrance."

"Maybe. Now all we have to worry about is how he behaves." Mandy shook her head. "I'm beginning to sound like Rachel."

"And we all know that he'll be fine." Cassie paused. "Won't he?"

Steve: "This is Y-96, I'm Steve Parker, and for all of you who are trying to work later than your manager, it's now 5:35! Speaking of working late, our own Roger Wonderful Weber and the Cass Woman are at Happy Twosomes. How's it going, Cass?"

Cass: "Just wonderful, Steve. Happy Twosomes really is Austin's new video dating club, with a difference! Right, Roger?"

Roger: "For once, I agree with you, Cass. If you're single and you've been thinking about joining a health club, why not take a look at Happy Twosomes? That's right, health club, because Happy Twosomes has a full line of Nautilus equipment, locker rooms and even a pool to keep you in great physical shape."

Cass: "The club is a lot like an exclusive country club. Greg Mayhew, the owner, has done an outstanding job of creating a special place to come and relax, workout if you want, and meet some terrific new people."

Roger: "I've even seen a few men looking at you, Sweet Cassie. Of course, if you don't get attention from the one you want, you can always go after him with a gun. (pause) What do you say about that?" (longer pause)

Cass: "So, uh, come on out; the big party is going on now, and if you decide to join tonight, you get a twenty-five percent discount on your membership. That's all at Happy Twosomes, on Research. Come join us."

FIVE

CASSIE STOOD in the ballroom shaking with anger and doing her best not to show it. Roger was in the upstairs lounge; he'd raced up there right after he'd put down the phone. He hadn't even had the decency to face Cass.

She couldn't believe that Roger had made that crack about the gun. How could he? And how did he know?

"Cass," a young man asked, boldly touching her arm, "Is Roger Weber as funny in person as he is on the radio?"

Cassie clenched her teeth, hoping it looked like a smile. "Roger is just one of those brilliant comedians; he can't help it, he's always funny." About as funny as a seven-point earthquake and just as destructive.

"You're so lucky to work with him," a woman said. She held a bottle of bubbles in one hand, and touched a floating bubble in the air, as she spoke.

"He'd love to hear you say that," Cassie said.

"And you're a lot prettier than I thought you'd be," the woman went on. "I mean, you know, the way Roger talks about you. I guess it's all in fun, though."

"Yes. Just for fun."

The band had been on a break and it started back in now with an old Chuck Berry song, "Johnny B. Good." Cassie pointed to the band, smiled a good-bye, and began to thread her way through the crowd toward the outer doors. She wanted out. She needed out.

She glanced at her watch, then stepped through the double doors into the reception area. The big room was bright in comparison to the ballroom, lit up like a stage.

Jenny was standing in front of the huge glass table, a drink in one hand. She wasn't alone. Standing less than a foot away from her was Roger. He was swaying, not quite steady on his own legs.

He's drunk, Cassie thought.

Roger had a supercilious smirk on his face as he leaned closer to Jenny and said something.

Jenny was already pale, and whatever he said goaded her further. "You asshole! I heard what you said on the air!" Then she lifted the glass in her hand and flung its contents toward him.

As if in slow motion the clear liquid rose out of the glass to form a perfect arc. It seemed to hang in the air, shimmering, before falling to splash on Roger. An ice cube grazed his ear and another bounced off his shoulder.

Disbelief flashed across Roger's face, then fury, while the liquid rolled down his skin.

"Damn you—" He raised his hand as if to hit Jenny.

Cassie flew forward, catching Roger's arm. "Stop it."

"Get your hands off me!" He flung off Cassie's grip, almost knocking her over. "You ought to teach your daughter some manners."

Jenny spat, "You don't have any manners, why should anyone else!"

"You little—"

"That's enough!" Greg was suddenly there, grabbing Roger in a hold that looked painful.

"Don't you ever," Cass gasped out, "speak to my daughter like that again!"

Roger ignored her in favor of Greg. With an effort he said coldly, "You can let go. I wouldn't waste any more of my energy on either of these...women." He straightened up as Greg released him.

With precise movements, Roger took a handkerchief from his pocket and wiped his face. He brushed off his tux. Then he looked at Cassie, his black eyes as small and cold as a viper's.

"Are you happy?" he asked her. When she didn't answer he stepped closer, his voice low and menacing. "I hope this little performance was worth it to you, because this is the clincher, lady. Don't even bother coming in Monday morning. You're through."

"You're drunk, Roger."

He smiled, an ugly smirk that Cassie wanted to slap off his fat face.

"No, I'm not, and it doesn't matter. You're finished at the station. You're finished in this business." He took a breath and started up the stairs, saying loudly, "Now, who do I have to screw around here to get another drink?"

Greg whirled around as if to go after him, but Cassie caught his arm. "It's okay, Greg, you can let him go. That was just for effect." Every nerve and every cell in her body was shaking.

Greg moved his shoulders stiffly as if he ached with pent up anger, then shifted his attention to Cassie. "Are you okay?"

"I'm fine." She turned around to get the same reassurance from Jenny and found that her daughter was gone. "Jenny?" Only Greg was with her in the reception area. "Where did she go?"

"Out the front door, I think."

"I'd better find her."

"I'll go with you."

"No, that's all right. You have guests. Oh, and Greg, I'm really sorry about that scene. It's not the kind of thing that normally—"

"Don't worry about it; it wasn't your fault. Or Jenny's."

"Thanks."

ROGER WEBER FELT like shit as he sat down on the couch in the small room they'd designated as a staff lounge. His stomach had been upset most of the day and now it was cramping ominously. He was even getting dizzy. It was that damn gout medicine; he was sure of it. The doctor had warned him it might have side effects. He should have eaten more today, but food wasn't appealing.

That little bitch Jennifer Ferris hadn't helped any, either, upsetting him like that. But he'd show her. And her mother. Come Monday Cass would be off his show for good. He almost smiled. Another one down.

His stomach cramped again and he looked at the tray of hors d'oeuvres with a scowl. Somebody had already finished off one tray, there were only a few canapés left on the second. *Pigs.*

He reached out and picked up two crackers at a time, not caring what was on them. He popped them in his mouth and swallowed after two chews. He had to get something in his stomach.

When the door opened, Roger looked up. Instead of someone who could help, he was faced with Scott Delany, the afternoon drive jock.

"Well, if it isn't the world's prettiest disk jockey," Roger said.

"Up yours, Roger," Scott responded. Even his scowl showed off his dimples.

Roger watched Scott move lithely around the portable bar as he began to fix a drink. *Damn kid.* He had everything Roger wanted: youth, an athletic body and a handsome face. He was even good on the air; any day now he'd be trying for Roger's job.

Scott reached for some ice cubes and the bottle of rum. "Are there any soft drinks around here?"

"I know you're not bright, Scott, but you can't be helpless, too."

Scott muttered something, then ducked down to rummage among the things behind the bar. He came up with a can of cola, popped it open, poured half into the plastic cup, then filled the cup with rum. He coughed on the first swallow.

"Can't handle it?" Roger asked. Maybe the kid would get drunk and end up getting fired.

"I can handle it."

Then a pain seared through Roger's stomach. He clutched at the cloth of his tuxedo pants, wanting to rip it away. Oh, God, he had to eat something. He couldn't take this.

"Are you okay?" Scott asked.

The pain began to ease, slipping from excruciating to almost bearable. Roger forced himself to suck in air and relax. "I haven't eaten. I just need food."

"Yeah, well, then eat."

"I intend to," Roger said. He waited until the pain eased further, then picked up the three remaining hors d'oeuvres and put them in his mouth at one time.

"Take it easy," Scott said.

Roger almost swallowed them whole. "Scott. Go downstairs and bring me something. A sandwich if you can manage that."

Scott just looked at him, then said, "Sure, Roger," and left.

Prick! Roger thought, *he has no intention of helping me. What good was it having a bunch of staff running around if they weren't taking care of him?* In a minute, as soon as he felt better, he'd go downstairs himself. Or maybe someone else would show up.

CASSIE STOOD OUTSIDE the door of the staff lounge. She'd already checked her car and the parking lot, and then she'd searched the two bottom floors of Happy Twosomes. Still no Jenny. She looked at the door.

Cautiously she eased it open a crack. The first thing she saw was Roger Weber sitting on the couch, looking like a stuffed toad in his tuxedo. He seemed to be watching the corner, as if there might be another person with him, but she couldn't be sure, and it certainly wouldn't be Jenny.

Cassie let the door close quietly. She'd take on Roger later, after she found Jen. Or maybe she'd save it until Monday. She pulled off her high heels and started up the stairs to the third floor.

Bill would have to do something about Roger now—he'd have to see that Roger had gone too far. Greg could refuse to pay the station, with justification, and Bill was always sensitive to threats to the bottom line. Unless, of course, Bill took Roger's side and blamed the whole thing on Jenny.

Cassie had the unwanted thought that it might be Bill in the lounge with Roger. Roger could be demanding her termination. And if Bill didn't agree to it, Roger would take it further. He'd call Walter Kraley.

Cassie's head began to throb as she opened the door to the third-floor gym. It was silent, echoing its emptiness.

She moved through it slowly, looking behind exercise equipment and in places where Jenny couldn't possibly be. After that she tried the women's locker room. Again, no Jenny. That left only the pool.

Cassie stepped through the open entranceway. The pool lights were on, bathing the area in aqua. Triangles of light and color danced on the walls and across the concrete coping, creating a surrealistic scene.

Sitting alone on the side of the pool was Jenny. Her skin was a ghostly white and her arms were clutched tightly around her chest. Her pantyhose, purse and shoes were in a pile at her side.

Cassie moved toward her. "Hi."

Jenny's head came up slowly, her feet moving rhythmically through the water. "Well?"

"Are you all right?"

"Yeah."

Cassie sat down. "You're shaking."

"I said I was fine." Jenny ducked her head again.

"Honey, I'm really sorry."

"I hate that man!"

"Let it go. It's over." She reached out a hand to touch Jenny, who jerked away.

"No, it's not! I threw a drink in the face of the great-god-of-the-morning and now you'll probably get fired."

"He doesn't have that power." The lie was for Jenny's benefit.

"If you don't get fired then Roger's really going to make your life miserable just to get back at me." Jenny kicked at the water.

Cassie didn't want to think about any of that. "You want to tell me what happened down there?"

"He pissed me off." Despite the tough words, Jenny looked young and scared.

"I figured that out."

"I don't want to talk about it, okay?"

"Okay."

They sat in silence for several minutes watching the patterns of light that flitted around the huge room. The only sound was the splashing of Jenny's feet.

After a while, Cassie checked her watch. It was seven. She tilted her daughter's head up so that she could see her eyes. "You ready to go?"

Jenny pulled her feet out of the water and stood up. She moved awkwardly, losing her balance. Cassie reached out to steady her, but Jenny ducked the outstretched hand. "I'm okay. I just want to go home."

"That's fine with me. We'll order a pizza." Cassie picked up Jenny's things.

Jenny reached down for a glass Cassie hadn't noticed before, swaying in the process so that she almost fell.

"Are you okay?" Cassie asked.

"I stopped off in the ballroom and got a drink." She held it out toward Cassie. "Bourbon and Coke."

The glass was empty, but from the smell Cassie guessed there had been a lot more bourbon than Coke. She'd never seen Jenny drunk before but this was a bad night all around, and not the time for a lecture on temperance.

"We'll talk about that tomorrow," Cassie said.

They walked side by side through the door into the empty gym, their bare feet silent on the tile floor. Cassie resisted the impulse to rub her throbbing temples.

"Mom," Jenny said, head down. "I want you to know I'm sorry."

"Thanks. And if it's any consolation, it could just as easily have been me who threw that drink on Roger. In fact, I wish it had been. He's always asking for it."

Jenny shuddered. "Yeah, well, tonight he got it."

SIX

CASSIE SPENT SATURDAY MORNING worrying about the consequences of Jenny's fight with Roger. It wasn't that she blamed Jenny, or even Roger. In retrospect it somehow seemed inevitable, and she berated herself for not seeing it coming.

By ten-thirty her psyche was thoroughly black and blue. She considered calling Bill, just to sound him out on Roger's threats, but vetoed the idea. When the phone actually rang, she let Jenny get it, and went to the kitchen for more coffee.

"Mom," Jenny said appearing in the doorway just a minute later. "That was Mandy. She's coming over to talk to you."

Cassie's head jerked upward. "To me?" On a Saturday morning? "Why?"

"I don't know. She sounded weird. Said they'd had some meeting at the station and she had to talk to you."

Meeting was always an ominous word at Y-96. "Who was at the meeting?"

"I don't know," Jenny said, as she went back toward her bedroom.

Cassie gripped her coffee cup. It had to be bad news. Really bad news, and she suspected she knew what it was: Mandy was going to fire her.

Since they'd lost their program director and only had a

consultant, Bill should be the one to do the firing. And he'd do it at the station. But Bill had been known to chicken out before. This time he was sending Mandy in his place.

When the doorbell rang, Cassie had moved to the dining room, but she still gripped what was now a cold cup of coffee. She rose reluctantly and went to the door.

Mandy was there, holding a large cardboard box.

Cassie's insides seemed to shrivel. *I'm fired all right,* she thought. *They've even cleaned out my office.*

"Look," Mandy said, her face white, "I'm sorry to bother you, but we just had a meeting—"

"Jenny told me," Cassie said, letting her in.

Mandy headed straight for the dining room table and set the box underneath it. Then she noticed the coffee.

"If you have any more of that, I could use a cup," she said.

"Sure." Cassie went to the kitchen.

When she returned, Mandy was rubbing her pale face. She wore no make-up and her blond hair was carelessly pulled back. She looked like a woman who'd already been through one ordeal and didn't have the courage to face the next. "Thanks, I need this," Mandy said, accepting the pottery mug with both hands. She took a gulp then held on to the cup as she spoke. "Walter's in town."

"Why?" Cassie asked as she sat down. The toe of her shoe brushed against the box. "Never mind. That isn't what you came to tell me."

"No, it isn't. There's something else, but I don't know how to say it."

Cassie waited, silent.

"I'll just say it." Mandy took a breath. "Roger Weber is dead."

Cassie blinked. "You can't be serious."

"I'm serious. I'm sorry if I was abrupt but I didn't know how to tell you."

"Oh my God." It wasn't possible. Roger? Dead?

She felt a wave of guilt. How many times had she wished Roger off the planet forever? And what was that but death?

"How did he die?" she asked. "When?"

Mandy drank more of the coffee, as if it might infuse her with strength. "He died last night. No, I guess it was early in the morning. At the hospital."

It took awhile but Mandy finally got the story out. Roger had left the Twosome's party early, saying he didn't feel well. Sometime after midnight he'd called EMS and was taken to Brackenridge Hospital, where he died less than an hour later.

"And the hospital called the station?" Cassie asked.

"No, they didn't notify us at all. Roger had an early meeting with Bill this morning, only he didn't show up." She paused for a second. "You know how Roger was about punctuality, so, when he was late Bill started calling his apartment. After an hour or so he went to Roger's place—just to check up. You know."

Cassie nodded.

"When he got there," Mandy went on, "there was yellow tape across the door and a policeman going around the apartment complex talking to the neighbors."

"Police?"

"They said it was just routine, but Bill was too shocked to find out much." She shook her head, as if none of it made sense to her, either.

"When will we know something?" Cassie asked.

"I guess after the autopsy. They said they'd keep in touch

with Bill." She paused, then said, We had a meeting, Bill, Walter and me."

Walter Kraley made his home in Chicago and at seventy-four he didn't travel to his stations unless there was important business. "How did Walter get here so fast?" Cassie asked.

"He didn't. The trip was planned—I picked him up at the airport this morning." She swallowed. "I had to tell him about Roger."

"Oh, Mandy, I'm sorry." She reached over and touched Mandy's hand. It was cold.

"Walter's taking it hard. He really loved Roger."

Cassie felt a lump in her throat. Poor Walter. He would be mourning Roger alone.

Walter had "discovered" Roger, as he told the story, in a small market station outside of Chicago. Since that day, almost fourteen years before, Roger had moved around the country, going wherever his mentor sent him, boosting the ratings of newly purchased stations and making Walter even richer. In return, Roger was the favored son who could do no wrong.

Jenny drifted into the dining room. "Hi, Mandy," she said, then stopped and looked at them. "What's going on?"

Cassie looked at Mandy then back at her daughter. "Mandy came over to tell me that," she paused and took a breath. "That Roger died this morning."

Jenny froze. "Roger? Roger Weber?"

"Uh-huh."

"But how?"

"They aren't sure," Mandy said.

Jenny turned a sickly white and seemed to sway. Cassie stood up and put an arm around her. "Are you okay?"

She nodded slowly. "I'm just…surprised."

"Here, why don't you sit down?" Cassie asked.

"No. No, thanks, I'm studying." Jenny looked at her mother. "I'm going to call Beth."

"Why don't you wait until I…" Cassie stopped when she saw how pale Jenny looked. "It's okay, call her if you want. Tell her I love her."

Jenny nodded, turned around and headed back for her bedroom.

Mandy frowned. "Is she okay?"

"I think so," Cassie said. Sometimes Jenny was merely a lovable stranger that Cass felt helpless to support.

"She's probably feeling guilty about fighting with Roger," Mandy said. "You know, right before he died and all."

"Uh-huh."

"Oh, I almost forgot." Mandy slid the box out from under the table. "You won't be on the air Monday. We've decided to do a silent morning show, just until Roger's memorial service on Wednesday. We'll play music and commercials, but no talking, just an announcement once an hour."

"And then what?"

"Then on Thursday, you know, big day for the ratings," she said, with a touch of sarcasm, "we want to do a special tribute to Roger. A show with all his best bits. Interspersed with music, just like a regular air-shift."

"Who's going to put it together?" Cassie asked. And then she knew what was in the box. With a plunk she put her cup on the table. "I'm supposed to do the show."

"Look, Cassie, Walter thought that you'd be the natural one and I agreed with him. You've got to do it." Even in the face of early morning death, Mandy was making decisions for other people. "I went down to Roger's office and got his airchecks. They're in here."

"But, Mandy, I can't get it done by Thursday! I've got to listen to all those tapes, and then it will take hours—"

"Walter wants it Thursday and so does Bill. You'll be off the air, so you'll have the time. Besides, it will be points for you in Walter's eyes. Big points."

"Who cares?"

"You do," Mandy said. "With Roger gone we've got to get someone else to do the morning show."

"I'm just the sidekick."

"Don't be stubborn, Cassie; listen for once. If you don't fight for the morning drive slot they're going to give it to Scott Delany and he'll want to pick his own partner. If that happens, you can kiss your job good-bye."

Mandy was right and the truth hit hard. The always-adorable Scott had an ego as big as his following of female fans, and he fought for what he wanted. He wanted that morning drive slot. If he got it, he'd never accept Cassie as a partner. He'd want someone young, cute, and totally, as he called it, twenty-first century.

Cassie rubbed her forehead. She could almost sense Roger hovering over her. Smirking.

"I'll do the show," she said.

"It could be worse; think of poor Roger." Mandy shook her head. "It's so hard for me to believe that Roger's dead. And what's it going to do to us?"

"We'll survive. The king is dead—long live the king."

"Maybe. But what if his successor isn't as good? The ratings could fall, and that would kill us. Do you have any idea how high my budgets are? How tough it's going to be to meet them without good numbers?" Mandy's agitated gesture almost knocked over her coffee. "My income is based on making sales quotas; I could end up with no money. Without a job!"

Cassie wanted to feel sorry for her, but Mandy had a six-figure income and the lifestyle that went with it. Surely there was money in savings.

"You'll do what we all do when things get tight: cut back on your spending. Besides, you've got David." Mandy's adored husband was a restaurant consultant, flying around the country most of the time. He had to be making almost as much as Mandy.

"Yeah," Mandy said, but she didn't sound convinced.

Cassie leaned forward. "Don't borrow trouble. It doesn't help and I ought to know; I do it all the time."

Mandy's smile was a weak effort. "Thanks." She stood up and moved toward the door. "And thanks for the coffee." Mandy opened the door to a stream of sunlight. She frowned and turned back long enough to say, "Oh, and Cassie, you might get a visit from the police."

The hairs on Cassie's neck began to prickle. "Why?"

"I don't know; Bill just said we should be prepared."

Scott: "The following is an announcement from Y-96 general manager, Bill Bankston."

Bill: "Roger Weber, Y-96's morning drive personality, died suddenly Saturday morning at Brackenridge hospital.

As you know, Roger was a great performer. His wit and zest added brightness to all our lives. He helped us laugh, no matter what the hour, and taught us to see the humor in ourselves and the world around us.

Thursday morning, from 6 until 10 a.m., we'll run a special tribute to Roger. You'll hear highlights from his past shows. The best of Roger Wonderful Weber.

In the meantime, we at Y-96 will miss Roger, just as you will. And despite the sadness of his death, we can all be grateful that we were enriched by his life."

SEVEN

Sgt. Wayne Root sat in a back booth at Coco's on I-35, waiting for his partner to show up. While he waited he watched the Saturday morning joggers mingled with people who looked like they'd just gotten out of bed.

Root had been awakened at 3 AM by the Senior Sergeant, sending him to the hospital to take on a new case. The case of Roger Weber, disk jockey, dead, possibly of an accidental overdose of a prescription medicine. Possibly not. Weber claimed he'd been poisoned. Practically screamed it according to the doctor, who couldn't believe a man so ill could be that violent. Maybe it was the drugs. Root wasn't sure and neither was the doctor who'd refused to sign a death certificate.

It was another high-profile case—just what he didn't need.

"You look tired." Andy Socorro slid into the booth across from his partner.

"You should, too," Root said. But Socorro's face looked as smooth as a baby's bottom. Maybe because he was overweight. *Stretched the skin or something.* "So, how'd it go?"

"Fine. I got one lucky break; Weber's boss from the radio station showed up at the apartment complex while I was there."

The waitress in a white blouse and burgundy skirt appeared. "What can I get you two?"

"Coffee," Root said. "Black."

"I'll take coffee, too," Socorro added. "And I'd like some cream, please." He waited until she left, then pulled out a small battered notebook and said, "According to the manager of the complex, Weber didn't have many friends visit him. He moved in there after his divorce about six, seven months ago."

Now that Root was going through his own divorce after seventeen years of marriage, he didn't even want to hear the word.

"Is his ex-wife in Austin?" Root asked.

"One is. Cynthia Weber is a teller with some bank. She's the most recent one. They were married only a year, then they moved to Austin and split up in about a month."

"She didn't go back home? Back to wherever they'd come from?"

"Atlanta." Socorro shrugged. "She must've liked it here."

"Where's his other ex?"

"Chicago. She has his two teenage daughters."

"New girlfriends?"

Socorro shook his head. "Not that anyone knows of. The manager's only seen one woman at the apartment, and she just stayed an hour or so. It was several months back, right after he moved there, and the manager says she hasn't seen any women since. No other visitors, either."

"What about the neighbors?"

"They didn't really know him, but I wouldn't have expected them to. There are only eight units, all occupied by retirees and widows in their sixties."

"Nice quiet place."

"Yeah." Socorro grinned. "Not quiet enough for Weber. Right after he moved in, he raised a stink about a party that was a little too loud one night. Bridge."

Root smiled. "Yeah, those bridge parties can really get out of hand."

"According to the manager, around nine-fifteen Weber came banging on the door, demanding they keep it down. Can you imagine? Two tables of sixty-year-olds playing bridge and this lunatic nearly breaks the door in because they're making too much noise."

"Nice guy," Root said. "Did you say nine-fifteen? Why so early?"

"Weber told her he went to bed at eight-forty-five every night, Sunday through Thursday, because he had to get up at four. And he liked it good and quiet so he could sleep. She said they cleared up the problem the next day. She apologized."

"Any possibility there?"

"I don't think so," Socorro said. "She's a nice motherly type. Knits afghans. I got that she really felt sorry for Weber. Although, it's apparent Weber wasn't the most congenial guy to have around. Blew up at any little thing. Somebody parked crooked in the parking lot and he threw a fit."

"Great. So, what about his boss? What did he have to say?"

Socorro bent his round face over his notebook and read, "'Roger was temperamental, as many talented people are. He wasn't popular with the rest of the staff.'" He looked up. "In other words, the guy was a jerk. So, what did you find out at the dating place?"

"Same thing. According to the owner of the club," Root pulled out his own notebook, "Greg Mayhew, Weber was a royal pain. Now, you want the bad news or the good?"

Socorro grinned. "Give me the bad first; you look like you'll enjoy that."

"There were over three hundred and forty people at that party. They all signed in with names, addresses and phone numbers, so we've got them in the approximate order they arrived. Still, depending on what Pritchard says, any one of them could have gotten to Weber." Pritchard was the Medical Examiner.

"I hope the good news balances that out."

"Yeah, well, it will help," Root said, watching as the waitress set their coffees in front of them. "Thanks." While Socorro poured cream and two packets of sugar into his cup, Root went on, "According to Mayhew, most of the people who were there didn't even know Weber. And Weber didn't mingle."

"So, what did he do?"

"Most of the time, he stayed in a little room they used as a staff lounge."

Socorro sipped his coffee. "What do you think the autopsy will tell us?"

"Pritchard still thinks it might have been an overdose of the gout medicine that Weber was taking. Did you find any at the apartment?"

"No, and I checked the pharmacy he used. There were thirty-six capsules in the bottle Weber picked up four days ago. It's the same one he had with him at the hospital. Weber had taken twelve pills, just the precise amount he should have."

"Well, Roberts said he'd finish the autopsy as soon as he could." Root took a sip of his coffee and almost smiled. "Good coffee this morning." He put the cup down on the Formica table. "I got a list of the radio station employees who were at the party last night." He looked at his notepad, and grinned. "And a little tidbit that I'm saving for last."

They were always doing that to each other.

"I've got one myself," Socorro said. "And I've got my own list. Got it from the station manager. He said that there were six people from the station, plus the daughter of one of them."

"Right. Weber, of course; Bankston, station manager. Mandy McCormick, sales manager. Rachel Sankey, salesman."

"Account executive," Socorro corrected. "That's what Bankston called her."

Root grunted. "Sales. Okay, then Scott Delany, disk jockey, and Cassie Ferris. You know, the Cass Woman? She was on the air with Weber. Oh, and Ferris's daughter, Jenny. She's young, about eighteen, I think. Mayhew made it real clear to me that the daughter wasn't a guest. Under-age."

"Same list of people I have." Socorro grinned, ready to give Root the best part. "And one of those people threw a drink on Weber."

Root beat him to the rest of the story. "It was Jenny Ferris. And her mother pulled Weber off the girl. Mayhew got involved, too. Unfortunately, he doesn't strike me as a poison kind of guy. He was pretty visible all night, too, but we'll need to look at the mother and daughter."

Socorro nodded. "I kind of got that Weber's whole life revolved around Y-96. When he went out it was on station business. At least we have a list for starters."

"And we'll take on the Cass Woman first," Root said. "I'd like to see what she looks like anyway after hearing her on the air."

"Maybe we'll get lucky and find out Weber's death was accidental."

"Dream on."

EIGHT

CASSIE SAT ON THE RUG in her living room listening to Roger's voice. Roger being funny. Roger being ironic. Roger being snide. She felt as if she were the one who had died and gone to a hell presided over by Roger Weber.

Jenny came in from the bedroom, her purse over her shoulder. "Mom, could you shut that thing up, for a minute?" she said pointing to the recorder. "It's making me crazy."

"Sure." Cassie stopped it. "Are you going somewhere?"

"In a little bit." She put her purse down on one of the couches.

"What's up?"

"Nothing." Jenny began to move around the room the way she did when she wanted to talk but wasn't ready.

Cassie watched her circling, and each time Jenny passed, she felt her own nerves tightening. "If there's something on your mind, Jenny, say it."

"Oh, right!" But she stopped.

"I know you're upset about last night, and I know how you feel—"

"No you don't! You don't know how I feel at all."

Cassie threw up her hands. "Fine. Then you tell me."

"You wouldn't understand," Jenny said, grabbing up her purse.

"Why don't you try me, instead of snapping my head off?"

Jenny whirled around and glared at her mother. "I threw a drink at a man, I called him names and now he's dead."

Cassie waited.

Finally Jenny said, "I'm glad I told him off. He deserved it. He was a terrible person, and all of you just let him walk all over you, like at the company picnic when he started that big fight…" She lost her momentum.

At times during her life Cassie had been a fighter, too, thinking she could slay dragons and right injustice. And how hard the discovery had been, that when you stand up to fight, you must be prepared to lose. But then, losing your daughter to an ex-husband is not an everyday battle, and it had taken much of the fight out of her. She suspected the events of last night were going to be just as hard a lesson for Jenny.

"Do you feel guilty because Roger died?" Cassie asked.

"No! He deserved to die. He was hateful, especially what he said to you on the air."

"About the gun."

"Yes." Suddenly Jenny looked confused. "But, I still feel…awful." The last was said pitifully.

Cassie stood up and slid an arm around her. "Maybe you just have to live through it, then let it go. There are things like that."

"I guess so," Jenny said, but she didn't sound as if she was ready to believe it. She started to say something, then shook her head. "Never mind. It's okay." She reached for her purse. "I'm going now."

"Are you sure? Where?"

"It's no big deal; I'm just going shopping with Brandi."

"Okay." There seemed so much more to say, but Jenny was already leaving.

"Bye, Mom," she said as the door closed behind her.

IT WAS LESS THAN an hour later that the doorbell rang, and Cassie reluctantly stood up, shaking out her stiff legs. The tapes were in three piles beside the recorder and she had only half-filled a page with notes of the bits she wanted to use.

She left everything as it was and went to the front door. There were two men on the porch, one in a gray suit, one in beige, and they reminded her of insurance salesmen.

"Yes?"

"Mrs. Ferris? We're with the Austin Police Department. I'm Sergeant Socorro and this is my partner, Sergeant Root." Socorro held out some identification. "We'd like to get some information from you on Roger Weber."

Cassie felt her muscles twitch. "What would you like to know?"

Socorro smiled. "May we come in?"

"Oh. Yes, of course."

Cassie led them to the living room, and she could feel the presence of the two men, heavy and powerful, behind her.

She gestured toward the couches, inviting them to sit down, then took a place on the loveseat. It was then she realized Socorro looked a little like Roger. He had the same round face and thin dark hair growing low on his forehead. His skin was smoother than Roger's, almost completely unlined and his dark eyes weren't small and vicious. They were large and innocent. Still there was some resemblance.

The other officer, Root, was taller and his body was lean. He had a neatly trimmed mustache the same color as his sandy hair. His eyes were a combination of goldish-green and gray that was probably listed on his driver's license as hazel. He was watching her.

"Mrs. Ferris, we appreciate your time on a Saturday afternoon and all," Socorro said, pulling out a notebook and moving his chunky body around to get comfortable. "We won't keep you long."

"We want you to understand that this is all preliminary," Root added, his voice deep and without much inflection. "A cause of death hasn't been determined, but we still need to find out about Roger Weber. His friends. His life. You understand."

"Certainly," Cassie said, although she didn't.

Root pulled out his own notebook, referring to it before he spoke. "Did Roger Weber have any particular enemies or close friends that you knew of?"

Only bits and pieces of Roger's personal life had filtered into the station. "He didn't have many friends that I ever heard about. I think he did before his divorce from Cynthia, when they lived in Atlanta. Couple friends. You know, married couples that he and Cynthia socialized with, but he didn't keep up with them after he moved to Austin. I guess that happens to a lot of people," Cassie said, thinking of her own divorce and the friends she'd left behind.

Root frowned and Cassie wondered if he didn't understand, or understood all too well. He asked, "What kind of man was Roger Weber? Was he a nice guy?"

"Well…" How could she say this delicately? "He was, sometimes, moody."

Socorro's big eyes were shining with what might have been amusement. "Would you say that you're putting it mildly?"

"Actually," she said, "Roger was very moody."

"I've been told he was a real jerk," Socorro said.

"Sometimes," Cassie said.

"Any particular incident stand out?"

When Cassie took too long thinking about it, Socorro said, "I know you don't want to say anything against your friends, but it would be very helpful to us if you'd just tell us what's on your mind. We'll hear everything eventually; you could save us a lot of time."

Cassie believed him. If everyone on the staff told the truth, this investigation would be over sooner and they could all get on with their lives. The problem was that she didn't know where to start.

"Roger, well, he threw tantrums and he'd involve anyone who happened to be handy."

"Was there one person he disliked more than everyone else?"

Cassie felt a tingle in her stomach. "Well, me. He didn't like having me on the show. Especially if I got any praise or fan letters."

Root sat up. "But you put up with him."

"It was my job."

"Did you two argue?"

Cassie nodded.

"When was the last disagreement you had with him?" Root asked.

"Friday."

"At the station? What happened?"

She had meant Friday night, but let it go. She much preferred to talk about the morning. "We were doing a promo, a promotional announcement, about the party at Happy Twosomes. When I mentioned that I'd be there, Roger went livid. He hadn't known that I was going to attend."

Socorro asked, "Why? Why would he get angry about that?"

"He said he could have made a fool of himself on the air."

"Was the exchange pretty heated?" Root asked.

Cassie nodded slowly. "Some."

Socorro leaned forward. "Is it always that way?" When Cassie shook her head no, he added, "Then, why that morning?"

"I don't know," she said slowly. "I didn't intend to have an argument."

"How did it end?"

"I left the control room."

"But you still had to finish out the show," he said.

"Of course," Cassie agreed. "Roger played commercials and music and I had a cup of coffee in the hall. In about ten minutes I went back in the control room and he didn't mention it again. Neither did I."

"Sort of an armed truce?" Socorro suggested.

"I guess."

"What about at the party?" Root asked.

Cassie had been waiting for that question, known it was coming, hoping it wouldn't.

"I had a few angry words with Roger. He was drunk."

Root sat back and Socorro took over. "Mrs. Ferris, we're just trying to get a picture of Mr. Weber and all his relationships. Especially during his last day. Would you go on, please? Tell us about him at the party."

Cassie suspected she was supposed to be lulled by his soft voice and gentle eyes. "I only saw him for a few minutes…"

"It's okay," Socorro said. "Just take a minute and tell us exactly what happened." Then he added the stinger. "We know he had a disagreement with your daughter."

Cassie stiffened. She wanted to leave Jenny's name out of it. "Roger was drunk. Or, at least he acted that way."

"Please, just tell us what happened."

Cassie realized that her hands, resting on her lap, were clenched together. She forced them to relax, as she slowly, reluctantly, told the police what she had seen, and been involved in, the night before.

When she finished Socorro said, "Sounds like he upset both you and your daughter."

"Yes. He did."

"What about the threat? Could he have gotten you fired?" Root asked.

She paused, then said, "Maybe. Probably. I don't know."

"Where is your daughter now?" Root asked.

The stiffness in Cassie's body shot out to paralyze every muscle. "She went shopping with some friends." They couldn't think Jenny had done anything. "Jenny's a student. She has a scholarship."

Socorro nodded, as if he understood perfectly how that would make Jenny innocent of any misdeeds.

"Did your daughter talk with Roger Weber after that?" Root asked.

"No, she didn't."

"You were with her the whole time until you left?" he pushed.

"Well, no. I, no. But I'm sure she didn't see him again. She would have said something."

Root stood up. He looked tall and frightening. "Mrs. Ferris, what time did the argument take place?"

"A little before 6:30, I think."

"And what time did you leave the party?"

"Just after seven."

"Where were you after the argument and before you left the party?"

"I was everywhere." Cassie realized her hands were clenched, again, making her ring, a gift from the girls, dig into her skin. "I went looking for Jenny and I found her by the pool upstairs. She was alone. We talked for a few minutes and then we came home."

"You spent a lot of time looking for your daughter. Was anyone with you? Did you talk to anyone?"

"No, I was alone. I was in a hurry."

Socorro looked at his partner, then back at Cassie. "That's understandable. The party must have been pretty well packed, and you can't go running around with other people in tow." He smiled. "Anyone else at Y-96 have problems with Weber?" he asked.

The switch left Cassie feeling off-balance. "From the station?"

"Yes. Did Mandy McCormick?"

Cassie nodded hesitantly. "I suppose so."

"What kind of problems?" he asked, as if Jenny and her argument with Roger were completely forgotten.

Cassie tried to concentrate on his newest question. Mandy and Roger were always at odds, how could she explain that to someone outside the business?

"It's an ongoing battle in radio. Roger felt he was being used to make money for everyone else. He blamed Mandy, but she just said it was her job to make money for the station and everyone in it," Cass said. "People don't see it's a joint effort."

"I see." Socorro was nodding. "Did anyone else fight with Roger?"

"Everyone." Cassie was beginning to relax. "If you worked with Roger, you were bound to cross him sooner or later. Usually when there were other people around."

"What about Rachel Sankey. How did she get along with Roger?"

Cassie wondered what it would take to make them really understand Roger. "Sergeant, Roger was rude to everyone. Sometimes a simple 'good morning' was enough to start a tirade. No one liked the man."

"He had two ex-wives," Root reminded her.

"And they probably really hated him."

Instead of smiling at her comment, Root frowned. He looked less happy with every word Cassie was saying. She began to think he disapproved of her for some reason, so she spoke to the heavy one, Socorro.

"On the air," Cassie went on, "Roger could be brilliant. In public he handled a crowd like a conductor handles an orchestra. He played them. Made them laugh, made them feel things. Like at the charity auction for underprivileged kids; Roger had everyone giving much more money than they'd planned.

"But he couldn't handle people on a one-to-one. He expected too much, and no matter how hard people tried to please him, it was never enough. He'd take that..." she struggled for a word, "failure...as a personal affront."

Socorro nodded, as if he wanted to understand. "But the station manager talked like he got along with Weber. Did he?"

"I don't know. Bill didn't have open disagreements with Roger like everyone else."

"I see." Socorro was beginning to look as unhappy as Root. "So, everyone in the station had arguments with Weber at some point. Probably on a regular basis."

"That's right," Cassie said.

He stood up. "Thank you for your time, Mrs. Ferris. As we told you, this is just preliminary work. We don't even know for sure that Mr. Weber's death was anything but accidental."

Cassie stood also. "I heard that there was some question of poison. Is that right?"

"Perhaps an accidental overdose."

Cassie walked them out. On the porch, Root turned around. "What school does your daughter go to?"

Cassie almost stopped breathing at the unexpected question. "The University of Texas."

Socorro smiled. "I went there myself; of course it's grown since then. How does she like it?"

"Fine."

Socorro nodded. "Well, thanks for your time. Oh, and don't be surprised if we show up again. This is slow work, and we prefer talking to nice people like you rather than some of the others we have to deal with." He smiled a sweet smile. "Then again, this may be over already, if the autopsy results are in."

NINE

CASSIE CAME OUT of the production room rubbing her aching shoulders; she'd spent all day Sunday listening to tapes, and the last six hours hunched over the console in the little production room. She passed by the control room and waved at Steve Parker who was on the air. The two of them appeared to be the only ones in the station who were working. Everyone else was discussing the latest news on Roger's death. Fact and rumor floated freely.

One almost verifiable fact was that Walter Kraley, wielding all the power of Northland Broadcasting, had pushed officialdom into a frenzy of efficiency. The autopsy had been completed in record time. Over a weekend, no less. Only no one knew the results. And the police had arrived at Y-96 over an hour before to talk with Bill. As far as Cassie knew, they were still closeted in his office. They seemed to be moving inexorably closer.

Her concern was that the police would talk to Jenny and that somehow Brad, her ex husband, would find out. He was perfectly capable of using Roger's death to his advantage. He'd claim that there were bad elements in Austin that might hurt Beth, and he wouldn't allow her to come for Thanksgiving. But that would just be the beginning.

He would go to work on Jenny, urging her to transfer to

the University of Washington in Seattle, on the grounds that she would be safer. He'd tried it before, and thank God, Jenny had been strong enough to resist. Cassie wasn't sure Jenny could withstand the pressure a second time.

Cassie was rubbing her forehead, trying not to think about it, when Rachel whizzed by, almost knocking her over.

"Oh, Cass. I'm sorry." She stopped in the middle of the hall. "Have you heard? The police just left Bill's office." She twisted a strand of red hair around her index finger. "Bill hasn't come out, though. Cassie this is horrible! What if Roger really was murdered?"

Cassie hesitated. "I don't know."

"Oh, God! And everyone knows he hated me," Rachel said, her body seeming to melt against the wall. "And I hated him."

"We all felt that way," Cassie reminded her. "If that's the criteria for being a suspect, they'll come after everyone, not just you. We'll have our own Y-96 cellblock."

Rachel tried to smile. "You're right, I know you are. It's just that you read about innocent people who spend years in prison. I can't think of anything more horrible!"

"Have a little faith. Tomorrow this will all be over and we won't see the police again."

"Maybe," Rachel said. "I hope so. I really do." She fanned herself with the envelopes in her hand, then looked at them. "I almost forgot, your mail."

"Oh. Thanks." Cassie took the small stack.

"No problem. I was on my way out. Bye."

Cassie shuffled through the mail as she went to her own office. First there were a couple of hand addressed letters, which she assumed to be fan mail. She set those aside. There were also the usual press releases and a couple of requests from charities for public service time.

Then she found an envelope with "Past Due" in blazing red on the outside. It was from the law offices of Feiner, Craft and Fitch.

Cassie sat down and grabbed up the phone, then thought better of it and put the receiver back. Firmly.

She had been sending Chris Feiner money for almost two years; money that amounted to a small fortune. All she had gotten in return was the knowledge that Beth was legally gone. And now, instead of accepting the monthly payments, he was making it clear to everyone at Y-96 that she was in arrears. This was the second bill she'd received at the station.

How did anyone have the gall to demand so much money for a job done so poorly? And why this latest insult?

With a calm that was the result of years of holding anger in check, Cassie carefully folded the offending envelope and put it in her desk, beside one exactly like it. She would throw them away at home, so no more people at the station would see them.

"Cassie," Mandy said, coming through the door without knocking.

Cassie closed the drawer. "What?"

"I need some advice—you've done news; you should know how to handle this." Mandy sat on the metal chair in front of the desk. "Greg just called from Happy Twosomes. The police have been talking to him about Roger's death and he's worried the club is going to end up on the news. Bad publicity, and all. He's talking about pulling all his advertising until this blows over. Do you know how much that is?"

It was a rhetorical question, so Cassie waited for Mandy to answer it herself.

"It's a bunch! I've got to help him keep his name away from Roger Weber's. If he cancels then other advertisers may cancel. I can't handle this." She sank into a chair.

"Come on, Mandy, get a grip. Call Greg and have him phone the police station. Chances are, if the reporters haven't gotten to him yet, they won't."

Mandy nodded, still agitated. "Really? Oh, that's great. I'll have Rachel call him right now." She reached for the phone pulling it closer, dialed Rachel's two-digit extension and waited. After a few seconds she said, "Damn! I got her voice mail—she must have left."

"I forgot—I saw her leave a few minutes ago."

"Maybe you could go down there," Mandy suggested. "You know, you could talk to Greg. Tell him what you told me. Reassure him, as a representative of Y-96, that we'll do everything we can to keep his name out of the press."

The request was pushing it, even for Mandy. "You have totally lost your mind. And don't think you can con me into it. You can't. Why don't you go?"

She seemed suddenly flustered. "I can't. I have to be somewhere in about twenty minutes. It's well, you know." She paused before her normal self assurance rose to the surface. "Anyway, Greg really liked you, and you have 'star power.'"

"You're amazing, you know that?"

Mandy straightened up and tried to look cocky, but her heart wasn't in it. "That's what I keep telling people, but no one listens. I'll call Rachel's cell phone and get her to go."

"Good thinking."

Mandy departed, and Cassie was still shaking her head when her office door swung open again.

Bill Bankston, his face pale and his tie askew, came in and closed the door behind him. "Cassie, have you got a minute?"

"Sure. What's wrong, Bill?"

He took off his glasses. "I'm telling the whole staff, just so everyone will know. The police now believe that Roger was murdered."

Cassie's head felt light. She leaned back in her chair for support. "I see."

"It's terrible. It looks bad for the station, and it's going to be hard on all of us. But especially, poor Walter. He's pretty upset. I'm worried he won't survive this; he's in his seventies."

Cassie sat forward and touched his sleeve. "It's okay, Bill. He can take it; Walter's tough."

"I hope you're right."

"Do they know what killed Roger?"

For a second Bill looked puzzled. "I'm not sure. Some kind of poison, but they aren't saying what."

"What *did* they say?"

"That they'll be doing a full investigation. They've asked for our complete cooperation and that means a formal statement from everyone."

"They already talked with me once."

"They'll be back. You can count on it."

THE THIRD FLOOR of the Austin Police Department had dozens of small cubicles made of bright yellow temporary partitions. While they gave the detectives some privacy they did little to baffle sound. There was a lot of sound that late Monday afternoon. Everyone seemed to be talking.

Root frowned at the noise, then looked out the window.

Almost directly across from him, I-35 was beginning to back up with commuter traffic. Above the cars the sky was a pale gray with patches of darker clouds. It was raining and it was supposed to become a real gusher. That would stop traffic completely. Root didn't envy the guys on the line; they'd be working late tonight. But then, so would he now that Roger Weber's death was officially a homicide.

He focused his attention back on his partner whose desk was beside his own.

"This is the weirdest damn thing," Root said, pointing at the file in front of him.

Socorro looked up, putting down his half-eaten cruller and licking his fingers. "Tell me about the weird part."

"This Rachel Sankey says that everyone was in and out of that staff lounge all night. Except she only went in there once, realized Weber was there and immediately left. The station manager, Bankston, says he went in one time. No one was there, so he got a drink, ate some hors d'oeuvres and went back out. Greg Mayhew says he never went in there."

"So?"

"So who are all these people that were in and out all night?"

Socorro picked up his cruller and took another bite, then carefully moved his notebook closer, using only the tips of his sticky fingers. "Scott Delany, the afternoon jock at Y-96, says he went there a couple of times to get drinks. Seems the drinks were free in there, but he had to pay at the bar downstairs. And there was no line in the lounge."

"Great. Did he see Weber?"

"The first time he didn't see anyone. The second time, after six-thirty he thinks, Weber was there complaining about his stomach. He was also drinking and eating."

Root watched Socorro finish off the donut and said, "Maybe he shouldn't have eaten so much."

Socorro smiled, shrugging off the words. "People got to eat, Wayne." He licked his fingers carefully then went back to his notebook. "According to the autopsy, Weber must have ingested the poison between six and seven."

"This poison is another weird part." Root flipped to different page of the file. "According to the autopsy, Weber died of an overdose of Colchicine. 'Derivative of colchicum, from plant Meadow Saffron.' It's the same base as the medicine Weber was taking for his gout. And they found this plant substance in his stomach." Root looked up at his partner. "Is that a coincidence or did someone plan it that way?"

"Well, the ME told me that if Weber hadn't been taking the medicine, then the amount of this plant he ate wouldn't have been sufficient to kill him. It looks like a pretty well thought out murder to me."

Root rubbed his face. He was tired and it showed in the slowness of his mental processes. He wanted to go home. Not to the apartment where he lived, but to his house where Lucille and he had lived. Where they had made a home together.

You can't go home again. Root wasn't sure who'd said it, but he knew it was true. He focused on Socorro. "Why the hell would anyone eat part of a plant?" he asked.

"I've been thinking about that," Socorro said. "According to the autopsy, it didn't look like Weber had dinner at home, which is why he was eating so much at the party. Lots of hors d'oeuvres. Maybe that's how he got it."

"Wait a minute. You think someone chopped up the plant and put it on one of those little crackers or something?"

"That's what I think."

Something Root had seen or heard earlier was coming back to him. He paused a moment to give it time to surface. It was something about plants. He rubbed his forehead, trying to force it out.

"What?" Socorro asked.

"Damn. My memory's going; I can't remember. Let me flip through the file, maybe that will help." Root went through the first of the evidence sheets, a listing of items collected at Happy Twosomes early Saturday morning. "I knew it! There were leaves in the trash at that video dating place."

"Better send 'em down and get them identified, I guess," Socorro said. "That'll tell us if we're right."

"Yeah, and we'd better check with someone who knows plants. Maybe someone in the Botany department at the University." If it could be accomplished on the phone, Root could save himself a trip out into the rain. "I never knew Meadow Saffron was poisonous. Did you?"

"I've never even heard of the stuff before."

Root felt a little better. Maybe he wasn't as far behind as he thought. "I looked it up, but I didn't find much. Has yellow flowers, blooms in the fall, right about now, and is not indigenous to Texas, but they bring it in for landscaping and such." He snapped his fingers. "I wonder if there was any in the garden at Happy Twosomes?"

"Well, I can't see someone carrying a plant around all night. It'd be a little conspicuous."

Socorro made it sound like someone had been toting an entire pot, but Root didn't think it had been that way. "All they'd have to have were a few bulbs stuck in their pocket or purse. Or leaves, or whatever part they used."

"Yeah, you're right. Oh, I got Martha Martinez calling the

guests—all three hundred and forty-two of them, so I'm not expecting instant results. If we get lucky, one of them saw someone go into that private lounge. Or, maybe pulling up one of the plants. "

"Maybe," Root said. "Or maybe the murderer chopped it up at home, you know, in one of those Cuisinart things." Root had given his wife a Cuisinart for her birthday just before they'd separated.

He thought about calling Lucille, but vetoed the idea. He was too busy to see her and that would only make her more sure that she'd done the right thing by filing for divorce. She was already pretty sure about it.

"You okay?" Socorro asked.

"Fine," Root said. "We'd better get moving on this. We're supposed to meet with the Case Agent in half an hour."

And, as they both knew, Senior Sergeant Jacobs, the agent on the Weber case, liked to see progress.

CASSIE STARTED TO LEAVE the station, but the traffic and rain on the street sent her back inside. With the odd hours she worked, she wasn't used to that kind of snarl on the roads. If she hung around for half an hour she could miss the worst of it.

She sat down at the receptionist's desk, watching the rain slide down the big front window. Outside was a dark and lonely twilight. Perhaps she should call Jenny to let her know she'd be late. She reached for the phone and saw a Happy Twosomes business card. It was in mauve. *Mauve and murder,* Cassie thought with a shudder.

She should call Greg to thank him for coming to Jenny's rescue. And, she could tell him what she knew about staying out of the media.

She dialed the number, half expecting to hear taps after Mandy's dire predictions. Instead she got a receptionist who sounded as professionally elegant as Mandy did.

"Happy Twosomes. May I help you?"

"Yes. This is Cass Ferris and I was calling for Greg Mayhew. Is he available?"

Another phone chimed in the background. "I'm sorry, will you hold a minute?"

"Sure."

Cassie was put on hold and another professional voice, this one tape-recorded, began extolling the virtues of Happy Twosomes.

"...all that, you can enroll in classes to help you make the most of your life.

"First, there's Single and Serene: Yoga and meditation to help you deal with stress.

"Single and Savvy is all about financial planning for your future.

"Single and Sleek is low impact aerobics to streamline your body.

"And don't forget Single and Self Confident. Just the class to prepare you to start a relationship. You'll learn that, whether you've been dating or not, you're pretty terrific. You—"

The receptionist was back. "Sorry. Who were you calling for?"

"Greg Mayhew."

"He's teaching a class right now."

"A class?" Cassie said. "Greg teaches the classes I heard about on your tape?"

"What tape? Oh, the on-hold tape. I forgot. No, he doesn't

teach all of them—just Single and Self Confident. He's a psychologist." The receptionist waited until a sharp crack of thunder subsided, then said, "Maybe someone else could help you. If you just want to sign up for a membership—"

"No, no. That wasn't why I called."

"But isn't this the Cass Woman from Y-96? I recognized your voice. Did they tell you that you get a complimentary membership?"

"Yes, but no."

"Are you sure? I could take your app over the phone, then you could come in to do your tape."

"Thank you. No."

Cassie didn't need someone to date. Although, she had to admit that there were times, like now with the rain and the cold, or when the police had come to the house, that she wanted someone to talk to. Maybe even someone to hold her. But men didn't mix with single parenthood.

She looked at the rain sliding down the glass doors.

She felt as if there was a hollow in her body. Some blank space that had just been pointed out; like a dent in her car or a spot on the wallpaper that she'd known was there, but had been able to ignore.

Cassie ignored it one more time. "What time will Greg be finished?"

"Six-thirty. Oh, wait, can you hold again?" This time she didn't wait for an answer.

Another voice picked up the phone within seconds. "Hello? Were you being helped?"

It was a woman's voice and Cassie knew it, although it took a moment to register. "Rachel? Is that you?" Rachel answering the phone at Happy Twosomes?

"Yes. Cassie? How are you doing?"

"Fine. How about you?"

"I'm okay," Rachel said. "A little shaky. The police already called me on my cell phone and asked for a formal statement. Can you believe that? They want me to come to the police station tomorrow at two o'clock. When are you making your statement?"

"I don't know. I don't think I have to do one. They came by the house on Saturday," Cassie said. "So what are you doing at Happy Twosomes? You aren't working there?"

"Oh, no. But the phone was ringing and I can't stand an unanswered phone. I just stopped by to talk to Greg. Get the results of the promotion; you know." Her smile could be heard in her voice. "And it was very successful. He's happy."

"Well, that's good. I guess I can go home with a clear conscience."

Rachel said, "Sure. Maybe tomorrow will be a better day."

"Right," Cassie said, wishing she believed it.

TEN

REGARDLESS OF THE CRISES that befell Y-96, and regardless of how ineffectual Bill might be in some areas, at least you could always count on him to remain calm. According to him, there was no reason not to, because, as he explained it: panic caused problems.

Even now, with his morning man dead and the police worrying everyone with their interminable questions, he was cool. If Cassie hadn't known better she might have suspected he didn't understand the situation, but Bill was exceedingly intelligent. With an IQ in the genius range, he had been one of the "Brilliant Children," as he had once explained. At age nine he had been taken away from classes with his friends and put in a special school for the mentally gifted. At the time he'd been hurt and angry with his parents and teachers. Over the years he had come to appreciate his gift, even if he was never sure their decision had been a good one.

Sitting around the glass conference table in his hunter green and gray office with Bill and Walter Kraley, Cassie realized that Bill's intelligence was a defense that was serving him well. The three of them had listened to the first half of Roger's tribute and Bill had analyzed the show without attaching it to Roger, or Roger's death.

The tribute wasn't finished, but Cassie was pleased with it

so far. She now realized it was for the living. The listeners who'd felt as if Roger were a friend. And, of course, for Walter.

Walter was nodding his gray head, his usually sharp eyes almost closed. The power that radiated off him seemed dim, like a light that was losing its source of energy.

"You've done a nice job with this, Cassie," he said. "I like the music you've selected, too. I like using it to help tell a story."

"Thanks. I've got the rest of the show worked out, including the songs we'll play." She slid a yellow tablet toward him. "If you've got any suggestions, I can make changes."

"No, that's fine. I trust you."

Bill nodded his agreement. "I'm glad you're doing this. Very nice job."

"Then I'll just finish it up. Would you like a copy of it?" she asked Walter. "I thought we might send a dub to Roger's daughters."

"That's a nice thought," Walter said. "I don't know if they'll be able to listen to it right away, but it will be something of Roger that they can hold on to. Send two copies. One to each of the girls."

"Certainly."

Walter nodded and moved on, addressing his question to Bill. "What about the police? Have you heard anything?"

"Not really," Bill said. "They've talked with all of the staff who were at the promotion. I gave them a formal statement last night, and I think Scott has an appointment with them sometime today. Unfortunately they just ask questions, they aren't giving out much information."

"Why the hell not?" Walter demanded, a touch of his fire

coming back. "This is not some goddamn game. A man was murdered. We have a right to know how their investigation is going."

"I realize that," Bill said, "but they consider us either witnesses or suspects. I'm not sure which."

Bill's words added credence to the thoughts Cassie had been having. As unrealistic as it was to her, they were suspects in the eyes of the police.

"It seems they want to find out about Roger's friends." He hesitated. "And his enemies."

"Preposterous," Walter said. "Roger was a brilliant man. A virtuoso at what he did. People like that step on toes, we all know that, but they can be forgiven their idiosyncrasies. Or should be. Only a terribly petty person would hold Roger's moods against him."

It was easy for Walter to feel that way, since he hadn't been subjected to Roger's moods.

Bill straightened. "I'm sure the police will tell us everything in their own good time."

"Have you figured out why Roger wanted to see you this weekend?" Walter asked.

"No," Bill said. "But, something was up."

Walter nodded. "I was in meetings all day Thursday and Friday, but my secretary said Roger was very agitated. He told her it was urgent that he talk with me Saturday. I made a special trip because of it." Walter slammed the palm of his hand on the glass table. "Damn! If only Roger had talked to us, he might not have died." He rubbed a veined hand across his brow, ruffling his gray eyebrows. He seemed to lose strength. "Or maybe not. I suppose it's one of those things we'll never know. I just wish there were something I could do, something to help the police."

Cassie stood up. "I'd better get back to work."

"Of course," Walter said.

Bill stood also, went to the credenza behind his desk and popped the CD out of the machine. "Do you need this?" Bill asked.

"No," Cassie said. "I've got the original." She shook hands with Walter, a polite custom that he'd instituted with his employees years before. "Thanks again, Walter."

"You're welcome, Cassie."

"You, too, Bill. And since you're both here," she said, "I wanted you to know that I'd like to stay on the morning show."

Without a program director on staff, Walter and Bill would be making the decision about the vacancy Roger had left. And they had to do it quickly.

Walter nodded and said, "Cassie, we assumed you'd want to continue on the air, but with everything that's happened, we haven't come to any decisions." His eyes were hooded. There were two things Walter prided himself on: he kept his own counsel and he never promised what he didn't deliver. "Cassie, you've always worked hard and been loyal to the station, and, of course, you're doing a fine job with Roger's tribute. Friendship and loyalty are rare in this business, and believe me, we'll do the best we can for you."

"And thanks for making your wants known," Bill added.

Cassie forced herself to smile. "Well, thank you, then." She turned and left.

As Cassie walked downstairs she kept thinking about Walter's words. Friendship and loyalty.

They were nice words, but Walter and Bill didn't base decisions on words—they based decisions on numbers. Numbers that showed up in the ratings, numbers that could be counted toward the bottom line. Numbers with dollar signs preceding them. Cassie had no idea how they ranked her when it came to numbers.

As she passed the control room she could see Scott Delany doing his regular afternoon shift. His back was to her.

Scott twitched the mike closer, then a little to the right—a compulsive gesture—then started talking, his head bobbing as he spoke. Scott had not pretended any sorrow at Roger's death. His show was even wilder, more upbeat, than before. Scott was pitching for the morning drive slot with every word he spoke on the air.

He started some music, threw the mike switch closed, pulled off his headphones and spun around as if expecting applause. When he saw Cassie he flashed his dimples in a grin and gestured for her to come in.

"I'm hot stuff today!" Scott said, as Cassie closed the door behind her.

"Well, it's nice to know that someone's on a roll."

"Hey, you shouldn't be complaining," Scott said. "I heard you got a private audience with the king. I haven't even been able to make my pitch for the morning slot."

"It wasn't really a pitch; I just told Walter and Bill that I wanted to stay on the show," Cassie said.

"Oh, right. You were in there for an hour."

"They were listening to Roger's tribute."

"See, and that's another advantage you've got," Scott said, turning away from her and pulling commercials out of the rack. "You're getting lots of brownie points for that tribute. I wish they'd asked me to do it."

"So do I," Cassie said. "A week from now no one will remember the damn thing."

Scott was double checking the names of the commercials on the log. When he finished he looked at her. "Listen, Cassie, this here's a war. A fight to the death. Winner take all, and all that rot." Scott's tone was light, but he wasn't kidding.

"You know, Scott, we could pull together on this one. End the war and settle for a win-win."

For just a moment he looked embarrassed. "Thanks, Cassie, that's nice of you, but I don't work like you do. My style is different."

"I'm flexible. I can adjust some, if it means a better result."

"You don't understand." He leaned forward, earnestly. "You worked with Roger, and he was like, well, his humor was old-fashioned. Predictable. I'm not like that."

"So what are you like?" Cassie asked, her words coming out slowly.

"Hey, I'm like Chris Rock, or Robin Williams. You know, hot, wild. Totally today." He grinned. "Roger was more like Bob Hope. I mean, I guess that style of humor was okay, but it doesn't cut it anymore."

"You realize that our audience is hardly composed of teens? As an oldies station we appeal to adults."

Scott winked. "I'm adult. It's just new humor. Not your style."

"Seems to me," Cassie said, "that the ratings have been very good in morning drive. Better than in the afternoon." Her voice had a little tartness beneath the sweet.

"More people listen to the radio in the morning; it's just a fact of life."

Scott was like a puppy: obnoxious, offensive and able to get away with it because he was cute.

Cassie had taken all she could. "I have to get back to work." She started out, and at the door she stopped long enough to say, "But I do agree with you on one thing, Scott."

"Oh? What's that?"

"This is a fight to the death."

She saw his dimples flash in a grin as she saluted him and left the room.

So much for joining forces, Cassie thought.

At least there wouldn't be anything underhanded about the battle for morning drive. Not that Scott was bright enough to think of anything too devious.

And she really didn't want to face Scott every morning, anyway. His cute-obnoxious behavior wouldn't be any easier to stomach than Roger had been. She was amazed she'd put up with Roger as long as she had.

In the production room Mandy was waiting.

"Looking for me?" Cassie asked.

Mandy shook her head. "I'm just hiding out." She looked at Cassie more closely. "Are you okay? You look about the way I feel."

"I'm fine," Cassie said. She was tired and it was time to quit. "Why are you unhappy?"

"Because life is shit." Mandy pulled out a tall stool and sat on it, her whole body slumping. She put her elbows on the console to prop herself up. "Everyone hates the morning show without a live announcer, and all the advertisers we had scheduled to run tomorrow morning want to switch to Thursday morning. Unfortunately, we sold Thursday at a higher rate. I've got a few slots open, but not many, and Louisa in traffic is ready to kill me, because I keep moving commercials around." She rubbed her forehead. "The sales people are pissed because their clients are pissed, and I don't have anyone to blame but myself, because I'm the one who came up with the idea of the silent morning show."

"Is that all?"

"There's more, but I wouldn't want to burden you with the whole load." For a moment she looked like she might cry, then she smiled. "I've thought of hara-kiri but I don't have anything to wear to my funeral."

"I wish I could help, but it doesn't sound like there's much I can do," Cassie said. "Wait, maybe there is. What if I make room for a couple of extra minutes of commercials every hour during the tribute? We'd have to clear it with Walter and Bill—"

"I already asked them, and they said yes, but if it throws all your work off and makes you mad, I really will commit suicide."

"Save your suit," Cassie said, glancing at Mandy's creamy Armani. "It's not a problem." Cassie pulled out the cardboard box she'd been carrying around ever since Mandy had delivered it Saturday morning, and began stacking tapes in it. "I don't have to hit any special newscasts, or network stuff, so it's no problem. You've just made my job easier by eight minutes."

"Thank God I've done something right. Are you almost done with the show?"

"I'll finish up by noon tomorrow." She laid things carefully in the box.

"I don't think so. We've got Roger's memorial service tomorrow morning."

"I'm not going. It might throw me behind and I've got to get this show finished."

"Then you'll work all night, but you have to be at the service."

"Why?" Cassie asked.

"It's expected. You were Roger's sidekick. The press will be there and his listeners will show up. Not to mention Walter and Bill."

Cassie put the last of her things in the cardboard box. She didn't want to go to the memorial service. It was like some cheap publicity stunt, and she found it offensive. Regardless of whether or not she'd liked Roger, his death deserved a little more dignity. "The memorial service is not a performance."

"Sure it is. This is radio. Show biz, remember?"

"The lowest form of show business. Or does that award go to snake farms?"

"It was a close vote, but snake farms won," Mandy said. "The whole staff is leaving at nine-thirty; I've arranged for limos."

"I can't wait to see the bribe you've got planned for St. Peter."

Mandy began playing with knobs on the console. "Did you get a chance to talk with Greg yesterday?"

"No, he was busy teaching a class," Cassie said, picking up the box. "Let's go in my office; I'm sure someone else needs the production room."

"Okay." Mandy slid off the stool and followed Cassie down the hall. "So, you didn't talk with Greg. Did you become a member of Happy Twosomes?"

Cassie put the box on the floor behind her desk. "No. I don't date."

"Well, you should. You'll never meet anyone unless you

take some chances. You'll be an old maid and shrivel up like a prune and die. Nobody will even care."

"My daughters will care."

"They'll be married with kids of their own." Mandy let out an exasperated breath. "You drive me crazy! Don't you ever get bored with radio? Want something more in your life?"

"Of course I do, but I've got Jenny…"

"And she's got friends of her own, but she probably feels guilty every time she goes out because you're sitting at home alone. Cassie, you've got to give her some room to breathe. Room to live."

Cassie didn't have a response; she was afraid Mandy was right.

"Well?" Mandy demanded.

"I don't know."

"I do. Give the kid a break and make some friends of your own before Jenny moves out and gets her own apartment. It could happen, you know. It will someday, because college kids do that."

Cassie wondered why women without children seemed to understand teenagers so much better than parents did. Maybe because they still identified with youth, instead of the parental role. "I'll think about it."

"Don't think about it, just do it." Mandy picked up the receiver of the phone and held it out to Cassie. "Here, call Happy Twosomes and tell them that you want to join."

"I'll think about that, too."

"Enough thinking. Call. Better yet, I'll call for you." She reached for the phone but Cassie stopped her.

"Don't," Cassie said. "This is not the right time. Do you realize that I may not have a job in a week?"

"What does that have to do with anything?"

"A lot! Life is serious right now. There's a murder investigation going on, and I may not have a job, and you're playing like life is a dating game."

"That's your problem, Cassie." Mandy leaned forward and spoke earnestly. "There are always going to be serious things. There's always a war somewhere. There are famines and floods, and death all the time. And yes, they're important, but so are laughter and fun. Every bit as important. And if you don't laugh, then you're missing life. You're not having fun."

"I laugh; I just don't date."

"Dating is part of life, too. It leads to love, and that's what life is all about, you know? And what about sex?"

"I think I remember the word. Oh, wait," Cassie said. "I've got it. Weren't the instructions something like 'Insert prong A into slot B?'"

"If that's all you know, Brad must have been some kind of lousy lover. Either that, or you need a refresher course."

"Well, when they offer it at the community college, I promise to go."

"Cassie," Mandy said seriously. "What we're talking about is what makes for a rich full life. The kind that you don't have."

Cassie was being pummeled into what Mandy would no doubt consider "right thinking." And the hell of it was that Cassie agreed in part.

"I'd better go home," Cassie said, reaching under her desk for her purse. "I'm starting to think you might be right."

Mandy stood up. "I am. And when you see those two policemen, take a good look at that Sergeant Root. He reminds me of a thirty-something Clint Eastwood."

"I guess they don't need to talk to me. They haven't been around since Saturday."

"That's weird. Especially because of the plants."

Cassie felt a ripple of chill. "What plants?"

"They asked me all about plants and I don't know anything about them, except how to make them turn brown. And they kept asking who knew about plants, and since you and Jenny are such experts, and since Jenny was even talking about them that night at Happy Twosomes…" Mandy's voice trailed off.

"Plants? They're asking about plants?"

Cassie wasn't really an expert on plants, although she probably knew more than most people. It was her mother, whom she affectionately called the Gypsy Witch, who was the expert. An herbalist. And Jenny had loved the idea of plants that cure. At age five she'd spent more time in the garden with her grandmother than she had in kindergarten. She was majoring in botany, and already had dried packages of herbs stashed in the garage.

But Jenny's interest went beyond just herbs. She could quote chapter and verse about almost any plant. Plants that cure. Plants that kill.

"The police haven't called me," Cassie said.

"Oh, well, maybe it's not important. I wouldn't worry about it."

Worry? "No, no. Of course not."

ELEVEN

CASSIE WAS WORRIED. Everyone who'd been at the Happy Twosomes party had talked to the police at least twice, and they'd all made formal statements. Not only that, the police were intent on plants, so why didn't they just come right out and ask her about them? Somehow the absence of the police was more ominous than their presence.

She had been pacing her living room, now she sat on the couch and Sly immediately jumped into her lap. Stroking his black fur soothed her.

She certainly didn't think the police suspected her or Jenny of Roger's murder; it would just be easier if the police let them make a statement and get it over with. She didn't want it dragging out. Brad would use the murder investigation as an excuse to stall Beth's visit, which was only a month away. He had put Cassie off in the past even without the police.

"Sorry, Cassie, but Beth has to get braces and the only time we could schedule appointments was during spring break. I know you understand the importance of that."

"Sorry, Cass, but Beth's grades have slipped a little and I've engaged a tutor. I know you wouldn't want her school work to suffer."

"Sorry, Cassie, but we're going skiing for Christmas and Beth wants to come with us. We promised her she could. I know you wouldn't want to deprive her."

Cassie could already hear Brad explaining patiently why Beth wouldn't be coming to Austin for Thanksgiving. "Sorry, Cassie, but you can't really expect me to let her fly out there with a murder investigation going on. In fact, it would be better if Jenny came out here. At least for a while. I know you see the wisdom in that."

Even though Cassie had grown accustomed to Beth's everyday absence, she counted on the twice-yearly visits. And there were still moments of intense pain at the loss of Beth. It didn't take a lot to bring them on—the sound of a little girl laughing, a card from Beth, and sometimes just a television commercial would be enough to move Cassie to tears.

She wanted so much to have Beth with her.

The worst of it was that Cassie suspected Brad wasn't just being cruel; he really believed she wasn't good for her own daughters. She wished she could make him see that it had been the divorce that had made her act so crazy.

She jumped up from the couch, almost knocking Sly to the floor.

That was over, long dead and past.

She went to the kitchen window, and looked out at the late afternoon sunshine. There was a beige Chevy on the corner, one she'd never seen before, and for just a moment the old paranoia came back. It could be someone Brad had hired to watch her. No one was in the car, but as she had good reason to know, private detectives were like termites, totally hidden while they gnawed away at the foundation of your life.

The front door slammed. "Mom? I'm home."

"Hi. I'm in here."

Jenny came in, dropping her knapsack on the table and pulling her denim jacket off in one continuous movement. "Is there any food?" She looked at Cassie. "You look like something's wrong."

"Well, not really wrong," she said. "I just found out something and I've been puzzling over it."

Jenny began foraging through the refrigerator. "So, what's the deal?"

Cassie watched as Jenny took out an apple, frowned at it and put it back. "Mandy told me that you were talking about plants the night Roger died. At Happy Twosomes."

"I'm always talking about them. So, why is that important?"

"Because it seems the police are asking about plants."

Jenny's hand, holding a cluster of grapes, stopped halfway to her mouth. "The police? Why?"

"I don't know. Maybe Roger died from a poisonous plant."

"And right after I was telling everyone about them that night," Jenny said. "We were all out on the patio. Weird."

"I'm sure it's nothing," Cassie said. "I just wanted you to be prepared. At some point, they'll probably want to talk to us about it."

"They'll want to get information? Like expert witnesses or whatever they call them?"

"No," Cassie said slowly. "I think more as plain witnesses. Because you and I were there, and we know about plants. What I can't figure out is why—"

Jenny wasn't listening. "It doesn't look good, does it? I hated Roger, and I threw a drink on him. But why would I tell everyone about poisonous plants if I were going to use one to kill him? That doesn't seem very bright."

"Jenny, let's not worry about it—"

"Maybe the police think I told the others because I wanted

to throw suspicion on them." She dropped the grapes to the counter and began to walk around the small kitchen. "Like I wanted to—"

"Jenny! For God's sake, would you knock it off?" Cassie looked at the counter. "Eat your grapes."

"I'm not hungry anymore. When are the police coming?"

"I don't know. Maybe they're not. You're making a big deal out of nothing." *Of course she is,* Cassie thought. *I taught her to be that way.* "Look, let's go for a walk; I could use some exercise."

"But what if the police come while we're gone?"

"Then they'll come back." She took Jenny by the shoulders and propelled her out of the kitchen. "Hurry up, change your shoes."

"I don't know…"

"Get moving."

Cassie hurried into her bedroom and pulled off her pants and shoes. A walk would do them both good. Some fresh air to clear the mind and clean away the worries.

She took her running shorts out of a drawer and then tossed them back. Just in case the police did show up, she didn't want to look quite that casual; it would leave her too little dignity. Instead she dressed quickly in white pleated shorts and a pink T-shirt.

"Jenny? Are you ready?" she called out, heading for the living room.

Jenny appeared. "Ready. Where should we go? The running path at Town Lake?"

"No, we'll just walk around the neighborhood." They locked the doors and Cassie began a stretch on the front porch.

"Let's be daring and run first," Jenny said. "Come on."

"Fine."

They started off at a quick pace. As they passed the beige Chevy, a teenage girl with spandex shorts and a tennis top was getting into it. Not a detective.

There was almost no traffic; the neighborhood was empty except for an older man watering a bed of bronze and yellow mums. It seemed as if everyone was tired of summer and had taken refuge inside their air-conditioned houses. They were nice houses, not large, but well kept, most of wood or brick, or a combination. The lawns of thick carpet grass were still green and while the flowers of summer were gone, a few mums were appearing.

At the corner they stopped for a faded green car that slid by so closely Cassie could almost reach out and touch the heavyset man who was driving. He was oblivious to them, his concentration apparently on the wheel he was turning in his pudgy hands.

Pudgy hands. Cassie thought of pudgy hands sliding something else. Roger. Roger putting something in his briefcase that Friday morning before he died. Hiding something?

"Mom? We can cross now."

"Right." They started across the street, but Cassie was focused on the scene in her mind. That morning Roger had been behaving strangely. And he'd lied about being in the bathroom. Cassie knew, she'd looked.

When a jock was on the air he, or she, didn't have the luxury of waiting in line for a bathroom. If the one of the proper gender was busy you merely knocked on the door of the other one and waited a few seconds before going in. Cassie had used the men's room that morning, and Roger had certainly not been inside.

So where had he been? Upstairs? And what had he so carefully kept from her view?

Then she remembered Walter saying, "If only he'd talked to us, he might not have died." Roger was killed to prevent him from telling them something?

Something that he'd found upstairs at Y-96? Something he'd hidden from Cassie?

But what was worth killing for?

THE SMALL, BARE soundproofed room at the police station was designed for privacy, and when necessary, for intimidation. It was working. A tiny line of sweat beads had broken out on Scott Delany's smooth upper lip. Or maybe the disk jockey didn't like the lights and camera. Root didn't care what was making the kid uncomfortable, he just knew that on some level he was glad.

Root had found that most of the people from Y-96 were just like everyone else. They had their quirks, but they were regular folks. Except Delany. Delany was the epitome of cool, as in with-it, making Root feel very out of it. Like a guy past his prime and missing the joke.

"Now, Mr. Delany," Root went on, "did you ever see Weber outside of work?"

"Only if we both had to go to a station promotion. The guy didn't like people much."

"And did you like him?"

"He was okay," Delany said. His voice sounded a little high.

Root leaned forward. "Are you saying that you got along well with Roger Weber? Didn't mind his sarcasm?"

"What sarcasm?"

"He called you 'The World's Prettiest Disk Jockey.' That didn't bother you?"

Delany frowned for just a brief instant, then shrugged it away. "He was jealous; a lot of people are. So what? I was on the air in the afternoon and he usually left by noon. I hardly ever saw the guy."

Root straightened up, letting Delany get away with what sounded like a lie.

Socorro took over. "Now tell us again about the evening at Happy Twosomes, Friday night," he said.

"Happy Twosomes was great. They signed up a lot of members and everyone had a great time."

Root could feel his face tightening. He didn't like being fed pablum by an infant. "*Everyone* had a great time?"

"Well, except for Roger, I guess."

Root and Socorro were deliberately silent, waiting for Delany's nonchalance to disappear. When it finally did, it was Root who said, "Go back to your first encounter with the staff. Tell us again what happened the first time you went out on the patio."

Scott Delany started to scowl and changed his mind. "Bill, Mandy, Rachel and Jenny Ferris were out there together. Rachel had that look on her face like she gets when she's determined to get her own way. Like she's going to start bossing someone around. Mandy and Bill were listening to Jenny who was going on about plants."

"Do you know who started the conversation about plants?" Socorro asked.

"No." He took a moment to weigh his answer. "They were already talking when I walked up. Besides, you don't have to say anything to get Jenny going. She's obsessed. A couple of weeks ago she was at the station, by Irma Belton's desk, babbling about how one of the plants in the office was poisonous."

Now it was Socorro who was leaning forward. He's too anxious, Root thought, as his partner asked, "What plant?"

"I don't know. Something with big leaves and some yellow on it." They waited him out. "It started with a D, I think. Dif something."

"Dieffenbachia?" Root asked.

A big smile with a flash of dimples. "Yeah, that's the name."

"What other plants did she talk about at Happy Twosomes?" Root asked.

"Mistletoe. She said it's poisonous, too."

"Any others?"

"I can't remember."

"Try."

He took his time, twisting his face like he was really working at it. Root wondered how much of that was for show.

After a while Delany said, "I don't remember. Sorry. But you could ask Jenny."

That was enough about plants for now. No need to tip their hand. They'd found leaves in the trash at the club, which had been confirmed as Meadow Saffron. After some intense searching they'd actually discovered the barren spot on the Happy Twosomes patio that the plant had come from.

"Okay," Root said, "you were in the patio, you talked to Jennifer Ferris. Then what happened?"

"Rachel sent Jenny back to work and they both left."

"Did you discuss Roger Weber on the patio, or did he come out there?"

"He didn't show up, but somebody said he was sick and they'd better make sure Cass knew about it so she could do the call-ins. I think that was Mandy. No, maybe Rachel. I decided to mingle."

"Where exactly did you mingle, and where was the rest of the group?"

"The others stayed on the patio and I went and danced for about ten, fifteen minutes. I saw Bill once. He wasn't dancing, just walking through the ballroom."

"What time?"

"I don't know."

"Try to remember," Socorro said. "A close approximation will help."

"I guess around 6:15."

"You're sure it was six-fifteen?"

"Yeah. Six-fifteen."

The too easy answer made the hair on the back of Root's neck twitch. "Did you see anyone else?" he asked.

"Yeah. Rachel. She told me to go upstairs and make a video tape, so I did. You know they put new members on video, so that's what I did."

Root felt better at that—Scott Delany had signed up for video dating. "And when was that?" he asked.

"That was a little later, maybe 6:30, maybe later. I went upstairs and stopped in the lounge for a fresh drink, and that's when I saw Roger."

"What was he doing?"

"Eating hors d'oeuvres."

"Tell us about the hors d'oeuvres."

"Well, there was only one tray left with anything on it. They were pretty small trays. The cheese things that I'd tried before were all gone and I didn't recognize anything else. Weird stuff."

"What color?"

"I don't know. One looked like a little fish. And one looked like little beads; it was red. Roger finished them all up."

"Tell me about the others."

His look held both disbelief and disgust. "Orange. Like pimento cheese. I don't like to watch people eat. At least not guys."

"Fine. So tell us everything that happened.

The sweat on Delany's lip was more visible now. Root wondered why he didn't wipe it away. Maybe he didn't think he sweated.

"Well, I went in and Roger was on the couch with a drink. He had a tray beside him. I said 'hi,' and he said 'hi,' and I fixed my drink. We didn't talk because he was eating and I was busy. As soon as I finished pouring my drink and was getting ready to leave, I noticed that he turned a funny color and I asked if he was okay. That's when he said his stomach was bothering him because he hadn't eaten lunch or dinner. I told him to finish up the food on the tray, and he said that was a good idea." He paused. "Then I left."

"That was all that was said?" Root asked.

"That was it."

"Did you see anyone near the lounge that you knew?" So far, of the nearly one hundred and fifty guests who'd been phoned, only four had seen anyone go into or come out of that small room. Three had seen Weber, one had seen Scott Delany. They had been vague on the times. Root added, "Anyone else on the Y-96 staff?"

"No. There were a bunch of people in that other room,

across the hall. You know, looking at books and things, but I didn't go in."

"Then how do you know what they were doing?"

Delany looked surprised again, perhaps that anyone would dare question him.

The disk jockey repositioned himself in the chair. "Well, I stuck my head inside, but I didn't recognize anyone, so I went next door and did my video with the owner. Greg. Then I went back downstairs and danced some more until I left."

The door opened and a uniformed cop stepped in. One of the new guys, Root didn't remember his name. "Root? Socorro? You've got someone outside."

"Thanks," Socorro said as the officer left. He looked at Root. "Why don't you handle the other one? I'll stay here."

"Fine."

MAYHEW SEEMED as comfortable as if the two of them were having a couple of beers. Root had been asking questions for over ten minutes and Mayhew just kept answering.

Root didn't trust anyone who was that relaxed.

"So tell me about the caterers," Root said.

"We had a professional firm do all the catering. Parties To Go."

"And who put the food in the staff lounge upstairs?"

"They did, but I'm the one who told them to," Mayhew said. "I had them take two of the trays of food there."

"Who replenished them?"

"No one. With everything that was going on, we simply forgot." Mayhew shook his head as if that whole evening had gotten away from him. "Luckily most of the staff, Happy

Twosomes' and Y-96's, spent their time downstairs with the guests."

"How much time did you spend in the staff lounge?"

"None," Mayhew said. "I was too busy. I worked the entire evening in the taping room. After people started arriving, around, I guess five-fifteen, I couldn't get away. I only took two breaks. I went downstairs at about 6:30, and then I got Elise to take my place for about fifteen minutes a little after ten."

"And what did you see at 6:30 when you went downstairs?"

Root had already asked that question twice, once the morning after the party, and once again on Sunday. Now he wanted to see if the story changed.

Mayhew went through his telling of the argument, making it concise and colorless. It was the exact same story Root had heard before from two other people.

Root accepted it with a nod. "What did Cassie Ferris do? How did she react?" He couldn't get a handle on Cassie Ferris.

"She was upset about her daughter. Especially since Jenny had disappeared."

"And then?"

"Mrs. Ferris went to look for her daughter and I went back upstairs to the taping room."

"When did you first meet Mrs. Ferris?"

"That evening around five." Mayhew's face remained impassive. Maybe he hadn't noticed that she was attractive.

"Have you talked with her since?"

"No."

Root moved on. "Had you ever met Roger Weber before that evening?" he asked.

"Yes."

Through years of experience, Root held his face placid so the surprise wouldn't show. "Tell me about that."

"It was back when I was in school. I worked part-time in a radio station outside of Chicago. Roger Weber was the morning drive personality. Since I worked evenings on the weekends, I only spoke to him a few times before he got a better offer and moved on."

"You were in radio?"

"I was still in school at the time, the University of Illinois, and I was living with my father who was a professor. Even though that kept tuition down my father thought that I should have a job like most of the other students."

"Did you like working?" Root asked.

"Yeah, I did." Mayhew smiled. "It made me one of the guys; I wasn't in a fraternity and all my friends worked. That was important to me, especially since my father was a professor. I guess I didn't want anyone to think I was different."

"And that's when you met Weber?"

"Right. Like I said, I didn't see him very often; even though we were about the same age, our status at the station was completely different. Roger was already married, already doing morning drive and that made him seem older. More mature. I was just the part-time weekend jock."

"How did you feel about that?"

"Truthfully, I didn't think about it all."

Root keyed into the word truthfully. Usually when a witness said something like that you knew they were lying, although in this case, he wasn't sure. Mayhew was awfully casual about it.

"You didn't resent that Weber was more important?"

"No." Mayhew leaned forward a little and laughed. "Maybe because my friends were so impressed that I worked in a radio station. They didn't know that the morning guy was more important."

"Did you ever have any disagreements with Weber?"

Mayhew shook his head. "No. I rarely saw him. In fact, the only time that I really remember seeing him, he seemed pretty mellow. Self-assured. It was during a staff meeting, and then Weber left a week or so later."

Root got up and moved behind his chair. With his hands resting against the back of it, he leaned forward and asked, "So, you never saw him after that?"

"Not until I saw him standing there by Jenny Ferris."

"He didn't come in and introduce himself?"

"No. Rachel told me that he'd arrived, but he wasn't with her. I was busy taping new members, so I didn't think much about it."

"Did you know when you hired him to come to Happy Twosomes that you knew Roger Weber?"

Mayhew shook his head. "No, Rachel handled all of that. I'd heard him on the air, of course, and I remembered the name, but I didn't know it was the same Roger Weber. Then when I saw him I recognized him."

"So it was Rachel Sankey who hired him to come out that night?"

"Yes. She said that if we were going to spend all that money on the promotion we needed to have the top Y-96 talent. It was also her idea to invite the rest of the staff," Mayhew said. Mayhew was just too damn open and Root didn't like it. Lucille always said Root would suspect his grandmother if she were too open; maybe Lucille was right. Or maybe that was why he was a good cop.

TWELVE

ROGER'S MEMORIAL SERVICE was quietly dignified and in Cassie's mind, slightly off key. At the foot of the altar was a table covered in starched white linen. On it flowers surrounded Roger's picture. Hs body was already being flown to Chicago for the real funeral to be held the following morning.

During the Catholic Mass those gathered in the church stood, knelt and sat, but rarely at the same time. Even the priest seemed unsure of himself, perhaps because he'd never heard of Roger Wonderful Weber. Walter, who delivered the eulogy, did appear focused on Roger and Roger's death; the pain of it was apparent.

Cassie wondered if the listeners who'd shown up were disappointed. Instead of some zany send-off for Roger, they were merely seeing a solemn ritual that had been repeated for centuries for farmers and disk jockeys alike.

She gave up trying to follow the service and as she did her real feelings rose up, surprising her. She felt like crying. Not for Roger, but for his daughters, and Walter. The people he was leaving behind, the ones who were hurt most by his death. She began saying her private prayers, although they were muddled, mixed with requests for Jenny and Beth as much as for Roger and his family.

As soon as the final benediction had been offered, Cassie filed out with the others and tensed when she spotted Root and Socorro in one of the pews. They nodded at her, and followed her progress through the church.

Outside she felt better. Mandy's four hired limousines were lined up along the curb waiting to take the staff back to the station, but it wasn't the limousines. It was the sunshine and the normalcy of a morning outdoors that boosted her spirits.

"You ready?" Mandy asked, tapping Cassie on the arm.

"What? Oh. Sure."

"Are you doing okay?"

"Of course. And you?" Cassie asked as Mandy hustled her toward a waiting limo.

"I'm fine. Fine."

Mandy didn't look fine. Her normally clear blue eyes were tinged with red as if she had been crying.

As they neared the limo Cassie wondered if this was the one that had ferried Roger to Happy Twosomes Friday night. Top Class Limousines had a trade with Y-96; they received advertising in return for providing cars for special functions. To her knowledge, this was the first time the station had ever used Top Class for a funeral.

As the driver opened the door for them, Walter Kraley came hurrying over. He looked better than he had earlier. Stronger. In fact, he looked annoyed, a healthy sign.

"I can't abide standing around in front of churches!" Walter said as he stopped beside Cassie. "My mother was the world's worst for talking to everyone in the congregation after the service. I spent half my childhood sweating in some uncomfortable damn suit. This time I've got an excuse to leave, I've got to get to the airport."

"You're flying out?" Mandy asked.

"I have to get back to Chicago for Roger's funeral service. I just wanted to say goodbye and tell you what I've decided to do."

"What is that?" Mandy asked.

"I'm offering a twenty-five thousand dollar reward for evidence that leads to Roger's killer. And a conviction."

Mandy whistled softly. "That's a lot of money."

Cassie noticed the two policemen come out of the church, look around, then thread their way through the mourners to get into a fairly new Mazda parked behind the limousines. After they had driven off she turned back to the conversation.

Walter was saying, "I think the police have been slow and inefficient, but this should help."

"Then you've talked with the police lately?" Cassie asked.

"Yes, and even after I offered the reward," he said with a snort, "they wouldn't tell me anything."

Cassie asked, "Do they know that Roger wanted to talk to you before he died?"

"Of course, but they didn't seem interested." His green eyes focused hard on her. "You look like you've got something on your mind, Cass. Just say it straight out, whatever it is."

Mandy excused herself on the pretext of needing to talk to Rachel.

"I remembered something," Cassie began. She told Walter about Roger's odd behavior the Friday morning before he'd died and then asked, "Do the police have Roger's briefcase?"

"Not as far as I know. I can have Ruth check the list of things they took. Whatever Roger had might be evidence of something wrong at Y-96. He was so insistent on talking with me."

"That's what I thought."

Walter let out a long sigh. "I still can't believe it happened. That Roger is…" He swallowed hard before he could even say the word. "Dead." He looked old and tired again.

"I'm sorry, Walter."

"Thank you." He wiped his mouth with a handkerchief, perhaps to hide the tremble in his lips. She thought about touching his arm, or hugging him, but she held back. The set of his shoulders was still rigid; it didn't invite sympathy.

Mandy reappeared beside them. "Are we ready to go?"

"Not yet," Walter said. "I need something from Cassie." He turned his eyes to her, and there was fire in them, green fire, as if created by some voodoo magic. "I want you to talk with the police in person and make sure they understand how important that briefcase is."

Before Cassie could remind him that she was still working on Roger's tribute, Bill Bankston came striding up. "I'll ride to the airport with you, Walter," he said. "We need to go over a few last minute things." Bill was carrying his briefcase even at the funeral. Surely he'd left it in the limo during the service.

"Fine," Walter said. "Cassie, Mandy, I'll be back next week sometime." They shook hands and then he reached into his pocket and pulled out a set of keys. They were Roger's. "Here, Cass, take these. Give them to the police."

Her fingers tingled as she touched them. She'd seen them so often in Roger's hand or lying on his desk.

Walter didn't wait for her response, instead he hurried off to the waiting limo with Bill.

"You think Roger's briefcase is important?" Mandy asked, as she followed Cassie into their own car.

"Maybe."

"I wish I could care."

Cassie was going to ask what ~~that meant, but~~ Mandy leaned back against the dark blue velvet seat and closed her eyes.

"SO, WHAT DO YOU think?" Root asked.

Socorro glanced down at the stack of videotapes they'd just reviewed and shook his head. "I think that what we have here is a real who-dunnit."

Root shuddered. Even though they used the term around the station, he'd once made the mistake of saying it off the record to a reporter. The next thing he knew he'd been quoted in the *Austin American Statesman*. He'd caught hell for it, too.

"Yeah, well, pick one of them," Root said. "Any one. How about that little redhead, Rachel Sankey? What did you think of her statement?"

Socorro frowned. "Well, she's hiding something, but I'll be damned if I know what. I asked her every question I could think of and she answered straight enough...still..."

"That's what I thought, too. It had something to do with Happy Twosomes. Or was it the owner, that Mayhew guy?" Root couldn't put his finger on it, but there had been nerves beyond the normal. "Let's look at her tape again. At least the first part."

Socorro slipped the cassette into the VCR and waited until there was a clear picture of Rachel Sankey.

"Fast forward it a little," Root said.

Socorro did, allowing them a speeded up view. Although they couldn't hear her words, they could see Rachel's mouth moving and her head tilting.

"Notice how she tips her head up to the right before she answers?" Root asked.

"Yeah." He hit the play button and the tape slowed to normal speed.

Rachel was saying, "I was all over Happy Twosomes that night. I stayed at the front desk for a while making sure that Jenny Ferris knew what she was doing. She's a nice kid and I didn't want to abandon her. Then I just seemed to be running everywhere." She smiled and again tilted her head to the right. "You know how it is. I sold them the advertising, so I felt responsible for everything working."

She was wearing a suit on the tape, an expensive one in black and white with a blouse that looked like silk. A cameo was pinned to the jacket. Lucille had a cameo pin, too, only not that large. Lucille had inherited hers from her mother.

Socorro's voice came from off-camera. "Did you spend much time in the private lounge that was being used for the staff?"

"Oh, no. I didn't have time," Sankey said. "I started to go in there once and I poked my head in the door…" Head tip. "But I saw Roger Weber, so I left."

"What time was that?"

When she bobbed her head this time, Root could see the clip that held her hair at the back of her neck. "I couldn't even guess. It seemed like the middle of the party, but that could be any where from six to eight."

"You didn't have any conversation with Roger Weber during the Happy Twosomes' party?"

Again her head tilted up to the right. "No, I didn't."

"I understand that you dated Roger Weber."

Her face turned pink, then white, and her lips formed a

straight, angry line. Finally she said, "I went out with him exactly twice. He'd only been in Austin a couple of months when he separated from his wife, and I felt sorry for him. It was over six months ago."

"Did he stop asking you out? Or did you quit saying 'yes'?"

"After a few dates, I realized he wasn't my type. I told him it would be wiser if we didn't see each other again."

"Why wasn't he your type?"

Her hesitation was brief. "My career is very important to me. It takes up most of my time and I don't have enough left to be a patient listener for Roger. Not at the office or after work."

"How did Weber take that?"

"He wasn't happy."

Socorro stopped the tape. "Seen enough?"

Root nodded. "She likes money, that's for sure. The jewelry, expensive suit, acrylic nails."

"Yeah, you'd know about that stuff, having a daughter; I don't."

Root didn't want to think about Angela now. He felt as if she were slipping out of his life and he didn't know how to prevent it. "But I don't see how killing Weber would get her any more money."

"How about fear as a motive?" Socorro suggested.

"Afraid enough to kill him?"

People did kill out of fear. Root just didn't figure that Weber had much to threaten Rachel with except public embarrassment. And while he'd gotten the distinct impression that Rachel Sankey was a lady who would fight for her dignity, he didn't think she would kill for it. "I don't know." He glanced at the black screen as if her image were still there. "Even though she didn't say much she made it clear what Weber had been like."

"Sounds like he hounded her at work and then called her at home with more of the same."

"And she didn't put up with it for long."

"Two weeks and he was out." Socorro picked up one of the tapes and waved it. "I don't like this other disk jockey. Scott Delany."

"Okay. Why?"

"I just don't like him. He's smug and cocky." Socorro put the tape back on the stack. "Hell, I wouldn't like him if I met him at a party. Not that he'd bother talking with me."

"Yeah, I don't think you're his type," Root said allowing his grin to show.

Socorro grinned, too. Then he said seriously, "I checked with Martinez on the phone brigade. With all the people they've talked to—they're up to about one seventy or so— only five saw Weber go into the private lounge, three saw Delany and no one mentioned anyone else."

"I wonder how come they remembered those two?"

"'Cuz Scott's so cute," Socorro said, poking his finger into his cheek to create a dimple. "It was women who spotted him."

Root smiled. "What about the times? Do they match up?"

"Vaguely, if you don't mind a half hour or so difference."

"Shit. Well, Weber wasn't cute, but they noticed him."

"Yeah, but he was the star attraction and the only glimpse the folks got of him was when he was going into the lounge. They were a little pissed off about it, too."

"And nobody saw anyone digging up a plant on the patio?"

"Nope, not so far," Socorro said.

"Well, then I think it's time to bring Cassie Ferris in," Root said. "And her daughter."

They'd been saving both of the Ferris women for last, until they could get a handle on the poisonous plants. After all the questioning they'd done there seemed to be only two people who had specific knowledge of plants. Cassie and Jenny Ferris.

While Root had investigated kids before, some of them a lot younger than Jenny Ferris, this time he was feeling protective. Maybe because his own teenage daughter was living with Lucille and he didn't get to see her every day.

Damn, he thought. The divorce was making him soft, making him care too much, and for the wrong people and the wrong reasons. He had a job to do and he wasn't getting it done as fast as he would have liked.

"Let's bring them in," Root said. "First the daughter, then the mother."

"Ten bucks says the mother wants to be here when we talk with the girl."

"Screw the mother."

"Maybe that's your problem, Wayne," Socorro said. "Maybe you want to."

Root growled. "Let's go. I'll drive."

CASSIE HAD SPENT all afternoon finishing Roger's tribute and it was with great relief that she had placed it in the control room with the morning's log and left the station just before five. The show had taken a lot of energy and a lot of time, but it was something she was proud of.

It wasn't until she was in her kitchen, fixing herself a glass of iced tea and looking out the window that she remembered she'd planned to call the police. What jogged her memory was the blue Mazda that pulled up in front of her house.

Root and Socorro climbed out of it.

Cassie waited for the bell, then went to the door. Sly, quick as only a cat could be, slipped in the door between the two policemen and gave Cassie a deprecating glance. Obviously he should have been let in earlier. Then the cat stalked off toward the living room leading the parade of Cassie and the two policemen.

"We were hoping to find your daughter at home, too," Socorro said. "Is she here?"

"Jenny?" Cassie had expected them to want to talk with Jenny, yet somehow hearing them say it heightened her apprehension. "I don't know what time Jenny will be home. I could try calling her friend's house, but I know they won't be there."

"That's okay; we'll catch her later," Socorro said. "If it would be convenient, we'd like you to come to the police station with us."

Cassie nodded. *Get it done, and do it before Brad finds out.* She looked at her watch. "Let me get my purse."

"We'll drive you and bring you back," Root said.

"Can I be there when you question Jenny?"

Socorro shook his head. "I'm sorry Mrs. Ferris, but that's impossible. We have to get statements from all witnesses, and we have to do that privately. It's standard policy, ma'am," he said smoothly. "We've questioned even very young children without their parents."

"I understand," Cassie said, glancing again at the clock. She paused in her movements. "Just let me leave a note for

Jenny. Can I have her call me at the police station? Is there a number?"

Socorro gave her the number and while she went to write the note, she overheard Socorro say to Root. "You owe me ten bucks."

"I didn't bet," Root responded.

Cassie had no idea what that was about.

THIRTEEN

As far as Root could tell, Cassie Ferris repeated her story much the same as she had the morning after Weber died. No surprises, no new information. She'd hesitated only once and that was during the description of Jenny throwing the drink. Other than that it had been a nice simple statement. It wasn't much help, but then, they had more to talk about. He let his partner continue asking the questions.

"Mrs. Ferris," Socorro said, "I understand that the night Roger Weber died, your daughter was on the patio at Happy Twosomes talking to the staff. Were you there at the time?"

She frowned. "Me? No."

"Did your daughter tell you about the conversation?"

"She mentioned it briefly."

"Do you know what time it took place?" Socorro asked.

Root knew that wasn't important, they already had the time pinpointed from other statements. What was important was finding out exactly which plants Jennifer Ferris had talked about. Socorro would get to that slowly without giving anything away.

"I really don't know what time she was on the patio," Mrs. Ferris said.

"Do you know who else was on the patio?" Socorro asked.

"I haven't any idea."

"Did you know they were talking about plants?"

She stiffened almost imperceptibly. "Yes, I think Jenny told me that."

"Your daughter is quite knowledgeable about plants, is that correct?"

"Not really. Jenny learned about herbs from my mother, but only the ones that are used for medicinal purposes. My mom was the real expert."

Cassie Ferris probably knew as much, if not more, about plants as her daughter. She could have killed Roger Weber just as easily as her daughter. More easily. She had more reasons and all the knowledge. It merely confirmed one of the possibilities they'd discussed in the case meeting, and it annoyed Root that he wasn't pleased about it.

"Was?" Socorro asked.

"My mother's older now, she was almost forty when I was born. She doesn't remember as much as she used to."

"I'm sorry," Socorro said. "Did Jenny ever gather plants? With your mother?"

"Yes, sometimes."

"Wouldn't she have to be able to identify poisonous plants, so she wouldn't accidentally get them mixed up?"

Cassie Ferris looked annoyed, perhaps even angry. "I guess so."

"And she is a botany major."

"Yes, but she's only in her second year."

"Does she make a habit of talking about plants?"

Root thought Socorro made the daughter sound like a bore. Or like her hobby was wrong; naturally a mother would get defensive, but Cass Ferris remained pretty cool.

"Jenny is an outgoing person, and plants are her..." she stopped. "They're her hobby."

"Who else could she have talked with about plants? And which plants was she currently studying?"

"I really couldn't tell you." Her face seemed guarded. "As for who she talked to, the answer is, anyone. All they had to do was ask one question and Jenny was off and running. She would tell anyone anything."

She said it firmly, making her point clear.

Socorro nodded before looking to his notebook. Cassie took the break to ask, "Have you found Roger's briefcase?"

"No," Root responded. "We haven't found any briefcase. Did he normally carry one?"

"Yes, yes, he did. And Friday morning, the morning before he died, he put something in it." She looked at Root. "He had some papers and I don't think he wanted me to see them. He was being secretive."

"Could you see what was on the papers?" Root asked.

"No. But they seemed important, and he wanted to talk to Walter and Bill about something. Maybe the papers were proof of something illegal or immoral going on at Y-96. Isn't it possible that he was killed for those papers?"

This was the first they'd heard of any briefcase, and if she was telling the truth, it could be important.

Of course, she could also be making it up to get the focus off her and her daughter.

"We'll check it out," Root said. "Can you think of anything else that might help us with our investigation? Anything else that Mr. Weber might have said to you that night at Happy Twosomes?"

"Yes." She reached for her purse and pulled out a set of

keys. "Walter Kraley asked me to give these to you. He thought you'd need them for the briefcase."

"I see." Root didn't take them. "You can return them to Mr. Kraley, if you like. We—"

He intended to tell her that they had copies of them, but a quick double tap at the door interrupted him. It meant that Jenny Ferris had arrived.

As soon as they'd gotten to the station with Cassie Ferris, they'd sent someone back to her house to wait for Jenny. It was procedure. Good procedure.

Socorro picked up his notebook. "I'll go. Excuse me, Mrs. Ferris."

After he left, Root turned back to Cassie Ferris. "I'd like to go over the party at Happy Twosomes, again," he said. "Is it accurate that you only saw Roger Weber one time? Downstairs, at approximately six-thirty?"

"That's right." Then her eyes went wide in surprise. "Well, actually, I did see him once more, but I didn't talk to him."

Root held himself still. New information. "When did you see him?"

"When I was looking for Jenny," she said, her voice careful. "I looked in the staff lounge and Roger was there. He didn't see me; I only opened the door a crack. He was on the couch, kind of looking toward the corner. That's all I saw before I closed the door and went up to the third floor."

"Was someone else in the room with Weber?"

"I don't know. If there was, I didn't see them."

"Was there food around? Trays of food?"

She looked down as if to collect her thoughts. "Roger had a plate beside him." She looked back up. "It was one of those small paper plates like they had downstairs. And he had a napkin in his hand."

"Exactly what time was this?"

"I don't know…maybe around six-forty, quarter of seven. Something like that."

"You didn't hear any other voices?"

"No. I closed the door and went straight up the stairs."

Everyone had been inside that little room between six and seven, meaning any of the Y-96 staff could have killed Roger Weber. Except not everyone knew about plants.

WHEN THE INTERVIEW WAS OVER, and Cassie Ferris had been sent home with another officer, Root finally got to sit down at his desk. He was bone weary and wishing he could go home, too.

He looked down at the pink message slips on his desk. His daughter, Angela, had called; he brightened a little at that, and then frowned. He hoped she didn't have a problem.

Next was a message for Cassie Ferris. Jenny was here.

Shit. He'd forgotten to tell her. As soon as she got home and found out, she'd be angry. It didn't make for good PR for the department.

He got up quickly and went out front to where their assistant sat. She was busy talking with the Sr. Sergeant, going over case notes. Root would have to make the call himself.

At his desk he flipped through some 3 by 5 cards, until he found Cassie Ferris's number. He glanced at the huge clock on the back wall. She'd only been gone five minutes. He dialed the number, and ended up with her answering machine.

"Mrs. Ferris, this is Sergeant Root at the Austin Police Department. I just wanted you to know that your daughter is

here, giving us her statement. I'm sorry I didn't tell you…"
He cleared his throat. "One of our staff will bring her home
when she's finished."

He hung up the phone. The problem, he thought, was that
people expected too much of him sometimes. Way too much.

He'd call Angela, now. That would cheer him up. Maybe
he'd get a chance to talk to Lucille.

CASSIE HAD JUST WALKED in the door, still holding her purse
and keys, when she spotted the note from Jenny. She dropped
her things on the kitchen counter, and read:

"I'm at the police station. Love—Jen. PS. It's only six, so
I should be home early."

The subtle anger that had begun during Cassie's interview
with Root touched her again. If they had told her Jenny was
at the station, Cassie could have waited.

She didn't understand what the police were doing. They
hadn't seemed interested in the papers Roger had slipped
into his briefcase. And when she'd offered them keys to open
the damn thing, in case they ever did find it, which now
seemed unlikely, they'd turned them down.

Sly meowed loudly and Cassie reached down to pet him,
before taking out the cat food and feeding him. As she did
so, the blinking message light caught her eye. While Sly
sniffed the food, Cassie pushed the button on the answering
machine and listened to Sgt. Root's message.

You damn sure will bring her home, Cassie thought, stuff-
ing the box of cat food back into the cupboard. But how
soon? She wasn't sure she trusted Sergeant Wayne Root, or
any of the police.

Even as she had the thought, the word *trust* jumped out at

her. It was an issue she had grappled with mightily ever since the divorce. The therapist she'd seen after the custody hearing had been very specific about the roots of her problem with it.

"It's because your father left when you were young," she'd said, in her quiet way. "It's very common to feel betrayed when a parent leaves."

Cassie had found that just so much psychobabble, especially taking the problem all the way back to childhood. "This has nothing to do with my father. It's Brad who betrayed me."

"Yes, this time. But you see, we're rarely very upset the first time something happens to us. It's later, when it happens again, and again, that we feel the feelings deeply and express them. It's usually in the repetition that we recognize how we're being treated, and then we get angry."

Cassie had certainly been angry then and she was beginning to feel it now.

"Trust is a choice," her therapist had said. "You choose to trust, or you don't."

Cassie pulled open the refrigerator door. She had trusted Brad, and he'd persecuted her relentlessly during the custody hearings. She'd trusted her lawyer and he'd lost Beth for her.

Yet, even in her mounting upset she realized that she was looking at history, while her problem with the police had no relation to it. Sergeant Root had said they would bring Jenny home, and yes, she did believe they would do that. But were they harassing Jenny in the meantime?

Cassie took a breath and closed the refrigerator door. The police had only asked to speak with Jenny once, which didn't qualify as harassment. Intellectually she realized the truth of that. For the moment, Jenny was safe. The questioning wouldn't take long—Jenny might even enjoy it in her own perverse way.

That left the issue of the investigation. The police hadn't been interested in finding Roger's briefcase, and they hadn't taken his keys so how could Cassie trust them to find his murderer?

During the years since the divorce and custody hearing, there had been only one person she'd really been able to rely on, and that had been herself. Somehow she had made a living, and a life, for both Jenny and herself. And now, she had to get this murder investigation over and done with, so they could get on with that life.

If she could find the briefcase…she felt a tingle of anticipation. If she could find the briefcase, she might discover who murdered Roger Weber. She would get the twenty-five-thousand-dollar reward, and she could spend every penny of it getting Beth back.

And if Brad heard about her involvement with the murder and tried his old tricks again? She could almost feel the fear pulling the strength out of her, like a cancer sucking the marrow from a bone.

She picked up Sly and stroked his fur.

How many times had she backed away from a challenge out of fear of Brad? Had she ever fought him, really fought hard, when he'd not sent Beth on a scheduled visit? Had she ever demanded that the time be made up on a later trip? No, she hadn't. And here she was, running away again because of the specter of Brad.

The very worst of it was that she was beginning to see that same behavior in Jenny. What kind of an example was Cassie for her daughters?

The thought was so abhorrent she squeezed Sly who protested and jumped out of her arms.

To hell with Brad. He had nothing more to take from her. Jenny wouldn't leave the university, or her.

She went back to the refrigerator, pouring herself a diet drink, while at the same time exploring the problem of the missing briefcase. There was one place where it might be, and she had a quick way of finding out. She picked up the phone, punching out the number of Happy Twosomes. "Greg Mayhew," she said when the phone was answered.

Her fingers tapped the counter as she waited.

"This is Greg."

"Hi. This is Cassie Ferris."

"Cassie, how are you doing?" She could hear his smile. "I understand I missed a call from you the other day."

"I was in a hurry, so I didn't wait."

"You sound agitated; is everything all right?"

"Of course. I just left the police station and it's given me a lot to think about."

"Being questioned by the police is enough to rattle anyone."

"I'm not sure I'm rattled," she said. "I just…" she hesitated.

"You just what?" Greg asked.

"Oh, I don't know." And then, she said, "Jenny is still there."

"Ah. I see. And you're worried because she had that argument with Roger the night he died." His voice came more gently. "Sounds like a good time to have a friend. Why don't I come over and keep you company?"

"No! No, I'm fine, that isn't why I called," she said. "But,

I do appreciate the offer. I'm trying to find Roger's briefcase and I wondered if there was any chance he left it at the club?"

"No, we didn't find a briefcase and we would have by now."

"I was afraid of that." But maybe they hadn't looked everywhere. "Could Roger have gotten a locker? You know, a gym locker or whatever they're called?"

"Actually, he could have. I never checked and the police didn't ask. I'll go look it up right now and tell you when I come over."

"I'm okay, Greg, honestly." Although the house did seem empty and hollow. "I wouldn't want to impose—"

"You're not. Not one bit, and I'm a great listener. I'll even bring a good bottle of wine." Cassie could hear the sound of something being moved. Then he said, "Give me directions."

The thought of having Greg there seemed incredibly comforting. An ally, when she needed one. "Okay," she said. "Take Research to Mopac and go South…"

JENNY STILL WASN'T HOME, and Cassie's resolve not to worry was being held in place only by the wine. She set her glass firmly on the coffee table. She didn't need a false sense of security.

"What if I called the police station?" she asked, glancing again at the mantel clock.

"I doubt they'd even tell Jenny about the call until they were finished getting her statement." Greg reached out and touched her arm lightly. "Jenny may have seen more during the party than you realized. It's probably just taking a while to tell them everything."

"Maybe." She started to lean back, realized how close that

would put them and changed her mind. "The problem is, I'm not even sure what time she got to the police station."

"You know, in my limited experience with the Austin Police, they've been very considerate. I really don't think you have anything to worry about."

Cassie stood up and moved to a spot in front of the fireplace, just a few feet from where Sly was lying. "I wouldn't be worried except for the damn plants."

"Plants?"

"Plants. The kind that kill," Cassie said. "They've been asking everyone about plants and Jenny is a botany major."

Greg's dark blue eyes suddenly comprehended. "They asked me about plants, too, but I never put it all together. How knowledgeable is Jenny?"

"Very. She's a plant fanatic. She was talking about them at the party. With the radio station staff."

"I see. So where does the briefcase come in?"

"I'm not positive it does, but it's missing," Cassie said.

"I'm sorry that I didn't find it." Sly jumped into his lap and Greg began to scratch behind the cat's ears. Sly purred with the attention. "Roger didn't even fill out the usual membership forms, so there's no way that he could have gotten a locker. I suppose the police checked his house and car?"

"I would think so. They said they didn't have it."

Greg frowned. "A safety deposit box? Another health club somewhere?"

"He didn't belong to a health club. He kept saying that he was going to join one to lose weight, but when he heard about Happy Twosomes I guess he decided that would be better." She began to pace around the room. "As for a safety deposit box, wouldn't the police have found that?"

"I'd think so; they're pretty thorough." Sly was now curled on Greg's lap, licking his hand.

"I just can't figure out where it could be," Cassie said, wondering if she could somehow track Roger's movements on that Friday before he died. Maybe she could find out if he'd gone to some bank.

Greg stood up, gently placing Sly on the couch, and reached out to catch Cassie's arm, stopping her movement. "I'm supposed to be here taking your mind off your worries and it doesn't look as if I'm doing a very good job." He smiled down at her, his eyes watching hers.

"I'm fine," Cassie said, gently drawing away. She was almost afraid of the connection she felt when he touched her. It only made her more aware of her need for human comfort. "And I do appreciate your coming by."

Greg started to say something, but the front door opened, and Jenny's voice called out, "Mom? I'm home."

Cassie jumped up and started toward the hallway. "We're in here. How are you?"

"I'm fine. Thirsty. Who's 'we'?" Jenny asked, then stopped in the dining room as Cassie came in, followed by Greg. "Oh, Greg, hi. What are you doing here?"

"I stopped by to visit your mother," he said. "Should I have gotten your permission first?"

They smiled at each other. "I give my permission," Jenny said. "Not that you needed it."

Jenny looked a little pale to Cassie. "How are you?" she asked, again. "How did it go?"

"Long. It wasn't at all what I expected. They were pretty nice; they just asked a lot of weird questions."

"Like what?" Cassie asked.

"Can I get something to drink? I'm parched!" She started for the kitchen.

"Maybe I'd better be going," Greg said.

Jenny turned around. "Don't leave because of me. Mom never has friends over; I'd feel terrible if I chased you away."

"Jenny!"

She shrugged and tried out the half-hearted smile again. "Just kidding. Anyway, as soon as I get something to drink, I'm going to bed. I have an early class tomorrow." She went into the kitchen with Cassie and Greg behind her.

"So?" Cassie demanded as Jenny reached into the refrigerator for a diet Pepsi. "What did they want to know?"

"Everything I saw and heard that Friday night," she said, closing the refrigerator. She popped the can top and took a long swallow. "Oh, that's better. I think I talked forever. I had to tell them who was there, and where I saw them, and what I did. You know, everything."

"Did they ask about plants?"

Jenny leaned against the counter. "Ad infinitum." She shuddered. "They wanted to know about every time I'd talked about plants with anyone from the station. And they wanted to know who was listening, which plants I talked about, and what questions everyone else asked. Luckily I'd only been around the station people a couple of times lately."

"So what did you tell them?" Cassie asked.

"God, do I have to say it again?"

"Humor me. You should have it down pat by now."

Jenny rolled her eyes and began rattling off information, "First there was the time at the station, just a week before the party. I was talking with Irma Belton at her desk." Jenny got an impish look on her face and went on as if quoting,

"Irma's desk is located at the end of the hall upstairs and it sits right in front of Bill Bankston's office, and at the corner is Rachel's—"

"Enough," Cassie said. "I know where all the offices are."

"Okay," Jenny said. "That day, I told Irma that the dieffenbachia in the building was poisonous, mostly to pets like cats and dogs. And then we talked about the other plants that are dangerous. You know, castor beans, oleander, and meadow saffron. Things that people plant all the time in their yards. And Irma said that when she was a kid she used to make leis out of oleander, and then evidently put her fingers in her mouth, because she'd get sick. She never knew what caused it and her parents always thought she got the flu."

"Why don't I bring in our wineglasses?" Greg said.

"Getting bored already, huh?" Jenny asked.

Greg smiled ruefully. "I've been interviewed by the police myself. I think I recognize their tedious technique."

"You know," Jenny said, "I thought it might be kind of fun being interviewed, I mean, even though I was a little nervous, but it really gets to be a drag."

"It's the repetition," Greg said. "I think I told them twelve times about the catering and what food was where."

Jenny nodded. "I had to talk about people and plants. And who I saw in the lounge and on the patio."

"I think I will get my wine," Greg said. "Cassie?"

"No, thanks."

"The only other time I talked about plants," Jenny said, "Well, I mean around the Y-96 staff, was at the party and I already told you about that."

"Which plants did you talk about?"

"You sound just like Socorro!"

"But I'm your mother—you owe me," Cassie said, as Greg returned.

"Fine. I talked about deadly nightshade, nettle, mistletoe, oleander and meadow saffron."

Greg looked curious. "Why those in particular?"

Jenny shrugged. "I don't know. I guess the mistletoe because Scott Delany saw some and asked what it was; it was on a tree in that empty lot on the other side of the patio. And you had some meadow saffron growing in the planters. I don't know why the nightshade. Oh, wait, yes I do. Mandy was quoting something, 'And on the darkened sky shades the night.' Something like that. She said it was the only thing she remembered from college English. It made me think of nightshade, and that's how the conversation got started."

Cassie looked at Greg. "As I said, fanatic."

"That was rude, Mother, so I'm going to bed." Jenny pushed away from the counter. "Nice seeing you, Greg." She waved, and said, "Don't be a stranger."

"Good night, Jenny," Cassie said firmly.

"'Night Jenny," Greg echoed.

"'Night," Jenny called as she left the room.

They sounded like the Waltons.

Cassie turned to Greg. "She seemed a little pale to me, but I guess the police didn't leave any permanent scars on her."

"Apparently not. How about you? Are you feeling better?"

She nodded. "Fine. Drained."

Greg set his almost empty glass in the sink. "Then I need to be going."

"That wasn't a hint."

"I know," he said. "And you do have to get up pretty early."

"Not tomorrow. We're airing Roger's tribute and it's already on tape."

"Then I won't be hearing you on the air until Friday?" Greg asked.

Cassie stopped. Her voice was uncertain. "I don't know. I...they haven't said."

"Why wouldn't you be on the air?"

"They might get someone else. Maybe a new team; I don't know."

Before Cassie even realized what was happening, Greg slid his arms around her in a hug. When their bodies made contact Cassie could feel the warmth all the way to her soul. She rested her head against his shoulder, letting her tense muscles relax.

Finally she straightened, reluctantly letting go. "Thanks."

"Thank you." He touched her cheek softly, then started for the door, pausing only long enough to flash her a quick smile before he left.

FOURTEEN

PINK MESSAGE NOTES with looping purple writing were scattered in not-too-neat piles all across the glass-topped receptionist's desk. Cardboard boxes of CDs and tapes waiting to be picked up by contest winners were sitting on the floor. Behind the boxes was a dark wooden partition that cut off the reception area from the other offices. The only real decorations were the rows of plaques and awards that Y-96 had garnered.

For once the phones were silent; perhaps, although Cassie doubted it, in memory of Roger. In the background she could hear the last hour of his tribute; the Grass Roots were singing, "In my midnight confessions..." Cassie had used two bits on marriage back to back, and had selected that song to go with them.

The rest of the staff was gathered in the conference room listening to the show, but Cassie had slipped out to talk to the receptionist, Jana Fitzpatrick.

"The day Roger died," Cassie said. "Ascertainments."

Jana frowned, her young face a study in puzzlement. "Huh?"

Jana usually watched the coming and goings of the station employees as if it were her own personal soap opera. She spent a lot of her time gossiping on the phone about the disk jockeys with her less privileged friends.

"The day Mandy and Bill were at ascertainments," Cassie said. "You know, the day of the Happy Twosomes' promotion."

"Oh, that day! Sure, I remember. Who could forget it? Roger threw that fit in the morning...of course, Roger threw a fit almost every morning." Jana rolled her carefully made-up eyes and flipped her long straight blond hair over her shoulder. "He was an ass, wasn't he?"

"Sometimes," Cassie said. "Now, what I was wondering is if you remembered when Roger left? If he might have said something to you about where he was going."

Jana looked at her with open curiosity. "What's up?"

"I can't give you details, but I'm trying to find something. And you can't talk to anyone about our conversation. Anyone."

Jana's eyes widened and she gestured for Cassie to sit down in the side chair. Then she leaned close, her voice a whisper. "Sound travels up here. Everything you say in the halls can be heard in all the offices."

"Got it," Cassie said softly as she sat down.

"Roger went to lunch kind of early that day. Even early for him. Here, I'll show you." She pulled a well-used legal tablet towards her and flipped through some pages, then pointed to a spot halfway down a page. "He checked out at eleven, and must have come back pretty soon, because he left for the day at one."

"Did he say anything to you?"

Jana concentrated for a moment. "He was huffy about something. He said would I please try to get his messages right, for once!" Her volume had crept upward, and she lowered it. "What a jerk."

"Did he have his briefcase when he left for lunch?"

"No. He never took that to lunch; he left it in his office. You know how fanatic he was about locking things up." She furrowed her brow for a moment. "He had his keys in his hand and said he was going to the dry cleaners to pick up his clothes. I noticed the keys because he was holding them close to his stomach, kind of bent over, like it hurt or something. His stomach, I mean."

"Do you know where he ate?"

"I don't think he did eat, because when he left later he said something about finally getting some food."

"And that was around one?"

"Uh-huh." She leaned even closer. "He did ask me where they were holding those meetings and he was bitching about his work never being done. The meetings were at the Driskill Hotel, by the way."

"Did he go to ascertainments?"

Jana shrugged. "I don't think so."

Cassie stood up. "Thanks."

Jana gave a thumbs-up sign as Cassie started off.

Cassie could now track Roger's day until almost one and if Jana was right, Roger's briefcase had been safely in his office until that time.

She passed Irma's vacant desk and Bill's darkened office behind it. There was something almost eerie about the emptiness of the station. Only Mandy's office was brightly lit, and through the window Cassie could see that Mandy was on the phone, her back to the door. Rather than interrupt, Cassie headed for the conference room.

"Hey, Cassie," Rachel called out as Cassie neared her cubbyhole, "I thought you'd be in there with the troops listening to Roger's tribute."

"I'm on my way," Cassie said, wondering why she couldn't make her own office look as good as Rachel's. On the back wall were wooden shelves with the more impressive mementos of Rachel's career. There was a signed photograph of Rachel with Wolfman Jack, Rachel with the Beach Boys, and Rachel with Walter and Bill at a broadcaster's convention. All the pictures were in brushed gold frames and between them were two, luxurious green ivies. It's the plants, Cassie thought. And the light and the paint, and the furniture and the accessories.

Rachel said, "I'm going into the conference room now; I'm sure Bill will have something pithy to say when the show's over."

"I certainly hope so," Cassie said. "Since I spent all that time on it."

"Oh, yeah." Rachel rose from her chair and they started down the hall together. "Did you hear that Walter is offering a reward for Roger's murderer? Do you think it will help?"

"I don't know. Maybe. "

"Have you made your statement yet?"

"Last night. So did Jenny, so I guess they're done with us."

"I hope they're done with all of us," Rachel said.

They stepped into the conference room as Roger's standard sign-off music was coming over the speaker.

"Ah, Cass, just in time for the accolades," Bill said, rising and joining her near the doorway. "You did a marvelous job and I want to thank you on behalf of the entire staff."

There was a smattering of applause and Cassie smiled. "Thanks, Bill."

"And now I have an announcement." Bill slid his arm around her shoulder and went on, "Tomorrow we will have a new jock in morning drive."

Cassie froze.

"His name is Tracker Forman," Bill went on, "and he's currently doing mornings in Kansas City."

The room was suddenly icy cold, and Cassie found it hard to breathe.

Bill nodded in her direction. "He will fill in here for one week as a test to see if we like him. His sidekick will, of course, be the lovely and talented Cass Woman."

Applause. Cassie felt the relief course through her as the blood began to flow again. She looked around the room. Everyone was smiling at her. No, not quite everyone. Not Scott Delany. He looked like he could murder someone and Cassie assumed she was at the top of the list.

CASSIE DREW A CHERUBIC little angel with halo and wings while she waited for the Production Director from K100 to come back on the phone. She drew another figure, this time attaching a forked tail and horns, then she shifted the phone to a more comfortable position.

"Cass? I'm sorry, it's crazy around here," Tony Hernandez said almost breathlessly. "Now, what was it you wanted to know? Something about ascertainments?"

"Uh-huh. Did you go this year?"

"Don't I always? It's my punishment for being a nice guy."

"What I was wondering was if you happened to see Roger Weber there."

There was a pause and Cassie could imagine the frown on Tony's moon-shaped face. "I didn't see him. Did he show up? That wasn't something he usually did, was it?"

"No," she said. Tony was wired into the broadcast community. As the saying went, he knew where all the bodies were buried, and who had done what to whom. He also knew where and why. It's the reason she called, and the reason she hesitated to say too much. "Look, Tony, I'm trying to find out if Roger went down to the Driskill that day. This is sensitive, and I don't want anyone else to know I asked. Anyone."

"I won't say anything."

"I'm glad," she said. "So, did you see him?"

"That was the day he died, right? No, I didn't see him. But, hey, you know, just because I didn't see Roger doesn't mean he wasn't there. While the meetings were going on anyone could have been outside in the hall, or in another room and I wouldn't have seen them."

"Any idea who else I might talk to?"

"What about our general manager? Or sales manager?"

"I don't know them…."

"I could ask around and see if they noticed him."

"Can you do it discreetly, Tony? I don't want people to know I'm interested. Oh, and I need to find out if he had his briefcase with him. That's really important."

"This is real secret-sleuth stuff, huh?"

"Very."

"No sweat, I'll keep it quiet. So, what's the story on the morning show? Who's going to replace Roger?"

"Bill just announced we're going to be trying out a guy named Tracker Forman from Kansas City. I'll be working with him, and that's a story you can tell everyone."

"Oh, yeah?" Tony laughed. "Think it'll squash some of the nasty rumors floating down the grapevine?"

"What rumors?"

There was a pause. "Well, you know…"

"No, I don't."

Tony couldn't hide the embarrassment. "It's just bullshit. You know how this business is."

"Come on, Tony, spit it out. What are people saying?"

He took his time. "It's just crap, Cassie, but I heard that Y-96 was bringing in a team because you were…well…the police were concentrating on you."

"Because I might have killed Roger?" Cassie asked.

"That's what I heard. Pretty stupid, huh?"

It was stupid. Baseless. And still…" Who did you hear that from?" Cassie asked.

"I'm not sure…"

"Don't do this to me, Tony. Who told you I was under suspicion?"

He hesitated, but not for long. "It was our sales manager. He said it came from someone at Y-96. Obviously it wasn't true."

And who at Y-96? *Programming people talked to programming people. Managers talked to managers, and sales managers talked to sales managers.*

But why would Mandy start a rumor like that?

"It's not true," Cassie said. "I gave my statement just like everyone else, and I haven't heard from the police since."

"I didn't believe it," he assured her. "Roger was a prick, but in this business you just put up with pricks; you don't kill them."

Aptly put. "But maybe you shouldn't ask anyone about Roger being at ascertainments."

"I'll be discreet; don't worry. And I'll call you this afternoon."

Cassie hung up the phone, and propelled herself up and out the door. Her father always said, you do what you have to do, and right now she had to talk to Mandy. Cassie hoped her words didn't come out like an accusation.

Mandy was at her desk, staring with great concentration at an opened manila folder.

"Excuse me, Mandy—"

She looked up, startled. Her nose was red and there were tears in her eyes. "Oh, Cassie. Sure."

Cassie faltered. "Were you busy?"

"No." Mandy shook her head, her voice rueful. "Come in."

Cassie sat down on a cream-colored leather chair. "Are you all right?"

"I'm fine," she said, but her voice cracked and a tear slid out. "Okay, that was a lie. I'm terrible." She leaned her head forward as more tears flowed down her face.

"What is it? What's wrong?"

"Oh, Cass, what am I going to do? David wants a divorce." Mandy began to cry harder.

Cassie moved behind the desk and put an arm around Mandy's heaving shoulders. There were more gut-wrenching sobs. Cassie made comforting noises, the same as she would if one of her daughters were hurt or scared. As Mandy continued to cry, Cassie continued to soothe, despite knowing that nothing she said could alleviate Mandy's pain. She had been through it and all the kind words in the world weren't enough to make a difference.

When Mandy's sobs slowed and she lifted her head, Cassie was still holding her.

"It's okay, Cassie. I'm better." She reached for a handful of tissues to wipe her face and blow her nose. Her delicate blonde features were red and swollen. "I'm going to be fine."

Cassie gave Mandy one more hug then slid around to the front of the desk and sat down. "I'm sorry," Cassie said softly.

"I know. It's just so awful." Her voice cracked like a little girl's. "It…hurts."

Cassie could only nod.

"And the hell of it is," Mandy went on, wiping her face determinedly, "I didn't do anything. I'm just the same as I was when he married me. Better. I'm smarter, I'm more caring…everything." She blew her nose, and her voice became stronger. "I knew he was unhappy lately, things haven't been great, but I didn't expect this."

"Maybe David will change his mind."

"That's what my mom says." Mandy took a long shuddering breath. "I hope he will." Her voice was small and hopeful.

"If he's got any sense he will. The important thing is for you to take care of yourself."

Mandy shook her head so hard that tiny tears flew out of her eyes. "I don't care about me! I don't even want to live right now."

Cassie leaned forward. "Don't say that. Don't even think it!" She had gone through blind craziness with her own divorce. The striking out had been a horrible mistake and it had cost Cassie dearly—it had cost her Beth.

"It's true."

"Mandy, you're beautiful, you're intelligent, and caring. And David's a fool." Mandy almost smiled and Cassie went on, "Why don't you take some time off? Go stay with your mom. Go to a spa. Something, anything, that will feel good to you."

"I'll think about it," Mandy said. She reached for another

tissue and blew her nose, again. "I don't want to talk about it anymore. Okay? I'm done crying. I mean it."

"Cry if you want, it's healing."

"No it's not! It's killing me. I think I'm dehydrating." Her voice almost sounded like the old Mandy. "Now, did you want to talk to me about something?"

Cassie stood up and shook her head. "It's not important."

"Yes, it is. Talk to me. Please. Distract me."

"Okay." Cassie sat back down. She had come here to ask Mandy about the rumors but the steam had dissipated. Instead she said, "I wanted to ask you about ascertainments. You were there all day, remember?"

"I remember."

"Did you see Roger at the Driskill?"

Mandy leaned back in her chair, meticulously folding a damp tissue. "He didn't go to those things."

"Not usually, but I think he was planning to show up. Not to sit in on the meetings. Actually, I don't know why he was going. Maybe to talk to someone."

"I didn't see—wait! I did see him. It was right after the lunch break and I was going in to chair the meeting with the Creative Rapid Learning Center. He was coming up the stairs when I closed the door to our room."

"Did he have his briefcase with him?"

"Is that what this is all about?"

Cassie nodded. "Yes."

"You think there's something inside that will help the police find his murderer."

"I'm hoping, but I don't know anything for sure. Did you see him talking to anyone?"

"No, he was alone."

"And the briefcase?"

"I don't remember."

"Are you sure?"

"I'm sure."

Cassie stood up. "Well, thanks."

"You know, I think this is a very bad idea. Hunting for that briefcase," Mandy said, standing also. "Leave it alone, Cassie."

Cassie frowned. "Why?"

"Why? Because someone killed Roger. There's a murderer out there. Don't get involved."

"I am involved."

"I'm serious about this; Cassie, for once in your life, just listen to me. Do what I say."

"I always do," Cassie said. "It's one of my major character flaws. On my tombstone will be engraved, 'I listened to Mandy.'" She looked at Mandy whose eyes were still moist and her nose red. She wasn't smiling. "Take care of yourself."

"You do the same."

FIFTEEN

ROOT WAITED PATIENTLY for his partner to get in and close the door of the Mazda. "What did you think?" Root asked as he started the car.

Socorro grinned. "Cynthia Weber is a real babe!"

"That's not what I meant."

"Lighten up, Wayne," Socorro said, still grinning.

So, Cynthia Weber was a soft and creamy blonde; for Root that wasn't enough. "A woman is more than a body. Or a face."

"Hey, in her case, who cares? The body and the face are enough to fulfill my wildest fantasies." Socorro leaned back, adjusting his seat belt. "And did you hear what she said? I look a little like Roger! Only better looking! You think she'd go for me?"

Root pulled out of the parking lot of the glass and chrome bank, and into the traffic on Burnet Road. "She said she was dating one of the assistant DAs. Burkhardt."

"A detail."

"And that she had spent the night at his townhouse both the Thursday before, and the Friday night when Weber actually died."

"So she sleeps around. I can live with that."

"You're sick." Root turned left on Anderson Lane, passing shopping malls on either side. "What do you think about her story?"

"Oh, that. Well, sounds like a pretty solid alibi to me. If everyone backs her up." He grinned again. "God knows I'd back her up."

Root ignored Socorro's last comment. "The day Weber died she went to lunch with three tellers. The other tellers confirmed that."

"And they were women; they had no reason to lie."

"All we have to do is talk with Burkhardt."

"One night with me and I could make her forget him."

"Get a grip."

"You've done enough mooning of your own over Lucille."

"No, I haven't." He waited for the traffic light to change. "I was afraid that Cynthia Weber was a longshot. After our first interview with her, I kind of figured she couldn't help. She just didn't have much association with Weber after the divorce. I guess that happens when you don't have kids." But he did have a kid. A daughter, and he wondered how that would effect his future with Lucille.

Socorro got down to business, flipping open his notebook. "Her supervisor told me that she didn't leave the bank at all that Friday, except for lunch. Even worked late. They had some computer trouble and she was there until almost eight o'clock. By that time Weber was already at Happy Twosomes."

"And had ingested the poison."

"We should have some info from NCIC on the rest of the people when we get back. You want to stop and grab a snack first?"

"I'd rather see those reports," Root said, watching traffic

carefully as he eased into the left-hand lane. "I just have this feeling that they're all clean. Nothing on any of them."

"There's bound to be something more than traffic tickets. We sent a lot of names." The list included Bankston, Delany, Mandy McCormick, Rachel Sankey, Greg Mayhew, Cassie Ferris and her daughter. Socorro knew the odds were in their favor. "I'll bet you one or more has some court actions against them."

"You're on. Divorces don't count; loser buys dinner at Castle Hill."

"Get a real date, why don't you, Wayne."

"Do we have a bet, or what?"

Socorro sighed. "I guess so. You'll have to do until I can convince Cynthia to go out with me."

"CASSIE FERRIS line four." The page came over the loud-speaker in the hallway, temporarily cutting off the pounding beat of the Rolling Stones' "Satisfaction."

Cassie, who had been headed for the production room, picked up her pace and hurried inside the cork-walled room. She swung the heavy door shut, hearing the whoosh as it cut off sound from the outside. Maybe Tony had some news for her.

"This is Cassie Ferris."

"Hi, this is Greg. How are you doing today?"

A pulse point in Cassie's wrist began to pound, and she reminded herself that she *should* be disappointed. After all, she'd been hoping Tony would call.

"I'm fine, Greg. Much better. And thanks for coming over last night; you made the waiting almost bearable."

Greg laughed. "Being called almost bearable isn't exactly what I'd hoped you'd say."

"You took that wrong on purpose," she said. "You know what I meant. You were wonderful—the waiting was difficult."

"So, what are you doing tomorrow night? If you don't have plans I'd like to take you to dinner."

"Well…I don't know. I haven't talked to Jenny…"

"This is an invitation for you," Greg said. "While I like your daughter, I would prefer we didn't have a chaperone."

"I didn't mean she'd come along; I just wasn't sure if she had some plans."

"Maybe she'll make some if she knows you're going out," Greg said.

It sounded like something Mandy had said. "Are you speaking as a psychologist or the owner of a dating club?" she asked.

"Neither. Just plain Greg Mayhew, adult male who enjoyed the company of a certain female disk jockey and who will go to great lengths to get to know her better."

"Uh…"

Greg laughed. "I think all you have to say is 'thank you.'"

"Thank you."

"And you might add that you'd love to have dinner with me. It would do wonders for my morale."

Cassie caught herself smiling. "I can't decide if dinner with you is exactly what I need or the last thing I need."

"Go with your first instinct. Say yes, and we'll eat out at the Oasis and watch the sunset over the lake. What could be better?"

The thought of sipping a margarita at the cliffside restaurant above Lake Travis was too much to resist. "You're on."

"Great. I'll pick you up at seven-fifteen." Greg added.

"Oh, and if you need to talk to me before then, just give me a call."

"Thanks."

"THIS CUSTODY THING involving Cassie Ferris counts," Socorro said. "You're buying dinner."

Root studied the computer printouts in front of him on his scarred desk. Dinner didn't seem relevant at the moment. "I want transcripts of this hearing," he said. "It isn't usual for a woman to lose custody of a daughter in Texas. The judge wouldn't have ruled against her, not in a town like Abilene, unless there was strong provocation."

Socorro raised an eyebrow as he stood over Root's desk, looking at the sheets. "You're right. Abilene's not all that big; something might have happened that didn't become official. No charges filed, but something that didn't make Cassie Ferris look like a very good mother."

"Exactly what I was thinking."

"What about Scott Delany's petty theft?" Socorro asked. "That was only a year ago, just before he left Phoenix and started work at Y-96. Think there was something more there, too?"

"Let's call Phoenix and find out."

"I'm going to order the Ferris transcript right now."

"I'll bet it's on microfilm, and they'll have to fax it. Or have them send it overnight mail," Root said.

Socorro moved to his own desk and picked up the phone, while Root pulled the accordion case file towards him. It seemed to be growing every day and still he didn't feel they were any closer to finding Roger Weber's murderer.

Slowly, one by one, Root went through the sheets of paper.

Next he flipped through the stack of Polaroid pictures of the witnesses, taken when they'd made their formal statements. The faces stared back him, but they offered no insight. If he had to pick someone, it would have to be Cassie Ferris, or maybe her daughter. Motive, opportunity and means were all there, but no concrete evidence. And the motive was weak, same as for everyone else involved with Weber.

Root pulled out the signed statement from Cassie Ferris and frowned. Every time he looked at it he worried more about that briefcase. The Ferris woman swore Weber had put something in it the morning before he died, something he'd been secretive about. After asking around all the other Y-96 staff, he'd learned that Roger Weber had carried a briefcase with him like a woman carries a purse. So where was the damn thing?

The hum of activity around Root was slowing down as the afternoon wore on. Root hated the pressure he was feeling to hurry and get an arrest. High-profile cases were always like that, and then there was Jacobs, the case agent. He was the kind of hardassed cop who got what he wanted—fast. He could scare a suspect so bad they'd beg to make a confession and be led off to a nice quiet cell.

He'd been known to scare a few detectives, too.

Root wanted the investigation over, but he wanted to be right even more. He wanted to hand over enough evidence to be sure the charges would stick. With that briefcase still missing, and liable to turn up later, he couldn't feel right enough.

He looked around the big room. Maybe he'd go down the hall and call Lucille. She always seemed to give him perspective. Not that she commented on his cases, but she zeroed in on his feelings when he couldn't wrap up a case fast enough to suit himself.

No, he couldn't call Lucille. This was Thursday and Lucille wouldn't be home. She was doing group therapy on Thursdays. Maybe it was a good thing; he didn't need to be calling her anyway. She'd only cut him off and refuse to talk. He hated that.

"COME IN, CASSIE," Bill said. "I want you to meet Tracker Forman."

Cassie walked across the office, looking at the man who didn't bother to move from his sprawled position on one of Bill's green chairs.

"How do you do," Cassie said formally.

"Hi." Tracker Forman was giving Cassie a very thorough going over with his eyes.

His blatant stare made Cassie want to cross her eyes or stick her tongue out. Instead, she moved the other side chair fractionally away from him before she slid into it. Then she did some staring of her own.

The most notable thing about Tracker Forman was his beard. It was short and elegant and reminded Cassie of a portrait of a young Italian nobleman she'd once seen in a museum. It was out of sync with his clothing, especially the scratched leather belt that looked homemade. The heavy buckle was like something from the 60s.

Tracker Forman had the air of a downtrodden Renaissance poet. It probably got him a lot of attention from women.

Bill leaned forward across his desk. "I wanted you two to have a chance to talk before tomorrow morning."

"Good idea," Cassie said.

"Tracker can use Roger's office temporarily and by the end of next week we'll make a final decision."

Bill's reference to the uncertainty of Tracker's job at Y-96 didn't seem to bother Tracker much. Nor did the stack of air-checks on Bill's desk, all from other disk jockeys who also wanted the morning drive slot. Tracker merely sat unmoving, his eyes taking in everything.

Bill reached in his top drawer and took out a key. "Here you go, Tracker. My secretary, Irma, is at her desk. Ask her to show you where the office is." The new disk jockey rose to take the key, and Bill went on. "You don't mind staying an extra half hour tonight to visit with Tracker, do you Cassie?"

"Not at all," Cassie said.

"Thanks," Bill said, then turned to Tracker. "She'll be down in a few minutes."

"Sure thing, Boss." Tracker nodded at Cassie, then slouched toward the door. "You want this closed?"

"Please."

Even with the door closed, Cassie could hear Tracker say, "You must be Irma. The boss says you'll show me to my new office."

Then Bill distracted Cassie by saying, "I wanted to ask you about the keys. The ones Walter gave you."

"Oh, of course." So, Walter had mentioned them to Bill.

"You did give them to the police?"

"No, as a matter of fact, they didn't want them. I meant to bring them in and leave them with you, but I forgot. I'll do that tomorrow."

"They didn't want them? That's odd." He frowned. "Did you tell them about Roger's briefcase?"

"Yes, but they didn't seem very concerned about that, either. Maybe they didn't believe me."

"Maybe the investigation is almost over. Maybe they simply didn't need the keys."

From the intercom Jana's voice came sweet and clear. "Cassie, line four, please."

"I'll take it in the other room," Cassie said, jumping up.

"You can get it here." Bill picked up the receiver and handed it to her. Then he punched the button for line four, leaving Cassie no choice but to take the call.

"This is Cassie Ferris."

"Hi, this is Tony. Well, I asked around like you wanted, and guess what? Roger was at ascertainments! Our GM saw him about 2 o'clock talking with Bill Bankston. So, what do you think about that?"

"I don't know what to think," Cassie said, very aware that Bill was sitting not three feet away from her.

"I just thought I'd better call and let you know right away," Tony said, "since I'm taking a couple of days off. I won't be back 'til Tuesday."

"That sounds like fun." *Get to the briefcase!* "What else?"

"That's all, isn't it?"

"What about the other thing?"

"What? What are you talking about?"

"You know…"

"Ah, wait a minute, I get it now. Someone is there and you can't talk."

Cassie forced herself to laugh lightly. "Yes, of course."

"Okay, so what other thing? Bigger than a breadbox?"

"Just make it *brief.*"

"Oh, shit, of course! The briefcase! Yes, Roger had his briefcase with him. God, I must be brain dead. That's what comes of trying to get four days work done in two, just to go out of town." Tony paused. "Does that help?"

"Yes, it does. And thanks," Cassie said. "Have a great trip."

"I will."

She hung up the phone and went back to her chair, knowing that Bill was watching her.

"Sorry about that," Cassie said.

"No problem." His tone was flat, but he looked curious.

"Was there anything else you needed me for?" Cassie asked.

"Yes." Bill nodded slowly, shifting his shoulders and looking almost uncomfortable. "Cassie, I…I hope you won't think I'm out of line."

"No, I mean, I'm sure I won't. What is it?"

"It's about Mandy." He shifted again. "She's having a rather hard time right now. Personally. And I was wondering if you could make an effort to…uh…" He cleared his throat. "Actually, I'm rather concerned about her, and I was hoping you might be able to spend some time with her this weekend."

She wondered if every management person in the entire broadcast industry believed they had the right to dictate their employee's private lives. Her annoyance at Bill increased when she realized he had just asked her to be a friend to Mandy.

"I have plans for Friday night."

"Oh. Well, maybe Saturday you could do something with her."

It was so out of character for Bill to be concerned that Cassie's curiosity began inching ahead of her annoyance. "Did Mandy tell you about the divorce?"

"I walked in on her while she was crying." Bill's ears turned pink as he said it. "I'd like to help her myself, but it, well…you understand."

"Why? She just needs a friend. Don't we all in bad times?" Cassie felt like a brat pushing Bill, but she was just now realizing that he wasn't being all that fair with her. She was still dangling over the morning show. What if Tracker didn't work out? Was she off the show? And then to ask her to be nice to a friend—she felt some satisfaction at seeing him squirm. "Don't you?"

"I'm not sure how to answer that."

"You don't need friends?" Cassie persisted.

"Well, of course. I just don't think that's enough to satisfy most people."

"What's more fulfilling?"

"Oh, you know, money, being well thought of for the job you do." He was sincere and it stunned Cassie.

"Bill, not everyone is like that," she said.

"Perhaps not, but if you look around the staff you'll certainly find many people who are. Especially the sales and management people." He stood up. "Well, that's all for now."

Cassie stood also, her mind whirling with amazement. She was working for an automaton and she'd never realized. It brought up a most interesting question: if people weren't that important, was it acceptable to kill one? An annoying one? Who periodically embarrassed you in front of others?

As she started toward the door she glanced one more time at Bill. He looked like a grownup version of the kid who'd won the high school science fair—but what had he grown up to become?

Track: "Hey, hey, hey, it's six o'clock in the morning on K...uh...Y-96 and I'm Tracker Forman."

Cassie: "Good morning, I'm the Cass Woman and this morning we've got some great music, some great stories and the great new Tracker Forman joining us. Welcome to Austin, Tracker."

Track: "Thanks, Cass. Hey, you've got a beautiful city here and lots of beautiful women. I wonder if all the men are mad because their wives are waking up with a new man?" Chuckle. (pause) "I've been wondering about your birthday, Cass. When is it?"

Cassie: "February 7th."

Track: "What year?"

Cassie: "Every year."

Track: "Okay. Hey, I bet you can't guess why they call me Tracker."

Cassie: "Boy, is that a lead-in if I every heard one! But, I'll bite—why do they call you Tracker?"

Track: "Because when I see a gorgeous woman, I can always 'Tracker' down."

Cassie: "Well, I guess everyone needs a talent."

Track: "And what's your talent, Cassie?"

Cassie: "Getting up at four-thirty in the morning. Now, let's check in with Captain Martie to see what's happening on the streets of Austin…"

SIXTEEN

CASSIE HAD SPENT the previous evening alternately worrying about her first day on the air with Tracker Forman and trying to figure out where Roger's briefcase could be. She hadn't thought of any new places to look for the case, nor had she come up with anything brilliant for the morning show. The proof had been four disastrous hours on the air with Tracker Forman.

"Did Bill hear the morning show?" Cassie asked Irma Belton as soon as it was over.

"I'm sure he did. Although, he's out right now. At a client's."

Mandy's office was also dark. "Where's Mandy?"

"She won't be coming in this morning."

"Damn."

Irma glowered at the swearing. "Is there something I can help you with?"

"No. No." Not unless Irma could send Tracker Forman back to wherever he'd come from. "Thanks anyway. I'd better go to work, too."

Irma smiled stiffly. "Excellent idea."

Cassie started off. At the front desk was a young man in a chauffeur's uniform, holding out a paper to Jana.

"If I could just leave this for Mandy..."

Cassie stopped and stared; an idea had popped full-blown into her brain.

"Sure," Jana was saying. "I'll go put it in her office."

Jana turned toward the back hallway, and the chauffeur headed for the front door. Cassie stepped toward him. "Excuse me." She was hardly able to breathe; this was the manager of Top Class Limo.

"Hi," he said. "Aren't you the Cass Woman?"

"Yes. And you're with Top Class Limo."

"Right. Corky Lederer." Big smile, white teeth.

Cassie sucked in air. "Wasn't it one of your limos that took Roger to Happy Twosomes last Friday night?"

The smile disappeared to be replaced by a somber gaze. "It was our service. We were all upset about Roger dying like that. I can't tell you how bad I felt when I read about it in the paper." His tone became more formal. "Lou, the driver, didn't realize how sick Roger was. Lou could have taken him straight to the hospital, but in a situation like that it's difficult to know the proper thing to do. Even Roger requested that he be taken home. We hope you don't think there was any negligence on our part."

"No, I don't think that," Cassie said.

"Lou just assumed Roger had too much to drink, and that night Roger was, well, out of sorts. I guess he wasn't thinking too clearly."

In other words, Roger was being his usual pain-in-the-ass self, but Corky wouldn't say so. Cassie didn't either. "I guess not." She paused. "Corky, I was wondering where that limo is right now. The one Roger used."

Corky shook his head in disgust. "In the shop. When Mandy called about that night, we were booked solid; you know, a Friday night and all. So, I had to send out the car we keep for emergencies. Dumb thing broke down after Lou dropped Roger off and it's been in the shop ever since."

"I see." Her hopes were rising. "I've been trying to locate Roger's briefcase, and it could still be in the limo, couldn't it?"

"Oh, yeah. We just towed it in and stuck it in the back since we've been so busy. You know, that Japanese delegation is in town about the new computer company and we've been running day and night until today when they flew out. This is the first free minute I've had."

"It hasn't been a problem, but, could I go with you now, and look for the briefcase?"

Corky, who had slipped from official to friend, became all business again. "That's not necessary. I'll go back and look right now; if it's there I'll bring it to you."

"I don't mind—"

"No, ma'am, I'd feel terrible causing you any more inconvenience. You just tell me where you'd like me to deliver that briefcase. Here at the station?"

"No, no. Not here. I'll be home early this afternoon. Say after two at my house?"

"Certainly. Just give me the address. Better give me your phone number, too, in case it isn't there."

Cassie took a slip of paper from Jana's desk and wrote the information. "Thanks again."

"Thank you for your understanding."

Cassie hoped the station's official position was just as understanding.

SOCORRO RETURNED to his desk, annoyance on his face. "Bad news."

Root looked up. "Well? Where's the transcript?"

"Somebody screwed up and sent it to San Antonio."

"Shit!"

"That's what I said. It's too big to fax, so they're sending it over by messenger. We should have it this afternoon." It was only eleven.

"Damn. I'm ready to haul them all in and start over again," Root snarled, referring to their witnesses. "Anything new from the phone brigade?"

"Nope. They've called two hundred and seventy-five numbers and talked to fifty people and over two hundred answering machines. I think Martha was kidding when she told me that, but I'm not sure. Anyway, no one was seen pulling plants up on the patio." Socorro sat down, and took a candy bar from his top drawer. "I got an idea. How about if we just bring in Jenny Ferris and talk to her some more? Sort of quiz her on plants. Generally."

"I thought we did that."

"Yeah, well, pretty much." Socorro took the wrapper off a U-No bar. "See this candy bar? It's as valuable as contraband, did you know that? Can't get 'em in Austin. Had to have my mother send me some from Colorado."

Root wasn't impressed. "Why Jenny Ferris?"

"We don't want to bring in the mother, yet, but Jenny could tell us a lot about her mom. Maybe like why Cassie Ferris didn't get custody of the other kid."

"We'll wait for the transcript."

"Jenny Ferris could also tell us how much her mom knows about plants. We might even lean on the kid a little. Just in case she suspects her mom did Weber in. We might convince her to say some things she wasn't planning to."

Root tugged at his mustache. They'd already decided not to talk to Cassie Ferris again until they had more information on her. Never ask a question unless you know the answer. Besides, she'd want a lawyer.

He paused for a new thought. If they brought Jenny in before her mother found out, they might avoid having some legal bullshitter getting in the way.

"What time do you think we could pick her up?" Root asked.

"I've got her schedule at the university. How about if we take her before class?" He dug through his notebook. "Today she's got one from three to five."

"What time is the messenger supposed to be here with that transcript?"

Socorro swallowed a bite of candy bar. "Didn't say. Before five."

"We'll get her before she goes into class."

"Wish I'd thought of that."

WHEN CASSIE GOT HOME at 1:45, she was feeling as anxious as she'd been when Jenny had gone out on her first date. She wished now that she had set a specific time for Corky to come by.

She poured herself a glass of iced tea and wandered around, poking her finger into the plants to see if they needed water. They didn't; obviously Jenny was doing her job. Then Cassie looked at the front door, waiting for the knock that would either bring her good news or bad.

Ridiculous, she told herself. She had things to do, although it took her some time to remember what they were. Ah, yes, she could call Mandy. David would be at work and Mandy was probably at home alone, moping.

After three rings the phone was answered by a male voice. "Hello?"

"David?"

"Yeah."

"This is Cassie Ferris. I thought you'd be at work."

David's voice, usually one of his assets, wasn't a bit charming. Instead there was anger, deep and bitter. "I'm home a lot these days," he said. "Mandy didn't tell you? I got fired. Three months ago."

"I'm sorry; I didn't know. Mandy hasn't said a word."

"Guess it isn't something a successful businesswoman would want to talk about. Having a husband who's a bum on unemployment!" The self pity was thick in his voice.

"It must be hard on you," Cassie said. "Is Mandy around by any chance?"

"Not here. She drove out to Lakeway to see her mom."

"Oh." Good for her, Cassie thought. While Lakeway was only forty miles or so from Austin, it was like another world with wild deer roaming the area and magnificent houses overlooking the lake. Cassie hoped Mandy could get away from her problems up there. "Well, thanks anyway, David," she said. "Good luck finding a job."

"Right. You want me to tell her you called?"

"No, no. I'll see her Monday."

Cassie hung up the phone. That had not been her most gracious, or diplomatic, moment but why the hell hadn't Mandy said something? She could understand if Mandy didn't want David's unemployment to become common knowledge, but why keep it a secret from Cassie? They were friends. Supposedly. And hiding something like that for three months?

And then Cassie remembered Mandy's recent concerns

about budgets. No wonder Mandy was worrying about money.

The doorbell rang and Cassie looked at the mantel clock. Two on the dot.

She hurried down the hall and flung open the door, letting a rush of warm air into the air-conditioned coolness of the house.

Corky was standing on the porch. In his hand was Roger's big brown briefcase.

"I found it," Corky said.

"I really can't thank you enough." Cassie stared at the case, almost afraid to take it even when Corky held it out to her. "This will help a lot," she said. She reached out, suddenly stiff and mechanical. The plastic handle was hot with the warmth of the day and slick with sweat from Corky's hand.

"Like I said, I'm really sorry for any inconvenience we caused." Corky took a step off the porch. A long white limousine was waiting at the curb.

"Not at all." She watched him get in the car, then turned inside, feeling the heaviness of the briefcase. Now she had to decide, did she call the police? Or did she open it first? She took it back to the dining room where she laid it on the table.

There were two combination locks, and Cassie tested each one, discovering, as she'd expected, that they were locked. She continued to stare at the briefcase. She still wasn't committed—

The phone rang and she jumped guiltily.

"Now what?" Cassie asked the empty room. With annoyance, she went into the living room and picked up the phone.

"Mom?" Beth's voice on the phone was stretched and taut.

"Beth?" Cassie said. "Honey, what is it?"

"I want to come home!" The words cracked with tears.

Cassie could feel her heart contracting. "Beth what's wrong?"

"Everything. Just everything. Please, Mom, make them let me come home." Cassie could hear a tiny sob over the long distance line. "Life is just awful. It's horrible here. They hate me."

"Talk to me, Honey. Tell me what's wrong."

There was a shuddering breath. "Tonight's the school dance, and Dad won't let me go."

Cassie felt an instant relief. Beth was all right. There was another tiny sob and Cassie's heart began to ache. School dances might mean nothing in a grown-up world, but when Beth hurt, so did Cassie. This was a crisis in Beth's life and Cassie wanted to be there with her. She wanted to hold her. See her face. Wipe away the tears. Be a real mother.

Instead, she held the receiver. "Did something happen?" Cassie asked. "Did you and your dad have a disagreement?"

The story came out slowly, tearfully.

At Beth's first mention of the dance, Linda, Beth's stepmother, had gone out and bought Beth a new pink dress to wear.

"It's got little ruffles on the neck! I'll look like some stupid baby!" Beth sniffled. "I told her no way."

Beth had insulted Linda's taste, which would bring out Brad's cruel streak. And his stubbornness. "Couldn't you just wear something else?"

"No! Dad got all mad and said that Linda had excellent taste. He said I dressed like a tramp. People would think I was a tramp!"

She knew how his words could hurt.

"It's okay, Honey, you dress differently from Linda, that doesn't make you wrong. You dress like Jenny and your friends."

"But he makes me feel so rotten. And now he says if I don't wear the dress I can't go to the dance tonight. They're just being mean. Especially Linda."

This is happening because strangers are raising my daughter.

That wasn't totally fair, obviously Brad was Beth's father. Still, Linda was flaunting her parental authority and Brad was allowing it.

"Can you do something, Mom?" Beth asked.

"Have you tried talking to Linda?" Cassie asked. Getting Brad to see another point of view was like reasoning with a rock. "What if you explained to her that you appreciate what she tried to do, but that the dress isn't the right style for you?"

"I did that, honest. I told her that it was nice of her, but we don't wear things like that anymore."

"And what did she say?"

Beth's voice sparked with anger. "She said that I was an ungrateful little brat and that I didn't deserve nice things. She can be so mean, Mom! Especially since she found out that she was pregnant." The bombshell of Linda's pregnancy was gone in an instant as Beth went on. "She's always saying that they ought to just ship me back to you. I told her that's what I want, but she won't let me go. It's because of Dad, but I don't know why it matters so much. He never listens to me; he just takes her side and tells me I'm lucky to have someone like her."

The implication was clear: Beth was lucky to have someone like Linda instead of Cassie. Even three years later Brad was punishing Beth for the sins of her mother.

Cassie had to stop herself from blurting out something she'd regret. It wouldn't help Beth, who needed a loving parent right now. "Your father loves you, Beth, but sometimes he forgets to show it." She threw out all caution. "I'll tell you what, I'll try to talk to him. I don't know how much good it will do, so don't get your hopes up. Are you at home?"

"No, I'm at school. I'm using Linda's long distance card. She gave it to me for emergencies. This is one, but I'll bet she blows her top when she finds out I called you."

"Look, Honey, antagonizing Linda isn't going to help any."

Now that Beth's anger was gone she sounded defeated. "I know. It's just things keep getting worse and worse. Stupid things." Her voice was choked with unshed tears. "I spilled some water in the kitchen and dad had a cow. He said that Linda could fall and lose the baby, and I was being totally thoughtless. It was an accident, Mom, but he wouldn't even listen! He's so mean when he says things like that. But then, sometimes I think maybe I'm a bad person."

"No! That's not true. You're a wonderful person. You're just very different from your dad and Linda. You're like Jenny." Beth idolized her older sister; maybe the image would help. But no matter what she said, Cassie felt useless, thousands of miles away from her daughter who needed her. "I wish I were there."

"Me too, Mom."

"I'll call your dad right now. Maybe by the time you get home, everything will be straightened out."

"Thanks. Just talking to you helped."

"I'm glad. Call me tomorrow and let me know what happened. Call collect. I love you."

"I love you, too." Beth's voice was soft as she finished. "Whole bunches, Mom."

"Whole bunches, Beth."

Cassie hung up the phone softly, realizing again that she had to get Beth back, home, where she belonged with Cassie and Jenny. But in the meantime Cassie had promised to talk with Brad, and no matter how much she dreaded that conversation, for Beth's sake, she had to do it immediately.

Cassie went for her address book and looked up the number of Ferris and Bork, Bond Traders. Brad's father owned the company and it would some day be under Brad's control. When Cassie had met Brad at the University of Texas, he had been the self-proclaimed black sheep of the family. He had refused to attend his father's alma mater, and instead had hied himself off to what his father referred to as the ends of the earth. After graduation Brad had stayed in Texas and married Cassie, another sign of his independence from his family.

Brad had always claimed his father was a despot, ruling the family with ridicule and money, and Brad had professed nothing but disdain for him. His parents had never come to see them, except for a one-day trip for the wedding ceremony.

During the years they were married, Cassie and Brad had only visited his family in Seattle twice.

Everything changed when Brad's father had a minor heart attack. Brad had flown home to Seattle and had been taken back like the prodigal son he was. After that his trips to Seattle became more frequent, although Cassie and the girls were always left behind. After one week-long visit Brad returned to announce that he'd fallen in love with someone named Linda and he wanted a divorce. It was the end of Cassie's life as she had known it.

Cassie sometimes wondered if Brad realized he'd grown up to be just like his father.

She dialed the number with determination and then spent time talking to the receptionist, two admins, and finally an assistant. Then she was relegated to hold, perhaps to prove her lack of importance with Ferris and Bork, Bond Traders.

Every delay gave Cassie an opportunity to become more nervous. She tried to think about what she was going to say and how she was going to say it, but her fear-clutched brain wasn't responding. The only thing clear to her was that she couldn't show emotion. Any unwise word and Brad would be quick to point out that she was becoming irrational. It wouldn't be true, but Brad would believe it.

That was his reality.

SEVENTEEN

"BRAD FERRIS." He snapped out the words, a busy man being interrupted in his busy day.

Just hearing those two words brought home a realization to Cassie: she had no hate left for her ex-husband. During the years since their divorce it had finally slipped away.

Nor did she harbor any love towards him. No secret dreams that he might change, or she might, and they could go back to the early days of their marriage. For the moment, Brad Ferris was merely something to be gotten around, like a detour sign that forced her miles out of her way.

Still, she had to be careful. "Brad, how are you? It's Cassie. I apologize for bothering you at work, but this couldn't wait. Do you have a minute to talk?"

"What is it you want, Cass?"

No "hello, how are you?", nothing. He was too important to waste trivial niceties on her; she wasn't on his level.

Cassie kept her voice even, not letting the anger reflect in its sound.

"I wanted to talk to you about Beth's school dance. She's very unhappy about not being allowed to go."

"She called you about that? Ridiculous. She can go on my conditions, but I won't have my daughter looking like a tramp off the street."

"Brad, Beth has reached that age where her tastes are different from yours and Linda's. And from mine. She's a teenager now and they don't dress like we do."

"She was also rude, did she tell you that? Letting her have her own way would be condoning that behavior."

"She told me about that, Brad, and she's sorry. Haven't you ever said something you wish you hadn't?"

He ignored that. "She will wear the dress or she will not go to the dance."

"Brad," Cassie said, carefully. "Tonight is important to Beth."

"It's just a junior high dance, for God's sake!"

"To us, maybe, but to Beth it's the most important night of her life. Oh, I know, there will be a lot more important occasions, but she doesn't see that. Not right now."

There was the bite of sarcasm as he said, "Just what would you like me to do, Cassandra?"

"Let her go to the dance. Dressed any way she wants."

"Like a slut."

"Like a teenager." Cassie heard the flash of anger in the words, and she took a long breath before she went on. "You know how they are. Think of the things that Jenny sends you for Christmas; Jenny picks those out herself, because she really thinks they'd look great on you."

"That awful, baggy purple shirt?"

"You didn't wear it, did you?"

"Never."

Cassie forced a small laugh, as if she were sharing a moment of discovery with her ex. "It's the same thing, Brad."

"I didn't throw it back in her face."

"Beth never meant to do that. She knows how much that

would hurt you and she loves you." Cassie paused, once again forcing the even tone she hated. "Brad, please just think about your decision. That's all I'm asking."

He cleared his throat. "I still don't like your interfering." But he seemed to be wavering.

"I don't like it, either, but I can't ignore my daughter when she calls me in tears. Could you, if Jenny had called you?"

"That's manipulation, Cassie."

"No, it's honesty. We both love our children and I'm only doing what you would do," Cassie said.

"I'll call Linda and discuss the matter, but that's all I'm promising."

She didn't push it, knew she didn't have to. "Thanks, Brad."

With shaking hands she replaced the receiver. It took her a moment to get her breathing back to normal. If she didn't hate Brad, she did hate how she had to behave with him. The dulcet tones, the constant need to turn the other cheek. And all because of one mistake.

"Damn it," she swore aloud, aware that she was still trembling with the effort of talking to her ex.

It was humiliating to have to act like a machine without feelings or caring. And Cassie knew there was only one way to put an end to it. Get Beth back.

Quickly and purposefully, Cassie went to the dining room. The briefcase sat waiting for her on the table.

THE PADS OF Cassie's thumbs were sore from turning the tiny locks on the briefcase. She had dialed in Roger's birthday, 6-2-0, and nothing had happened. She had tried the date as 6-60, for June '60, and again the latches had remained firm.

After that she had moved on to numbers that related to the

radio station. The station's actual frequency was 96.4. She tried those numbers with no success.

Cassie was getting frustrated and anxious. Some part of her knew the briefcase should be in the hands of the police, but she wasn't listening to that. Instead she intended to keep it until she had seen what was inside. *So, why wouldn't the damn thing open?*

She stared at the locks, willing them to open, but something else caught her attention. Keyholes. Tiny keyholes beside the combination locks—and she had Roger's keys!

It only took her a moment to pull them out of her purse, and select the key small enough to work on the briefcase. Then she raced back to the briefcase, and held her breath as she slid the key into the lock. It clicked and the latch popped open. She tried the other lock, holding her breath. It opened, just as easily as if Roger Weber's hand held the keys.

Before moving to the next logical step, Cassie ran to the kitchen for plastic sandwich bags that she put over her hands. She was ready. She faced the briefcase, and with great care pulled the top upward.

"We have lift-off!"

"IT'S ALMOST THREE. You about ready?" Socorro asked.

Root replaced everything in the case file and stood up. A dull pain throbbed in his back. Maybe it was from bending over the desk, or maybe it was from the tension he was feeling. Maybe it was just middle age.

"Yeah." Root automatically reached for his keys and notebook. "You have any idea where her classroom is?"

"I looked it up on the map; it's not far from Twenty-fourth."

Root grunted. On the UT campus, there were a lot of

places not far from Twenty-fourth, and they were all part of a maze of buildings surrounded by big trees. He couldn't tell one from the other.

There were never any convenient parking spaces at UT, either.

"Hope y'all weren't planning to leave," Ruth, the department's admin said as she whizzed around the corner.

"We're going out to question a witness," Root said.

Ruth shook her head. "Sorry, but Jacobs wants to see you in his office."

"Now what?"

"Somehow the transcript you ordered on that custody hearing was delivered to him."

Root almost threw his notebook on the desk. "He want us now?"

"If you can't make it any sooner," Ruth said with a grin.

"So, we'll pick up the Ferris kid later," Socorro said as he reached for his own notebook. "Let's go, Wayne."

Root followed him down the hall until they reached the large permanent offices at the end of the building. He was trying not to anticipate what Jacobs was going to say.

Socorro knocked on the door.

"Come in," came Jacob's voice.

As they entered, Sr. Sgt. Jacobs looked up and gestured toward chairs. The furniture was new, real wood, and Jacobs' certifications were all framed and hung on the walls.

Both detectives sat down, facing the big window on the opposite side of the office. Root could see the sky over 7th Street, as well as the old buildings that housed antique shops and gay bars below. He thought the view wasn't bad if you didn't look down.

Jacobs held out a hand and showed them the transcript they'd been waiting for.

With the light behind him, Jacobs seemed even bigger than usual and he was a big man. He was also almost bald. The department joke was that the hair missing from his head had slipped off and now covered the rest of his body. He had heavy black eyebrows that formed one dark line above his eyes when he was angry. Coarse hair grew on his arms below his short sleeves.

"I've been looking this over," Jacobs said. "Hope you don't mind."

"Not at all," Socorro said.

In Root's opinion, reading the transcript first was way out of line and yet typical of Jacobs. He didn't say anything.

Jacobs said, "I think we've got something here. You can start reading where I have it marked."

CASSIE STARED INTO Roger's briefcase, still unable to accept what she was seeing. She reached out a hand and touched the paper. It was real. Here in black and white was recorded the most horrible moment of her life.

Her body went cold with shock, then flamed with fury and shame. Somehow Roger Weber had gotten the transcript of Beth's custody hearing and had tucked it away in his briefcase. Cassie couldn't believe that any human being, even Roger, would use something like this against her. But he had once already—she saw that now.

Cassie's stomach began to tighten into a hard knot just as it had the day of the hearing. She sat back in a chair, suddenly weak and sick.

Thank God she had found the briefcase and opened it. If only she could make that whole terrible time of her life disappear as easily as she could, and would, dispose of the transcript. Some things were just too painful to be brought out for the rest of the world to see.

ROOT PICKED UP the computer pages of the custody hearing and Socorro scooted his chair closer so he could read at the same time.

Atty. Drake: Mrs. Ferris, as a mother, have you always acted wisely?

Mrs. Ferris: I've tried.

Atty. Drake: And have you succeeded? All of the time?

Mrs. Ferris: No, not all of the time. I've made mistakes, like all—

Atty. Drake: And those mistakes, do you believe they ever endangered the lives of your children?

Mrs. Ferris: No, of course not.

Atty. Drake: I would like you to tell us about the afternoon of April the 14th. Specifically, what you did from approximately 3:30 on.

Mrs. Ferris: I, that wasn't a typical day.

Atty. Drake: I didn't say it was. Now, your children got home from school at approximately 3:45. Were you there to greet them?

Mrs. Ferris: Usually I'm there when Beth and Jenny get home, because I get off the air early. That day I had gone to the grocery store.

Atty. Drake: Did you know that you wouldn't be back in time for your daughters' arrival?

Mrs. Ferris: Yes, but their father was going to be there.

Atty. Drake: You weren't thinking about your daughters, or their being home alone, is that correct, because their father was coming to the house at your request?

Mrs. Ferris: Yes.

Atty. Drake: But you did see him.

Mrs. Ferris: When I got home he was there with his—

Atty. Drake: He had a friend with him, and he was picking up his things as you had requested. Still, you started an argument.

Mrs. Ferris: I just asked him to leave, that was all. He wasn't alone—

Atty. Drake: So, after telling your husband to come to your jointly-owned home to get his things, and arranging a specific time for him to do so, you changed your mind. You ordered him to leave.

Mrs. Ferris: You're making me sound crazy.

Atty. Drake: That's your interpretation, Mrs. Ferris. Now, where were your children during this time?

Mrs. Ferris: They were in the backyard.

Atty. Drake: Where did the argument take place?

Mrs. Ferris: In the den.

Atty. Drake: And you left the den during the discussion. Is that correct?

Mrs. Ferris: Yes.

Socorro pulled the next page out from the stack so that he could read ahead. Root scowled but went on where he was.

Atty. Drake: And where did you go?

Mrs. Ferris: I went to the bedroom.

Atty. Drake: For what purpose? You weren't leaving for no reason.

Mrs. Ferris: I went to get something, but—

Atty. Drake: And what did you get?

Mrs. Ferris: Do I have to answer this?

Atty. Drake: Yes. And I remind you that you are under oath to tell the truth. Now, what did you go get?

Mrs. Ferris: (mumble)

Atty. Drake: We can't hear you, Mrs. Ferris. What did you go into the bedroom to get?

Socorro whistled softly. "That's a killer."

EIGHTEEN

CASSIE HAD GONE from shock to full blown fury.

She stared at the transcript page.

Atty. Drake: Yes. And I remind you that you are under oath to tell the truth. Now, what did you go to get?

Mrs. Ferris: (Mumble)

Atty. Drake: We can't hear you, Mrs. Ferris. What did you go into the bedroom to get?

Mrs. Ferris: I got a gun. But it wasn't what you're thinking—

Cassie crumpled the page; it smelled of Lagerfeld, Roger's after shave. The nearly full bottle had been wedged at the side of the case and some had leaked onto the transcript. The smell sickened her.

Roger hadn't just casually made that crack during the call-in at Happy Twosomes. No, it had been carefully aimed and he'd been delighted it hit the mark.

Her hands shook as she searched the rest of Roger's briefcase. She removed four spiral notebooks Roger used for show preparation and slapped them on the table. Under the notebooks she found a stack of magazines. Articles were earmarked for use. Roger wasn't funny on his own—he was always funny at someone else's expense.

Cassie was nauseous. She wanted to be done with this whole mess—especially Roger. With her baggie covered hands she replaced everything. Unfortunately there was one more spot that she had to check. Carefully she moved on to the pockets in the lid. She was calmer now; her anger had turned to ice.

In the top pocket she found copies, no doubt the ones Roger had stuffed away, out of her view, that Friday morning. One was a copy of her over-due bill from the attorneys Feiner, Craft and Fitch.

There were bits and pieces of other people's lives, too. Copies of Mandy's credit card bills, alongside a corporation agreement for Happy Twosomes. It had to be damaging to someone, maybe Greg.

Besides the personal papers there were pages from the Y-96 accounting ledger and several more from daily logs with listings of commercials to be played on the air.

Cassie didn't know which of the papers Roger had planned to talk to Bill and Walter about, but she knew that they would never see them all now. She set aside all the papers, then page by page crumpled the transcript before burying it in the bottom of the kitchen trash sack.

The other papers she carried into her bedroom where she made copies on her fax machine. Ah, the conveniences of the modern world.

Then she returned the rest of the originals to the briefcase, and wrote a note for Jenny, "Be back in an hour or so. Love, Mom."

Last, she relocked the briefcase. The click sealed her duplicity.

Now, she would deliver it to the police.

THEIR FOAM COFFEE CUPS littered Jacobs' desk and the sky outside the window was not as bright as it had been when Root and Socorro arrived. The sounds in the hallway had quieted too, now that most of the office staff had gone.

"They never really proved that Cassie Ferris meant to shoot her ex-husband or his new girlfriend," Socorro said, gesturing to the transcript, now folded and laying across his knees.

Jacobs was rubbing his bald head with the palms of his hands. "No, they didn't. But you don't get a gun unless you plan to use it."

"They didn't prove a damn thing," Root said.

"They didn't have to," Jacobs said. "They only had to show that she was unstable. Not a good influence on her kids. I'm surprised the judge let her have the older one."

"Jenny," Root said. "Except that, according to this, Jenny was determined to live with her mom and the judge did order Cassie Ferris into therapy for six months."

"And like you said," Socorro added. "They didn't prove much of anything."

Jacobs leaned forward. "The woman got her father's revolver, ran downstairs and confronted her ex-husband and his new girlfriend. She sure as hell had something in mind."

"What about suicide?" Socorro asked.

"She denied it, remember?" Jacobs said.

"No," Socorro said. "She didn't really deny anything. She just kept saying that she wasn't sure what she intended to do."

"You think the woman's psycho?" Jacobs asked.

Root made a sound.

"You got a problem, Root?" Jacobs asked.

Root had a lot of problems. "No." He wasn't sure how he felt about this new evidence, if that's what it was, against Cassie Ferris. He wanted the Weber thing solved, but he wanted something hard to present to the DA, too.

Root put his hands on the desk. "If you take this whole incident in context," he said, "I'm not sure what it means. First her husband leaves her. Then, within a month he announces his intention of marrying his new girlfriend who was years younger."

"Happens all the time," Jacobs said.

"Yeah, but that wasn't all she was dealing with. Her husband didn't give her any child support before the end of the divorce, so she was in a financial bind." Root felt a sympathy for Cassie Ferris that he was trying not to show. "And then Ferris got private detectives to follow the woman night and day so he could go after his kids."

Jacobs shrugged. "That was after the incident with the gun."

"Okay, but I still think she'd just reached the breaking point."

"And maybe she'd reached the breaking point with Weber. So, this time, she got smart and planned her murder more cleverly," Jacobs said. "You got anybody else in mind?"

"There's that disk jockey. Scott Delany," Socorro offered. "He stole some stuff from the last radio station he was at."

"Like what?"

"Typewriters. A computer—"

"Bring the Ferris woman in," Jacobs said. "Lean on her."

It wasn't a suggestion. Root and Socorro stood up, taking their coffee cups and the transcript with them.

"Oh, and I'll come in tonight after bowling," Jacobs added. "See how it's going."

Once they were outside, Socorro said, "I think we ought to eat first, then pick her up."

Great, thought Root. *Just great.*

CASSIE PULLED ONTO the on-ramp and stomped her foot hard on the gas peddle. She wanted the briefcase in official hands, and she wanted to be home again—as if she'd never seen the thing.

Small worries nagged at her. What if she had left her fingerprints on one of the papers? No, that wasn't possible; she'd been too careful. What if they asked if she had opened the briefcase?

She whipped around a slow moving car and cut over to the right lane.

If the police asked, she would simply lie.

Traffic was light; everyone else was moving away from the downtown area, not towards it. She took the Fifth St. exit, staying on Fifth until she was almost at I-35. Then she cut across to Eighth. By the time she found a parking place near the tall, sand-colored building of the Austin Police Department, Cassie's heart was pounding hard.

It's guilt, she thought. Maybe even well-deserved guilt, but for her, it was worth every irregular heartbeat to keep the transcript away from the police.

She pulled out the briefcase, locked the car and crossed the street, heading toward the double-wide glass front doors.

Once inside, air conditioned air chilled her over-heated body and Cassie stopped.

Sweeping circular counters, in varying shades of orange, formed a reception desk in the center of the room. Cassie sucked in a breath and crossed toward it; her footsteps were muffled by the echoing voices of police and citizens alike.

At the desk she waited behind two others.

Eventually it was her turn and a uniformed officer asked, "Can I help you?"

"I need to leave something for Detective, I mean, Sergeant Socorro," Cassie said. *Maybe they'll think I'm a lawyer.*

The man pointed to her right. "Other side. Keep going and tell them back there."

"Thank you." She moved further along the desk until she found a woman in civilian clothing wearing an identification badge.

"Yes, Ma'am? What can we do for you?"

"I need to see Sergeant Socorro." Cassie tried to lift the briefcase but her arm trembled so hard she couldn't. Instead she set the case on the floor. "I have something I need to give him."

"Socorro?" The woman clicked something into a computer, then picked up a phone. "Hey, is Socorro up there? Yeah. Yeah. Now isn't that typical!" She laughed as she put down the phone and turned to Cassie. "Sorry, but he went for dinner just a few minutes ago. Should be back later, though."

"That's all right. I'll just leave this. Do you have something I can write a note on?"

"Sure, here," she said, flipping over a piece of paper and handing it to Cassie. "You got a pen?"

"Yes, I do."

Cassie slid the paper along the counter, and fumbled in her purse for what seemed like a very long time until she could grasp her pen.

In a scrawl that looked nothing like her normal handwriting she wrote, "Sgt. Socorro. This is Roger Weber's briefcase. It was in the limousine that he used last Friday. Cassie Ferris."

She gave the note to the woman and with a shaking arm, finally got the briefcase up on the counter.

"He can call me," Cassie said. "If he has any questions."

"Okay; I'll handle the rest."

Cassie said thank you and started for the door. It seemed miles away. Her back twitched as if expecting someone to grab her. She wouldn't allow herself to run. Instead she took slow steady steps until she reached the warmth of the early evening sunshine. Once outside, she lengthened her stride as she walked to the car. She could almost breathe again.

It was Friday night. She would go home and order pizza for Jenny and herself. And while they ate, they would figure out why Roger had collected all the documents he had. And if any of them had brought him to his death.

LEMON MERINGUE PIE, its topping stiff and lightly browned, was placed in front of Socorro.

Root watched as the waitress scooped up their empty plates and stacked them expertly on her arm.

"More coffee?" she asked.

"No, we're in a hurry," Root said.

"I'll take a little," Socorro said.

As she moved off, Socorro cut the tip off his piece of pie and brought it to his mouth.

Root said, "That stuff will kill you."

Socorro savored the bite and swallowed. "This isn't bad for me. Eggs, lemons, it's all healthy stuff."

"Believe what you want," Root said, glancing around the coffee shop. The orange plastic booths were filled with the dinner crowd. "What time you think we ought to get her?"

Socorro looked at his watch. It was just before seven. "Soon as I finish this. Don't worry, she'll be home all evening. This'll just give her a chance to eat some dinner, too. Make it easier for us later."

They were at I-35 and Ben White, at least twenty-five minutes from Cassie Ferris's house. Still, if the questioning went on late into the night, and it could, Root knew he'd be glad that Socorro had talked him into eating.

"YOU STOLE THESE?" Jenny demanded.

"No, I didn't steal them," Cassie said, denying the act as well as her stab of guilt. "These are copies of what I found in Roger's briefcase and I don't want to talk about how I got them."

"How convenient."

Cassie hadn't mentioned the transcript to Jenny, nor would she. That had been a painful time and there was no need to dredge it up.

Jenny was on the floor, skimming a handful of papers. Sly was on the loveseat washing himself thoroughly, a task he usually saved until company was present. Cassie was on the couch studying the corporation agreement from Happy Twosomes.

Whereas, wherefore.

Cassie must have made some sound. "What?" Jenny asked.

"Lawyer talk."

Cassie skipped along the page until her eye caught on a name. She sat up straighter, reading slowly, forcing her brain to understand.

After a few minutes of concentration she had figured it out.

"I don't believe it," she said.

"What?"

"Rachel Sankey owns five percent of Happy Twosomes."

"No wonder she was bossing everyone around," Jenny said. "But why would Roger care? Is that bad?"

Cassie thought about it. "I don't think anyone would have cared if Rachel had mentioned up front about her association with Happy Twosomes, but to keep it secret was a mistake. It could be construed as a conflict of interest. You know, selling air time, and buying it herself for Happy Twosomes. And setting up the promotion. You have to make those things public. Or you should."

Apparently Roger had hated Rachel enough to run straight to Walter with the information, perhaps hoping it would be enough.

"Would she have gotten fired?" Jenny asked.

Cassie closed her eyes and tried to imagine Walter's response to this news. "Walter would cheer Rachel on. Oh, he'd give her a bad time at first for putting the station in a precarious position, but eventually he'd come around. He liked to see people make money. He liked to see them advance."

"Didn't Roger know that?"

"I don't know. Maybe Roger thought he was the only one Walter encouraged."

The more Cassie mulled it over, the more she thought Roger had been blinded by his anger. He probably had thought he could get Rachel fired with this ammunition, which only proved how stupid anger could make a person.

"This is a log, isn't it?" Jenny asked, holding up a sheet.

"Yes," Cassie said.

"Why would Roger want a list of the commercials you guys play? '7:10: Catalyst Training, Street Corner Productions, Petry, CPA. 7:25: N & S Chinese Restaurant, Highland Mall, Classic Oldsmobile-Pontiac.' Big deal. What's so important about this?" Jenny asked.

"I don't know." Cassie was tired; the long shower and washing her hair had helped, but she wasn't thinking as quickly as she wished she were.

"Someone wrote something on it," Jenny said.

"Where?"

Jenny handed up the sheet. There was indeed something written, but it was merely an additional commercial at 7:50 for Street Corner Promotions. "I don't think it means anything," Cassie said.

"Then why'd they write it in?"

"Probably because the client bought extra commercials after the log had been printed. Or maybe one was aired, but something was wrong with it."

"Boring," Jenny said. "And there are more logs."

"And accounting pages," Cassie offered, continuing to study the paper she held. It was actually part of an 'aging', showing the amounts due from various clients in columns marked thirty, sixty, ninety and over one-hundred-and-twenty days. Some clients were past due, that much was obvious. "What's the date on that log you have?" Cassie asked.

"May 25th."

Cassie looked at the aging. "This is from September."

"Last month." Jenny stood up and sat beside her mother,

whose curly hair was still damp from a shower. "I like the way your hair smells. What shampoo did you use?"

"I don't know and don't take it," Cassie said. "You have your own. That very expensive stuff."

"Don't go postal." Jenny looked over at the aging Cassie was holding. "Somebody wrote all over that, too."

"They do all the time," Cassie said. "They have collection meetings and they decide who will make the next phone call to try and get the money owed by the client. Either the sales-person, Mandy or Bill."

"How do you know?"

"Mandy comes down to my office and complains after the meetings. She hates them."

"Oh." Jenny stared at the paper, pointing to a notation. "That says 'write-off'; what does that mean?"

"It means that they gave up trying to collect the money and wrote it off as a bad debt."

"Wish people would do that with our bills," Jenny said with a grin.

"We pay our bills."

"Yeah, but wouldn't it be nice if we didn't have to?"

"No, because then we couldn't get any more credit."

"So, why aren't these people worried? These Street Corner Productions?"

Cassie shifted around to look at Jenny. "Where's that log page? I just had an idea."

Jenny flipped through her copies and handed one to Cassie. "What?"

"Look! Street Corner Productions, here on the log. This is when they ran, last May, and this is when the debt was written off. September."

Jenny looked puzzled. "Obviously, if they had a past due account they had to run commercials. So, what?"

"I don't know." Cassie frowned. It had to mean something, but she had no idea what. She felt brain-dead. The day had simply been too long and she couldn't think.

"While you're figuring it out, I'm going to order the pizza," Jenny said, rising from the couch. "I'm starved."

Cassie needed a break. "Order it with sausage. And extra cheese. And *no* jalapenos."

"I know, Mother," Jenny said as the doorbell rang. "You want me to get that?"

"Please. But let me put these things away first."

Cassie couldn't imagine who would be at the door on a Friday night. In a quick movement, she scooped up all the papers and slid them under the couch.

NINETEEN

"MOM, IT'S GREG," Jenny called from the front door.

"Greg?"

His voice came down the hall. "We have a date, or am I early?"

Cassie shot up from the couch and looked at the clock. It was seven-fifteen and she had forgotten that she had a date. As Greg and Jenny entered the living room, she was trying desperately to stand still, when her inclination was to run for the other room.

"Are you ready?" Greg asked. His eyes traveled from her damp hair down to her red shirt and white shorts, finally reaching her bare feet. "Not quite? Soon?"

At least he was in shorts, too.

Cassie was aware of how silly she was going to sound. "Greg, I'm sorry, some things came up and I totally forgot we had plans for tonight."

"Nice going, Mom," Jenny said.

"Does this mean you can't go?" Greg asked. "Or do you just need a few extra minutes?"

Cassie looked at the clock again, then at Jenny.

"Go ahead," Jenny said. "Just leave me some money for the pizza."

"Well," Cassie hesitated. She thought about the papers shoved under the couch. Maybe if she went out and thought about something entirely different, her subconscious would take over. By the time she got back, she might be able to make sense of what she'd found. "Give me five minutes," she said.

"Take more if you need it. Sunset isn't for another thirty minutes or so."

"Jenny, fix Greg something to drink; I'll be right back."

Cassie broke all land speed records getting ready, in part to make up for the rudeness of forgetting a date. Although she noted with some interest that Greg hadn't taken her forgetfulness as a sign of anything lacking in him. Nor had he seemed angry. Brad would have thrown a fit if he'd come home and found she wasn't ready for some planned event. Was that the difference between the two men, or the difference between a husband and a date?

She picked up a brush and began working on her hair. It was actually going to cooperate. A good omen, she thought, as she slipped on sandals. Then she brushed some blush on her cheeks, added lipstick and headed for the living room.

Greg stood up.

"Ready." Cassie picked up her purse and pulled out a twenty-dollar bill. "For the pizza," she said, handing it to Jenny. "We won't be late."

"Don't hurry home on my account."

"We'll be at the Oasis if you need me," Cassie added.

Jenny rolled her eyes. "And I'll be here if you need me."

TWENTY MINUTES LATER Greg and Cassie were sitting on one of the wooden decks at the Oasis, watching the fiery pink sun highlighting the sky as it slipped closer to the horizon. Below them the lake glistened like liquid silver.

A young waiter in T-shirt and shorts placed their drinks in

front of them. Greg was having iced tea, Cassie a tall, crisply green frozen margarita. One sip and she realized how potent it was.

"Whew! This might be more than I bargained for."

"Luckily you have a designated driver." He held up his tea glass and clinked it with hers. *"Salud."*

"Prosit." She took another big swallow, then glanced out at the horizon and the shimmering sunlight. "It's beautiful."

"Agreed. Beautiful," he said.

She turned to find he was watching her rather than the sunset. Her mind, tied so totally into her day, stopped. "Are you flirting with me?"

"Isn't that allowed?"

"I'm sure it is," Cassie said. "I just don't know the rules."

"Not to worry. Just follow my lead."

She thought about it. The old reflexes had to be there, slow perhaps, but not dead. "Is that a good idea?"

"Sure, just trust me on this."

Cassie made a face "Not my strong suit."

The waiter returned and took their food order. The sun began to sink even lower, leaving only a half circle of glowing red color in the deepening sky. Just below them Cassie could see a sailboat gliding into a cove. It made a graceful tack and headed out toward the other side of the lake. She could just make out the name. "Mirage."

Cassie felt as if she were in a mirage, a shimmering spot of calm that would disappear all too soon, leaving her in the midst of the papers she'd shoved under the couch.

"So, tell me why you have a problem with trust," Greg said, picking up his glass.

She dismissed the suggestion. "It's an old story. Very old."

"We make a lot of decisions about life and who we are, based on things that happened in childhood."

Cassie turned to look at him in the fading light. "I forgot that you're a psychologist."

"Pretend I'm not," he said.

"And you promise not to make any insightful remarks?"

"That's easier than you think," Greg said with a half laugh. He saw her face, and grew serious. "I'd still like to hear about you and trust."

What was she going to tell him? About her father? About her piece-of-shit ex-husband? She just might, especially with the margarita easing away her tensions, not to mention inhibitions.

Cassie sat back in her chair. "It's just that my father left us when I was eleven. He was a Lieutenant Colonel and I thought he was the most important man in the world. When he left, well, he left…" her voice trailed off and she took another swallow of her drink. "I didn't see my father again until I was nineteen."

"What was your father like?"

Her image of him was clouded, except one characteristic. "Militant."

"Abusive?"

"You promised you wouldn't have any insights," Cassie reminded him.

"Sorry," Greg said. "When I'm not being insightful I can be terribly slow."

"Why do I doubt that?"

"Trust, again?"

"Could be." There was an easy acceptance in Greg that she was beginning to like.

"You were telling me about your father," he reminded her.

"Ah, yes." She sighed. "As you guessed, he could be unkind. But it was more than just that. He somehow made us feel we deserved whatever we got because he was right. And I was always…" She shook her head. "Wrong."

She regretted saying that and looked up into Greg's face, expecting pity. Instead, he was nodding, waiting to hear more. "Anyway," she went on, "I've been told that having a parent who leaves like that, even an abusive one, removes some of your ability to trust."

"Not your ability. Trust is a choice," Greg said, his voice without any criticism. "But it does make the right choice a little harder. What was your husband like?"

"Like my father. Rigid. Oh, he wasn't physically abusive, but he was the master of ridicule. Still can be."

"Do you have to see him much?"

"No, but it's not me I worry about. It's my daughter, Beth. She's the one who suffers."

Greg looked surprised. "I thought you only had Jenny?"

"No, I have two girls. Beth is thirteen, and she lives with Brad. In Seattle." Cassie thought about Beth and wondered if she was at the dance right now. Cassie hoped so. And she hoped that soon, Beth would be in Austin.

"How often do you get to see her?"

"Only once or twice a year. And if Brad isn't happy about something—" Cassie couldn't say the words.

The sun disappeared behind a distant hill, leaving a brilliance of color that tinted the sky a vibrant red.

"I'm sorry I asked so many questions—I didn't mean for you to be unhappy."

Trying to be flippant, Cassie said, "I'm just following your lead."

Greg rewarded her effort with a smile.

ROOT SLAMMED the palm of his hand down on the steering wheel. "Damn!"

Socorro reached for his seat belt. "So, we missed her. Shit happens."

"Jacobs isn't going to buy that."

It was growing dark as he looked back at Cassie Ferris's house. The kitchen windows were bright with light. Her car, an older gold Datsun was parked in the driveway, but when they'd gone to the door they'd learned that Cassie was out for the evening.

"We could wait here for her to come back," Socorro said.

"Jenny said it would be late."

Socorro shrugged. "We don't know what late is for Cassie Ferris. If she usually gets up at four o'clock like Weber did, she might get tired by ten. That's not so late."

A call for them came over the radio and Socorro picked up the mike. "This is two-oh-four."

They were on a non-emergency frequency and the words came back casually. "You got a package at the station."

"What is it?" Socorro asked.

"Briefcase, delivered by a Cassie Ferris. Her note says it's Roger Weber's briefcase."

"I'll be damned!" Root said.

Socorro grinned, as he said into the mike, "She still there?"

"Nope. Delivered earlier, but you were out."

"We're on our way."

Socorro replaced the mike and looked at Root. "We'll see what's in that briefcase and by that time Cassie Ferris will be home. We'll bring her in." He added, "It'll be an all night party; hope there's some popcorn in the vending machine."

"So, HOW DID YOU end up owning a video dating club?" Cassie asked.

"Now that's a long story." He wiped his face with a crumpled napkin and pushed away his plate.

"I'm up for it." It was his turn.

"Are you sure?"

"Sure."

"Well, I was in private practice up in Illinois and my two partners decided to start an alcohol and drug rehabilitation center," he began. He cocked his head, looking out over the dark lake with its path of moonlight stretching across it. Then he turned to Cassie. "The center didn't seem crucial, to me—there were plenty of re-hab centers around. The people who check into them have already taken their first step toward recovery." He took his time, trying to explain. "I know they still need help, but I wanted to reach people who weren't that far along."

"So you started Happy Twosomes?" It made no sense whatsoever to Cassie.

"It sounds crazy, but I had a friend who'd opened a club like Twosomes in Dallas. He was doing very well, except he kept telling me about people repeating the same patterns in their relationships. One man would date ten different women, always choosing the same type, always unhappy when he didn't find what he wanted. I saw that kind of thing in my practice as well—people doing the same thing over and over again expecting different results. That's one definition of insanity." He looked at Cassie. "Do you know much about therapy?"

"A little. I saw a counselor for almost a year."

Greg nodded. "This friend of mine suggested I come and teach some classes on relationships. I thought it would be a way of getting to people who wouldn't ordinarily seek out counseling. So I moved to Dallas. I was newly divorced and ready for a change."

"But it didn't work?"

"Oh, it worked, I just wasn't making enough money to support myself." He smiled a boyish, almost sheepish, smile. "Besides, my friend seemed to be getting richer and richer, while I was struggling to pay my child support. Hardly seemed fair, so I decided to try a club in Austin with his help. Sort of a franchise deal. And it looks like it's going to work."

Cassie thought of the corporation agreement. "And your partners are happy?"

"They're going to make money."

"How many partners do you have?"

"Two, actually. The friend in Dallas, and then at the last minute, when some of the short-term financing fell through, I ended up with one down here." He didn't mention who that other partner was. "The interesting thing is, I hate running the club. I don't like managing a staff that large, and frankly, the image thing, you know video dating, bothers me. So I've decided to sell Happy Twosomes."

"You're kidding! Already?"

"It's on the market now. That's confidential, by the way," he said. "When it sells, I'll stay in Austin, but I'm going back to private practice. And tennis and all the things I like to do."

"You certainly made a quick decision."

"A selfish one. I don't even like thinking about Twosomes anymore," Greg said. "Next subject."

During dinner the light had faded, and as the sky had darkened. their conversation had become more open. Cassie ticked off the things she'd learned about Greg. "Okay," she said. "So, you've been divorced for three years and you have two boys, one sixteen, one nineteen. Jason and Kevin?"

"Very good," Greg said.

"When do you see them?"

"They were down here most of the summer. They helped with the club, setting up equipment, making suggestions." He laughed. "We probably could have opened two months earlier if they hadn't been involved, but it was worth it to have them around."

"What about your ex-wife, Penny? You told me she drove you crazy, but you never said why. Why did she?"

"Now there's a question!" Greg said.

"You can answer it anyway you want."

"How about with the truth, at least my version of it? Penny is one of those perpetually unfulfilled people, and I couldn't convince her that I wasn't enough to fill the empty spots in her life." He let out a breath, as if letting go of some annoyance at the same time. "And I probably didn't help much because I was always busy. On purpose." He shook his head. "At least I knew where to get help."

"I think exes bring out the worst in us."

"Does yours?"

"Sometimes."

"Was your divorce difficult?"

Cassie leaned forward, putting her elbows on the table. She looked toward the lake, taking a moment to think about her answer. "At first I was relieved that I didn't have to face Brad every day."

"That's a healthy sign."

She sat up. "Not so healthy; it didn't last very long. Then I..." she paused and picked up her napkin. "The day Brad announced he was re-marrying, just a month after he'd left, I didn't behave too well."

"I've told you my guilty secrets. Yours can't be any worse."

It was fully dark now and the umbrella above their table kept both their faces shaded from the lights of the patio. It made Cassie feel anonymous and safe.

She took a deep breath. The past seemed so close all of a sudden—as if the custody hearing had been that morning. She wanted to explain it to someone, and maybe justify what she'd done.

"One afternoon," she said, "about a month after he'd left, Brad, my ex, was coming over to get some of his things. I went to the grocery store so I wouldn't have to see him, avoid the whole situation. But, then I had this crazy idea that he might come home for good. That somehow we'd talk, and he'd realize that he still loved me. Want me back."

"That's pretty normal."

"Is it? I don't think anything I did was normal. I left the half-filled grocery cart in the aisle and ran home."

"And what happened?"

Cassie looked again at the silken water of the lake. In the distance the deep thrum of a power boat added a discordant note.

"When I got home, Brad wasn't alone." Cassie's voice caught. "A woman was with him, and he introduced her to me as his fiancée. Linda. He'd brought her along to meet the girls. I felt like such a fool. He hardly even looked at me, he was so busy talking to Linda, touching her..." she stopped. Even three years later she could feel the pain if she poked at it. She took a breath. "Then he told her to help him pick out the furniture they wanted. He ignored me like I didn't even exist and they walked around…shopping in my home. As if it were some damn department store! I couldn't believe it! And finally Brad said to me, 'Don't worry, Cassie, we won't be taking much. Linda has excellent taste.'" Cassie realized she was shredding her napkin, and tossed it on the plate in front of her.

"You had a right to be angry. He was invading your privacy, and bringing an intruder into your home," Greg said. "Anyone would have been furious."

She had come this far with the story and she couldn't stop now. "But not everyone would have done what I did. I told them to get out, and when Brad laughed at me, said I was being ridiculous…I went upstairs and got my father's gun. His military pistol. I pointed it at them and said some of the stupidest things I've ever said in my life." Cassie could feel her skin prickle with embarrassment. "Things like, 'I'll shoot you both if you don't leave my house.' Oh, and the really memorable, 'When you're dead I'll stick the gun in your hand, Brad, so it looks like a murder/suicide pact.'" Cassie rubbed her hot face in her hands. "Not my favorite memory." She looked at Greg. "Brad just kept sneering at me—that's when I pulled the trigger."

"And you shot…?"

"The front door."

Greg watched her. Finally he said, "And nobody was hurt and it didn't matter in the end."

"Not quite," Cassie said. "That's when Brad hired a private detective to follow me. That's why he filed the custody suit, and that's how he got Beth. That's why he still has Beth. Because, you see," she took a breath. "I wasn't rational."

THE BRIEFCASE sat open in front of them. Each item was now encased in a plastic bag, and smudged with fingerprint powder.

Socorro grinned. "You know what I think? I think our boy, Rog, was raiding desks when he wasn't on the air. A flip of the old credit card and most inside doors are easy. Or maybe, he knew where they kept the master keys. He sure took lots of financial stuff." Socorro wasn't known for his quick thinking, but he was methodical and had a good memory. "The owner of the station, Kraley, said that Weber wanted to talk to him and made it sound urgent. Any of this look urgent?"

"As blackmail material, maybe."

A long shadow fell across Root's desk and he looked up to find Sr. Sgt. Jacobs standing over them. Jacobs was in his green and white league-bowling shirt and he didn't look happy. Must have lost that night.

"Where's the Ferris woman?" Jacobs asked.

"We missed her," Socorro said. He indicated the briefcase and Cassie's note. "She dropped this off earlier when we were out. The briefcase was Weber's."

Without saying a word, Jacobs pulled a chair from a nearby desk and sat down. First he read the note from Cassie Ferris. Then he picked up the papers in their plastic bags. Root and Socorro waited as he studied each one, then laid it face down.

Finally, when Jacobs had finished with all of the papers, he said, "So, what's it all mean?"

"We were just discussing that," Root said. "The Ferris woman told us that Weber hid some papers in his briefcase—"

"I know all that," Jacobs growled. He knew everything they did. "Get to the point."

"We aren't sure," Socorro said, "but I've got an idea. There are a lot of accounting papers here. Maybe someone was pilfering money from the station and this was Weber's proof. That sort of thing."

"Well, I think this whole briefcase thing is some cock 'n bull story that Cassie Ferris made up to throw us off."

"But—"

"It's as plain as the nose on your face. Weber fights with the Ferris woman Friday morning and that night he fights with her daughter. She's had enough. She goes out to the patio, sees that plant, the poisonous one, and chops it up to feed him. Then she gets her daughter and high-tails it home."

Socorro said, "Martinez and her partner have called most of the guests, they're up to a little over 300, and so far, none of them saw Cassie Ferris go into that private lounge."

"Have them keep after it. Someone will remember." Jacobs stood up. "And get the Ferris woman in here. We'll find out if I'm right. Now." Root looked at his watch, and Jacobs added, "Don't worry about her missing a little beauty sleep, Root. She can make up for it with a few years in maximum security."

"Yes, sir," Socorro said, as Root reached for his keys.

TWENTY

CASSIE DIDN'T INVITE GREG IN. They stood on the porch steps under the dark night sky and she said, "Thanks again for the evening, Greg. I really had a nice time."

"You're welcome and so did I. I'm just sorry I didn't realize how tired you were."

She'd been up since four and her muscles seemed to have given up the fight against gravity as she leaned against the porch pillar. "That's all right."

"Well," he said, "You have a friend, anytime you need one. Just give me a call."

Cassie smiled. "Thanks. I'll remember that."

Greg reached out and gently touched her chin, tilting her face upward. A tingle rippled along Cassie's spine as he brushed his lips lightly against hers.

Something rustled in the neighbor's pyracantha hedge. She straightened up. *Probably Sly,* Cassie thought, *and what lousy timing.*

Greg took a step backward, still watching her face with the small boyish smile she was beginning to know. "Sleep well."

"Good night."

"I'll call you tomorrow," Greg said as he moved across the lawn toward his car.

Cassie waited on the porch until he had driven off, his wave and the wonderful smile just a memory.

Then she called, "Sly?"

No sound came from the hedge. Now she'd have to play hide and seek with the silly cat. It didn't matter. Cassie wasn't quite ready to face Jenny and all her questions, anyway.

And she had to admit, despite her protests about dating, it had been a wonderful evening. Almost like a recess from real life.

She straightened up and called again, "Sly? Come here, you big monster cat."

From the hedge came a sound like a cherry bomb exploding. Something whizzed through the air past Cassie and slammed into the front door. Her head snapped up. There was another crack and then something else flying past. She whirled around and saw a dark spot on the front door. The blunt end of a bullet.

Cassie fell to the ground and crawled the few steps to the door, reaching up to open it. There was another report. Now she knew it was a shot. The door opened in front of her.

"Mom? What are—"

"Get back!" Cassie pushed Jenny inside and fell through the door. "Close it!"

Jenny did as she was told and Cassie jumped to her feet. "Go!" Cassie snapped, locking the door and shoving Jenny down the hall.

"What's going on?" Jenny demanded when they reached the living room. Sly was there kneading the carpet.

Cassie picked up the phone and threw it to Jenny. "Call the police. Some crazy person is out there with a gun."

Then she raced off to check that the back door was locked. She knew the windows were secured; they locked automatically when closed.

In seconds Cassie was back beside Jenny.

"Someone is shooting a gun in front of our house," Jenny was saying. Then in a voice that sounded more bewildered than frightened, she gave their address. "Yes, ma'am, we will." She hung up.

"Is someone coming out?" Cassie asked.

"Yes. She said to stay in an interior room and make sure everything is locked."

"It is." Cassie hugged Jenny and pulled her down on the couch. Sly jumped up on Jenny's lap. No sounds from the outside reached them. Cassie hoped that meant the person with the gun was gone.

"So what happened?" Jenny demanded. "I heard Greg's car, and I was coming to unlock the door when I thought something hit the house. It was a bullet?"

Cassie nodded. "I saw it. It's still there."

"That's crazy!"

"Kids," Cassie said. "It has to be. Probably drinking too much and showing off. They probably didn't even see me." But some part of her didn't believe it.

ROOT GOT OUT of the car and walked around the blue and white to get to Cassie Ferris's yard.

"This could work to our advantage," Socorro said, trotting along beside him. "Maybe Weber's killer is getting sloppy. Maybe this will be a break."

They started up the two steps to the porch. "Maybe," Root said.

Socorro rang the bell. Jenson, one of the line patrolmen, answered the door immediately.

"You guys made a trip for nothing," Jenson said. "Nobody's dead. Nobody's even hurt."

"Cassie Ferris is a witness in one of our cases," Socorro explained.

Jenson whistled. "Then let me show you what we've got." He stepped outside and shut the door behind him, pointing to the bullet in the door, then at another two on the front wall of the house. As he explained what he'd been told of the shooting, Root looked around.

"You find anything in the bushes?" Root asked, pointing at the hedge with its clusters of orange berries. It was almost as tall as he was.

"Not a thing."

"So, nobody was around except Mrs. Ferris?"

"That's right. Her friend had already driven off."

"Who was the friend?"

"Some guy who owns a video dating club." Jenson said. "Grilkey's inside; he's got everything written down. You coming in?"

"Give us a minute to look around," Root said.

"Okay." Jenson went back inside the house and shut the door.

Root and Socorro went to their car and got big flashlights, then they walked Cassie's front yard and finally the neighbor's. The grass was thick and springy; there was no chance for footprints. Nor did they see anything else that might be called evidence. There was no convenient scrap of mate rial clinging to the prickly pyracantha hedge and no cigarette butts. In fact, there was no evidence at all that someone had hidden near the bushes, or anywhere else.

Socorro flicked off his light as they headed for the front door. He frowned at the bullet, sticking obscenely out of the wood. "Well, someone did shoot at her; that much at least is obvious."

"No, someone shot a gun," Root said. "Not necessarily at Cassie Ferris."

"What are you saying?"

"Jacobs is going to think she did the shooting herself to distract us."

Socorro started grinning. "And she could have."

Once Jensen let them back inside they joined Grilkey and the two Ferris women in the living room. Two pairs of dark brown eyes widened as they saw the detectives.

"Mrs. Ferris, Jenny," Root said with a nod.

She was wearing shorts and a red shirt. She had nice legs. Must do some kind of exercise. The red should have been good with her dark hair and eyes, but she was pale, almost waxen. "Mrs. Ferris, we'd like you to come to the station with us."

"Now?" She looked surprised and wary.

"Yes, Ma'am."

"But, I don't see what else I can tell you."

"We don't know either, until we talk with you. It might help us solve Roger Weber's murder."

She looked at Jenny. "I don't want to leave Jenny by herself."

"I could spend the night at Brandi's," Jenny offered. Then she frowned. "But then when you got back, you'd be alone."

"If we think there's any danger, we'll put a patrolman out front of the house," Socorro offered.

"And Jensen can drop Jenny off at her friend's," Root added. "We won't let anything happen to you."

Cassie seemed to hesitate, but finally nodded. "Jenny, you'd better call Brandi right now. It's already eleven."

While Jenny Ferris went to the other room to call, Root told Jensen to get a forensic team to check the yard. Never knew what they might find. Then he turned to Cassie Ferris. "Are you okay? Not hurt are you?"

"I'm fine." She seemed tired and confused. "Should I take my car?"

"No," Root said. "We'll drive you. We'll wait to make sure Jenny has things arranged."

Cassie nodded. "Let me see what she's doing."

When she was gone Root noticed Socorro was already moving around the room; he picked up the pillows on the couch and looked behind them. He opened a door on the bottom shelf of the TV stand and bent down to peer inside.

"We could get a warrant," Root said.

"Takes too long. Why don't you look in the hall closet?" Grilkey grinned. "You want me to check the kitchen?"

Root nodded and Grilkey moved off. Root didn't like what they were doing, but if it did turn up a gun, it wouldn't matter. They'd seal the house and get a warrant.

He went to the hall and opened the closet door. There were some wool skirts, sweaters and heavy coats in plastic cleaner bags. Pretty much what was in Lucille's front closet. Two tennis racquets, a badminton set, a stack of used textbooks and a pair of running shoes with a coating of mud were on the closet floor.

In the kitchen he could hear Grilkey quietly opening and closing cabinets. Root looked down the hall toward the living room. No sign of Cassie Ferris, but he could still hear her daughter on the telephone. He also thought he heard running water, but he wasn't sure.

Root checked the shelf above the hanging clothes. More

books, some Christmas wrapping paper and a fuzzy wool hat. No gun there.

"Wayne," Socorro called. "Come here a minute."

Quietly Root closed the door and went to the living room. Socorro was holding a sheaf of papers.

"Look at these," Socorro said, his voice low but urgent. "I'd swear these are copies of everything we found in Weber's briefcase."

Root took the papers and looked them over. "I'll be damned. Where'd you find them?"

Socorro was grinning. "Under the couch."

"Son of a bitch."

"We got us a breakthrough!" Socorro was still smiling as he slid the papers back under the blue and white striped sofa. "Hope Jacobs went home. I'd like to greet him in the morning with Weber's murderer."

"Don't count your chickens," Root said.

"Yeah," Socorro said. "Until they've signed a confession."

Grilkey returned shaking his head. "No gun."

"I didn't think you'd find one," Root said.

They were all standing in the living room when Jenny Ferris returned. "Mom's out of her shorts. Then we can go."

ROOT LED CASSIE FERRIS through the shooting. Her story was straight-forward, but then she must have figured out that was the best way to tell it. If she didn't embellish, she didn't have to remember those little details if someone asked her later. She was getting very clever, Root thought. No, not clever, devious. Or was she? He just couldn't decide.

He glanced up toward the corner of the sparse, sound-proofed interrogation room, the same one he'd questioned her in before. On the wall there was a small piece of mirror, a one-way mirror, and Grilkey was behind it. He'd listened to everything she'd said. Root excused himself to confer with Grilkey.

"Well?" Root asked him in the hall.

"Same thing she told me."

"What about the daughter? Did her story match?"

"Close. She heard the car pull up, figured it was her mom and waited for her. When her mom didn't come in and the kid heard the car drive off, she figured her mom had forgotten her keys. She was unlocking the door when she heard the shots. At the time she didn't know what they were, thought it was just something hitting the house."

"Then what?" Root asked.

"The girl opened the door and saw her mom on her knees in front of the door. Her mom pushed her inside and slammed the door. That's when the daughter found out there'd been a gun."

"But she didn't see one? Or someone who might have fired it?"

"Nope."

Root did some fast thinking. If Cassie Ferris had fired the shots herself the gun still had to be somewhere in the front yard. Maybe in the bushes. He'd checked the hedge on one side of the house, but he hadn't searched the other side as carefully.

"Grilkey," Root said, "Send someone back out. Have them look everywhere for a gun. Both neighbor's yards, too."

Grilkey nodded. "You think the Ferris woman did the shooting?"

"I don't think anything," Root said.

"Yes, sir."

As he hurried off, Root checked on Socorro who was behind the small room, also watching through the one way mirror. A camera was beside him.

"You got everything on tape?" Root asked.

"Got it all—not that it's worth anything."

Root frowned. He had asked her every question he could think of, tried every ploy, and he had nothing. He had hoped she would say more than she intended to cover for her daughter, but she hadn't given away a thing. Not about plants, motives, her movements, nothing. "I guess we'll talk about the papers from the briefcase."

"She'd better say something brilliant." Socorro said. "Jacobs went to change shirts, but he'll be back in a few minutes. He's in a bad mood."

"That's not news."

Root stepped inside the interrogation room and found Cassie Ferris slumped in her chair as if she'd been napping. When she looked up her face was pale and Root wondered if it was tension or exhaustion.

"Now, Mrs. Ferris," Root said, taking a chair across from her. "I need to ask you about something else."

She straightened up without enthusiasm. "Do we have to do this tonight?"

"I'm afraid so. I'll go through things quickly." He picked up a folder from the floor and placed it in front of him. He pulled papers out of the file folder and held them up for her to see. The papers from Roger Weber's briefcase. Her eyes seemed to widen slightly, but he couldn't be sure.

"But I thought we were just going to talk about the shooting. I'm really tired—"

"These could have something to do with the shooting."

She nodded but said nothing. Root slid one sheet closer to her. "Can you tell me what this is?" he asked.

"It's a page from a commercial log. Also known as a traffic log."

"So, what exactly is that?" he asked.

"It's a listing of all the commercials we play on the air," she said. She explained in detail and finished with, "Can I go now?"

"Just a few more questions. This is very helpful." He took another sheet and slid it toward her. "Can you tell me about this?"

"It's an aging." Her voice became flat, almost singsong. "Every month a new one comes out showing all of the station's clients, how much money they spent and if it's been collected. Mandy or Bill could tell you more about it."

"What do you know about this Street Corner Productions and this write-off?"

Cassie leaned forward to look more closely at the aging. "It seems that it was Rachel's account and it was over 120 days old. They owed over four-thousand dollars."

"So, these people owed Y-96 all this money and the station just decided to write it off? Forgive the debt?"

"Not forgive," Cassie said. She let out a long sigh as she began the explanation. "My guess is that this company was a promoter. You know, they come into town with a truckload of stereo equipment or waterbeds or plants or something. I don't really remember. Maybe it was a carnival. Anyway, after they ran the advertising, they left Austin and no one could track them down."

"Why would the station give those kinds of people credit?"

"I don't know. Maybe there was a check and it bounced. Maybe it was a company that comes into town all the time, or has some corporate headquarters somewhere that's done business with us before. If you went back to some older aging, maybe you'd find some notes on it."

Root looked through the other papers in front of him, but before he could slide one out there were two quick impatient knocks at the door. "I'll be right back."

He stepped outside and closed the door behind him, sealing off all sound. Jacobs was waiting for him.

"What the hell are you doing in there?" Jacobs demanded.

"I'm—"

"You're pansy-assing around! Socorro tells me that this woman had the briefcase all along. So what the fuck do you think you're doing with all these stupid questions?"

"Interviewing a witness."

"Bullshit! It's time to interrogate a suspect," Jacobs snapped.

"I don't see—"

"You don't see shit lately, Root! She brings you the goddamn briefcase and you don't think that's a little strange? Socorro tells me she's got copies of the papers under her couch and you don't think that's suspicious? What the fuck is with you?"

"I just don't see that we have any hard core proof that Cassie Ferris killed Roger Weber."

"And we'll never get any the way you're handling things," Jacobs said. "I'll get a damn confession and we'll get this thing over with."

He went inside, slamming the door behind him.

TWENTY-ONE

ROOT WENT INTO the viewing room to watch; it wasn't going to be pleasant.

"Now the picnic really starts," Socorro said.

"Yeah."

Inside the room Cassie looked up as Jacobs sat down beside her. He moved his chair close; he was already invading her space. Root noticed that she didn't respond to Jacobs' closeness. Maybe she was just too tired.

"Mrs. Ferris, I'm Senior Sergeant Fred Jacobs," Jacobs was saying. "It's late and I know you're tired; we need to get moving on this questioning, so I won't waste time."

"That's fine with me."

"I want you to look at these papers and tell me if you've ever seen them before." He fanned the papers in their plastic bags in front of her.

Cassie Ferris didn't look like she'd been expecting that. "Yes. Sergeant Root just showed them to me."

"Ever seen 'em before that?"

"I don't know. I may have. I see a log every day at the station."

"And this one?" He slid the aging toward her.

"I've seen several like it."

He voice got louder. "I'm talking about this specific page."

"I don't know."

"Mrs. Ferris, do you know where these papers came from?" He was leaning toward her, intimidating her.

"Sergeant Root said they came from Roger Weber's briefcase."

Good answer, Root thought. She was cooler than he'd expected.

"Right," Jacobs said. "And do you know how we got that case?"

"I dropped it off at the station."

"Well, isn't that convenient!" His voice bristled with sarcasm. "And where did you get that briefcase?"

"I got it from the manager of Top Class Limousine Service." She was moving her shoulders now, inching them away from Jacobs' heavy body. "Roger had left it in the limo the night he died."

"And very conveniently, you just happened to remember that."

"No, I," she swallowed forcibly. "I saw the manager of the service in the station and that made me think of it."

"But you didn't call us, did you?"

"I wasn't sure the briefcase would be there. The manager of the service wasn't sure. The car had been in the shop. It broke down." She took a breath. "He said he'd look, and then when he found the case he brought it to my house."

"Why didn't you call us then?" Anger had fused Jacobs' two eyebrows into one, like a furious bank of thunderheads. Root had seen that look all too often.

"I dropped it off," Cassie said.

"Maybe you had that briefcase the whole time!" Jacobs slammed the words into her face.

Cassie Ferris flinched and Root thought he saw a glistening in her eyes.

"You can call the manager of Top Class Limo," she said. "He'll tell you that I didn't get the briefcase until this afternoon."

"Oh, we'll do that. You can bet on it." Jacobs rose and repositioned himself in the chair. He put an additional six inches between the two of them and Cassie seemed relieved.

Socorro twitched beside Root and said, "Here comes a little trickeration."

Trickeration was the department's word for the slightly underhanded moves that would make a suspect break down. Root tensed himself to watch.

Jacobs gestured casually to the papers. "So, you saw the manager of the limo service and figured that Weber might have left his briefcase in the car, is that right?"

"Yes."

"And the manager dropped the case off at your house," Jacobs said.

"That's correct."

"What time was that, Mrs. Ferris?"

Her body twisted slightly. "I'm not sure exactly."

"You don't have to be exact, just give me an approximate time." Jacobs' voice was low, deceptively soothing.

"It was in the afternoon. Mid afternoon, I think."

Root wondered if she knew that she looked away when she lied.

"Would you say that was four o'clock?" Jacobs asked. He sat up, which put his body closer to hers. "Three? Maybe, two?"

Her right eye twitched. "Closer to two, I think."

Jacobs smiled. "So, we'll say between two and three. And you didn't deliver the briefcase to us until after five. I guess you were pretty busy this afternoon. Since you didn't get downtown until so late."

"Yes, I was busy." Her hips shifted almost imperceptibly, as if she wanted to stand up and run.

"And what were you doing that kept you so busy, Mrs. Ferris?" Jacobs' voice was still smooth.

"I don't really remember; my daughter was there and I talked with her a little."

"And what else?"

"I cleaned house and did some laundry. And my other daughter called; she had a problem that she needed some help on."

"Oh, and that took so much time you didn't have any left. Just a few minutes to use the phone?"

She licked her lips. It didn't look like she was breathing. "I guess I forgot."

Jacobs reached for a paper and held it up to her. He kept his tone even. "You know what we found on these papers, Mrs. Ferris?"

She shook her head. "No."

"Fingerprints, Mrs. Ferris. Fingerprints."

Oh, God, Root thought, he's doing the old fingerprint routine. The fingerprints had been Weber's, but she wouldn't know that.

Jacobs smiled. He twisted his heavy college ring face down as he said, "And guess whose fingerprints we found?"

Her voice was barely audible. "I don't know."

Jacobs rose up and punched his fist into the table; Cassie jumped. "Guess again," Jacobs roared in her face. "Whose fingerprints do you think we found, Mrs. Ferris!"

"I don't know…"

Jacobs was towering over her. "Bullshit! You're a liar, Mrs. Ferris!" Jacobs' voice resounded off the walls like a cannon roar.

"I don't know anything about fingerprints."

"Do you want me to tell you what really happened?" Jacobs demanded.

"Yes, I mean, no…"

"You got that briefcase early in the afternoon, Mrs. Ferris, and you spent all afternoon opening it! You had to get it open because you knew what was in it. Evidence. Evidence that you destroyed." He took a breath and spat out the last words, "Evidence that proved you killed Roger Weber!"

Root waited for her reaction, his stomach tight.

"No!" Cassie said the word loudly, the tears that had threatened earlier, disappeared.

"You're lying! Don't fuck with me!"

Jacobs was still above her, his face mottled with fury. Cassie wouldn't allow herself to flinch. She raised her head to meet his eyes. Black eyes, glittering with violence that made even her stomach tremble. Jacobs reminded her of her father, and she expected to see him raise his arm and strike. She expected to feel the pain of a fist against her face.

"I didn't kill Roger Weber." Her voice shook.

"The hell you didn't!"

Something inside Cassie was screaming. *I don't have to take this!* She sucked in a long breath, feeling the air pump through her quivering cells.

"I didn't kill Roger Weber," she said again, this time more firmly. Then she lost her nerve and her voice became quick and breathy. "I did open the briefcase, but I did it because I didn't think the police were interested; they didn't want Roger's keys. I thought they wouldn't follow through."

Jacobs sat down and Cassie could see his dark, sweaty, chest hair sticking to the inside of his thin shirt. He pulled his chair forward, closer, more invasive. His face was shiny with perspiration.

"I'm sick of your bullshit, lady; you don't even know how to tell the truth!"

"I told you the truth!"

"Then tell me about that night at Happy Twosomes. The night Weber died."

"I've told everyone! I got there a little before five and I only saw Roger twice. Once in the reception area, when he had a disagreement with someone, and once when he was in the lounge." She took in air and let it out, trying to calm herself. "That was all. I didn't even talk to him the second time."

Jacobs slapped the table again. Cassie jumped and her chair nearly fell over. Jacobs' voice bellowed and she could smell his foul breath in her face. "I want the fuckin' truth! What's it going to take to get it out of you!"

"You don't understand," Cassie said. "I'm not here to talk about this. Someone shot at me tonight. Didn't they tell you that?"

"Now we're back to guns again. Just like last time?" he sneered.

"Last time?" Cassie felt a tingle of new fear.

"Yeah. Don't tell me you forgot?"

"What last time? I've never been shot at—"

"But there was a gun, wasn't there? In Abilene. When you threatened your ex-husband and his new girlfriend."

She was stunned. "I didn't...I didn't hurt anyone."

"Maybe not that time, but you sure as fuck did this time!"

Cassie stood up. She was trembling so hard that the chair rattled when she grabbed it. "You can't talk to me like this."

Jacobs rose slowly, menacingly, until he was towering over her. "This is pussy stuff, lady; I ain't even started with you!"

She clutched at the strap of her purse and yanked it up. "You can't keep me here."

"You aren't going anyplace." He moved in closer, his face inches from hers. "SIT DOWN!"

Cassie tried to move but her foot tangled with the chair. She straightened. "I want a lawyer."

He couldn't keep her here without a lawyer and he couldn't harass her like this. She didn't have to take it. She wouldn't take it.

"I said, 'sit down!' Now SIT DOWN!"

She sucked in air, then roared out, "Fuck you!" She was standing as tall as her jelly-like knees would allow. "I came down here to help you and I don't have to stay; this is harassment."

"You sit your ass down!" He pointed to the chair.

She took a step backward, free of the chair now. "I'm leaving. If you try to stop me, I'm calling a lawyer. And the media." She heard her own hysteria.

"You listen to me, lady," he said, moving closer, almost pinning her against the wall with his bulk. "You're going to talk to me, you got that? You're going to tell me the truth! All the truth. All about you and Roger Weber."

Cassie stared up at him, feeling the heat coming off his sweaty body. He wasn't going to hit her. The thought helped her nerves and her voice. "Listen, Sergeant, I told you the truth. I didn't kill Roger Weber. I don't know who did, but you're wasting your time with me."

Maybe it was her hard-won control that made him change tactics. He took a half step backwards. "Sit down." It was a command, tossed off curtly like so many from her father. It expected compliance.

Cassie's anger coursed again, and she shook from it. She moved forward and waited until Jacobs was out of the way. Then, instead of going to the chair, back to her subservient position, Cassie lifted her chin and stepped to the door. She grasped the knob firmly. "I'm leaving."

Jacobs' fury boiled. His face was red, his black eyes lethal. "Like hell you are!"

"You haven't got a warrant. If you want to talk to me again, you call my lawyer." She swung open the door and stepped out into the hallway.

She began to run through the maze of empty offices. Behind her a door opened and she heard footsteps. In front of her were the elevators. She ran past them to a door marked "stairs." Cassie hit the bar that opened it and began to stumble down the cement steps. Her legs were so weak she had to grasp the handrail. At the second level she felt stronger.

Never again! Never again would she take that kind of abuse. Not from anyone. She'd put up with it from Roger; she'd let her father abuse her, and she'd let Brad rule her with ridicule.

Never again.

She raced through the lobby, not even caring about the guard who watched her. If they came after her she would file charges. If they got a warrant, fine. She'd fight them through the legal system. She would call a press conference, too. She had enough friends in the media to create a storm and Senior Sergeant Fred Jacobs would feel the heat from it.

Outside the night was dark and the air cloying. Cassie felt the warmth mixing with the sweat of her body. She stood under the bright lights of the building and began to shiver. She looked at her watch. It was after two and she didn't have a car. Damn.

In front of her was the elevated freeway and all around her were parking lots and deserted buildings. Two blocks away was Sixth Street, Austin's answer to the French Quarter. At this hour there would be no one partying, though. The people still out would be drunks or punks or the bag people who scoured the trash cans. Still, she went in that direction. People and lights were better than what waited in the shadows.

Somewhere in the distance a siren sounded and tires squealed as a car peeled around the corner.

Cassie began to walk, moving from streetlight to streetlight, thinking quickly. Maybe she could find a phone. She crossed the street and began to walk faster. Out of the corner of her eye she saw a man lurking in the shadows, watching her. Cassie clutched her purse closer to her body.

Footsteps sounded behind her—Cassie looked up the street frantically. The old buildings seemed dark and dangerous.

Where the hell was a phone? A cab?

At the sound of a motor Cassie looked toward the street. Two cars raced towards her, one a convertible filled with drunken college kids.

"Hey, Baby, want a ride?" a kid yelled out as the car whizzed past.

Then the footsteps were back, still behind her, but faster now. Cassie began to run.

"Mrs. Ferris." The voice was male, breathless. Cassie didn't stop, and the voice called again. "Mrs. Ferris. It's me, Patrolman Grilkey."

She spun around. The uniformed officer was running towards her. Cassie called out, "What do you want?" He stopped. There was still half a block between them. Enough for her to get away if she had to.

"I'm supposed to give you a ride home."

"How do I know that?" Cassie demanded.

He looked around at the darkness of the street and put his hands on his hips. "Sergeant Root sent me. He said to take you home."

Cassie debated, looking over at the shadows where the other man had watched. He was gone. She looked back toward Grilkey and saw that he hadn't moved. Which was the lesser of the two dangers? Cassie wasn't sure, but she nodded.

"Okay," she said.

"My partner's coming around with the car."

She waited, twenty feet away from him, until the blue and white patrol car slid around the corner.

"I WANT A TWENTY-FOUR HOUR tail on her," Jacobs snapped at Root and Socorro. "And I want that gun found. The one she used tonight."

"The yard has been searched thoroughly," Root said. "Nothing there."

"Look again."

Socorro looked puzzled. "Wouldn't her daughter have seen it?"

"Maybe her daughter helped kill Weber! Maybe she's in on this, too."

The interview with Cassie Ferris had given him a personal grudge, Root thought. Nobody had ever walked out on Jacobs before.

Tomorrow, Root decided, Jacobs would calm down and go back to being the hard-nosed asshole he usually was. Maybe not a good guy, but a good cop. They'd be talking to all the other witnesses again, but in the meantime they'd humor him.

"You think we have enough for a search warrant?" Root asked.

"No, goddamnit, I don't! Or an arrest warrant, but I want enough. I want you to hound that woman. Follow her everywhere until we get the evidence. Her ass is mine, now."

He whirled around and left.

TWENTY-TWO

"I THINK WE OUGHT to call the cops and tell them what jerks they are!" Jenny stomped through the living room, threatening to shake loose the towel wrapped around her wet hair.

"It wouldn't do any good," Cassie said.

She had picked up Jenny a little after eight that morning, and after hearing about Cassie's experience with the police, Jenny had fumed continuously. Finally Cassie sent her to take a shower and cool off. Now she was back with a vengeance.

"They aren't even trying to catch the guy with the gun!"

"We don't know what they're doing," Cassie said. "And 'frankly, my dear, I don't give a damn.'"

"So what are you doing?" Jenny asked, indicating the litter of papers that were spread across the couch.

"Figuring things out. These papers have to mean something, or Roger wouldn't have collected them."

"Who cares about the papers?" Jenny flung her arms out in an angry gesture. "I'm concerned about the police. Aren't you worried about that? Shouldn't we be filing some kind of charges against them? Call the newspapers? Do something to show them they can't treat people like that?"

"But obviously they can; and I will call the news media if it happens again." What was left of Cassie's anger didn't flame, it smoldered slowly, fueling her to action. She stood up and gestured to the papers. "In the meantime, I have a very simple mission—I'm going to find Roger's murderer. Then I'm going to hand him over to Walter Kraley. That will not only put an end to all of this, it will also get us the reward that Walter Kraley is offering."

"Reward?" Jenny stopped her furious movement. "What reward? Is it a big one?"

"Twenty-five thousand dollars."

"We'll get a new car!"

Cassie cocked her head at Jenny. "Oh, no we won't. We'll put that money to much better use than that."

"What could be better than a car? Ours is a piece of junk."

"Agreed, but I'd much rather get Beth back."

"Beth?" Disbelief mixed with just a touch of hope. "Are you serious? Do you really mean it? Do you think we can get her away from Dad?"

"Yes, I do. We'll have enough money to hire another lawyer, and we'll get one who's a hell of a lot better than Chris Feiner. Then we'll initiate another hearing." She felt as if molten liquid had been poured into her spine last night and this morning it had hardened to steel. Nothing could daunt her now—not the thought of someone coming after her with a gun, or more interviews with the police, or even Brad. "And this time I'm not giving up until we win," Cassie finished.

Jenny stood stock-still, watching Cassie. She said quietly, "You know, you never used to say things unless you were really going to do them."

"Oh, I'm really going to do this," Cassie said. "I'm not giving up this time, Jenny. Not until we have Beth with us in Austin."

"But what if we get another terrible lawyer, and what if Dad comes down here?"

"Very simple: I'll fire the lawyer, and battle your father on every level including hand-to-hand combat if that's what it takes." Every muscle, every fiber of her being was ready for this fight. "I don't care what it takes, we're going to do it."

Comprehension spread into a slow grin across Jenny's face. "You're back."

"I've been here all morning."

"No, my mom went away after the divorce."

Cassie stared, at first not comprehending the words, maybe not wanting to. Then she understood what Jenny was saying, and it twisted something inside her.

God, what she'd put the girls through. Three years of cowering. Three years of watching their mother hide. She whispered, "I'm so sorry, Jenny."

Jenny shrugged as if it didn't matter. "It's okay." But the glitter in her eyes, said otherwise.

Cassie straightened. That was over, as of now. She made her cheek muscles move, forced herself to smile. "What you need to know, is that I am back. For good. And I'm mean as hell and tough as nails!"

A tear rolled down Jenny's cheek, and then she laughed. At first it was a tentative sound and Cassie realized how seldom she had heard it in the last few years.

"It's just too bad that Roger isn't still available," Cassie said. "Because I owe him one. No, I owe him several and it would give me great pleasure to kick his fat butt around the block a few times."

Jenny laughed again; this time it had a young, happy quality to it. It reminded Cassie of Beth. "Wouldn't I like to get that on video tape!" Jenny giggled.

It made Cassie think of how things used to be. She put an arm around Jenny and said, "However, since we can't do that, we have to get constructive."

"Okay, Commander," Jenny said, standing straighter. "What do we do first?"

"First," Cassie said, "we figure out why Roger had these papers."

"Boring."

"At the moment, it's all we've got. Take care of the small things and the big things will take care of themselves." Cassie unconsciously quoted her father. She sat down on the couch.

Jenny took a spot on the floor. "Okay, I'll help. What do you want me to do?"

"First, we can eliminate these." Cassie set aside all the personal past due bills. "Everyone goes through a period when bills don't get paid on time. It isn't something you kill over."

Jenny sorted through some papers. "What about this?" she asked. It was the Happy Twosomes' agreement.

"Put it with the bills. I think it was just more of Roger's nastiness." Cassie picked up the agings. "These have to be important. I'm not sure why, but they are."

"Why?"

"Because there's one thing I know—you don't screw with Walter Kraley and his money. These make me think that somebody was." She glanced over several pages. "What I didn't realize before is that the write-offs go back to when Northland took over Y-96. Some of the debts were from the old ownership. According to my figures," she picked up an envelope with her scribbled calculations, "management has written off over twenty-seven thousand dollars in the last eight months. Fifteen was owed to the old ownership."

"Twenty-seven thousand! That's a lot of money."

"Yes, it is. There were a total of fourteen clients involved. Some were pretty small, just a couple of hundred dollars. A couple of them owed several thousand dollars each. Rachel handled the majority of the accounts with write-offs, but she's the top biller; since she brings in more clients, she'd have more bad debts."

"So, you think someone pocketed the client's payment instead of turning it in to the station?" Jenny asked. "But wouldn't the client get a bill?"

"I've thought of a way around that. The salesperson could explain to the client that the invoice was a mistake. Clerical errors. You just say, 'the computer screwed up.' I hear that all time."

"But after awhile, the salesperson would get caught…"

Cassie nodded. "Unless the client closed down or left, and that's exactly what happened to most of these accounts. This Tootles Restaurant went out of business. Street Corner Productions left town. Since the station doesn't use a collection agency there's no skip tracing. After a couple of months, the salesperson would say they couldn't get the money, so there would be a write-off."

"Then it has to be the salesperson."

"There's more." Cassie picked up a page and held it out for Jenny to see, pointing to a handwritten notation. "This note says that the salesperson had given up trying to collect the money and Mandy was going to take over." She pointed to another. "This one says Bill. Actually it would be easier for Bill or Mandy to embezzle. The salesperson had already stopped trying to collect, so Bill or Mandy go out, get the money and keep it. No one's going to question them. And there wouldn't be any invoices by that time."

"That's impressive, Mom."

"Thank you. That's also all I know about agings." Cassie put them face down on the edge of the couch and picked up the logs. There were over twenty sheets; she had counted. "I still don't understand why he had these."

"Let me see some of those," Jenny said, and Cassie handed her half the stack. After a few minutes of scrutiny, Jenny said, "Every page shows at least one commercial for the write-off clients. Some ran in the morning shift, some in Scott's show, and some aired in mid-day or evenings."

"But it isn't really important."

"Why not? You're completely ignoring the jocks. They write commercials on the logs, all the time. Look at this one; Scott wrote on two commercials for Tootles restaurant."

"Those are late orders," Cassie said. "The salespeople race into the control room waving an order, demanding that we write additional commercials on the log. It happens all the time. They can't put the extra spots on, because they don't know which breaks have room."

"Could a disk jockey make money from that?"

"No, of course not—" Unless they were working with one of the salespeople. "Wait, there is a way! If the salesperson got the client to pay for the spots, they could split the extra dollars with the jock."

"But doesn't someone look at the logs?"

"They're reconciled in accounting…"

"And they'd send a bill wouldn't they?" Jenny asked. "Oh, wait, I know what would happen. Computer error."

"Exactly," Cassie said.

Jenny groaned and stood up. "The list of suspects just gets bigger and we still don't have any proof."

"We will," Cassie said. "Now, who at the radio station needs money?" She answered her own question. "No one. Except, maybe, Mandy. Although she has to have some savings. Bill makes a very good salary and Rachel is the top salesperson, so you know she's doing okay."

"What about Scott?" Jenny asked.

"He just bought a new car. Well not new, but fairly new, and it's a BMW." A quote that Cassie had learned in college popped into her mind. "'...the greatest crimes are caused by excess and not by necessity.' Aristotle."

"Greed not need?" Jenny asked. "So, who's the greediest?"

"Anyone in sales. That's why they go into sales."

"I guess you can't measure something like that."

Cassie put the papers aside and did some hard thinking while Jenny studied the logs.

"Well, we know for sure that all this stuff," Jenny gestured to the papers now scattered along the couch, "has to mean something or Roger wouldn't have taken them."

"That's right," Cassie said, sitting upright. "And he called Walter and talked him into coming into town, so it was big." Cassie gathered the copies together, put the stack on a side table and reached for the phone.

"Who are you calling?"

"Mandy. She's the expert on this; maybe she can help. After I talk to her let's fix some breakfast; I'm hungry."

"Mom, what if Mandy is the one who killed Roger? That could put you in more danger."

"Jenny, I've known Mandy for twenty years. We were in

college together, remember? I might complain about her," she stopped, "and complain to her, but I know her. I know she couldn't kill someone."

Jenny looked uncertain, but said, "Okay, if you say so. Here, let me." She gathered up the rest of the papers, but one got away from her, sliding out from the bottom of the stack. It was the overdue lawyer's bill.

Jenny picked it up, and looked at it. "You know, Mom, when I see something like this I think that maybe Roger didn't know what he was doing, after all."

"ROGER WEBER was not stupid," Cassie said as she rinsed dishes and put them in the dishwasher.

"He was an asshole." Jenny wiped the counter.

"Yes, he was, but he still wasn't stupid. And by the way, your language is becoming as bad as a disk jockey's."

"I'll work on it," Jenny said.

"I'd appreciate that."

"I'll say stamen instead of asshole; pistil instead of dick; anther instead of—"

"Enough! I've got the idea," Cassie said. "Why don't you get your things; you can go with me to the station. Mandy said she'd meet me—"

"Oh, no!" Jenny said, suddenly. "I just remembered!"

"What?"

"I've got that botany field trip today! It's a fourth of my grade."

Cassie straightened up. "What time do you have to go? Where is it going to be?"

"We're meeting at eleven at Wild Basin Wilderness area, but I can't go," Jenny said.

The concern of being late for an important school event was almost immediately overshadowed by greater worries. Last night someone with a gun had shot at the house. Would Jenny be safe if she went on the trip? Cassie looked out the window at the porch, now flooded with morning sunshine. Shootings didn't seem possible in sunshine. "Maybe we can figure a way," she said. *But how?*

Jenny came to stand beside her at the window. "Mom, I don't think it's a good idea to leave you alone. What if you needed me?"

"Let's think about this for a minute." Cassie put the last cup in the dishwasher. "What time are you supposed to go?"

Jenny stiffened. "Mom," she said quietly, "There's a strange car down the street."

"Where?"

"Look outside, just beyond the hedge. There's a man in the car."

Cassie straightened up and was looking hard. "I see him."

"He's watching our house."

"I see that, too."

TWENTY-THREE

ROOT PICKED UP his "Fishing is Reel" mug from the shelf in the coffee room, and said, "Delany was at a club until almost one. It was a Y-96 promotion, like the one at Happy Twosomes, so a lot of people saw him." Root was talking fast; they had a lot to accomplish that morning. "After that Delany had 'company' who came home with him. The 'company' was still at his house this morning."

"Was she cute?" Socorro asked from the doorway as he pulled the cellophane off a pack of donuts he'd gotten from the vending machine.

"Yeah, she was." Root poured coffee from the stained pot. "A little blonde who couldn't have been over nineteen."

"Lucky guy. I guess that clears him." He began to eat.

"I don't know," Root put the pot down. He didn't even have time for a cup of coffee this morning, but he was having one, anyway. "The club wasn't more than five minutes drive from Cassie Ferris's house, so he could have left, done the shooting and been back before anybody missed him. Oh, and you'll be happy to know that he's thoroughly pissed. He didn't appreciate my early visit. In fact, he was rude." Root took a swallow of the coffee and puckered his mouth while he thought about spitting it out. Finally he swallowed. "God, this is bad."

"I think it's been there all night. You could make a fresh pot," Socorro said. "Or, throw in a lot of cream and sugar and you'll hardly notice."

"I could take it intravenously and I wouldn't taste it at all. It'd be faster, too." Root left the cup there and headed back to his desk, Socorro following. "I asked Delany about the logs, and he told me the same thing Cassie Ferris had, but he didn't even know what those accounting pages were." Root got to his office, noticed the stack of messages, and folded his stiff body down into his chair. "While his guest was taking a shower I asked Delany about the charges in Phoenix and he claimed he was innocent. Said he'd had a friend with him at the radio station one night and the friend stole the stuff while he was on the air. Delany says he didn't know about it."

"Right. So, how come he pawned the stuff?" Socorro began making notes while he ate the chocolate donuts.

"Claims the typewriter he pawned was a gift from the same friend. Delany says he had no idea it had come from the station."

Socorro didn't even look up. "I think the guy's full of bullshit."

"That's what they pay him for," Root said. "And I discovered that he has a nice BMW in his carport. That kid's been spending some money lately. Of course, he doesn't have a family, so I guess he could have saved it." Root thought of Lucille and his former family, pushed the image aside and concentrated on the case.

He wanted something solid. Anything.

"What did you find out?" Root asked.

Socorro stopped writing. "Mandy McCormick was at her mother's house at Lakeway. I phoned and she's coming in later. I need to verify that she was there all evening, but I

wanted to wait until the mother was alone to call and ask her."
He put the last donut in his mouth and swallowed without
chewing.

Root thought of his own breakfast, an Egg McMuffin he'd
swallowed almost whole. Right before he'd checked on Wilson.

"I talked with Wilson," Root said. Wilson was watching
the Ferris house.

"Anything yet?"

"Not yet. He says that Cassie Ferris went out to pick up
her daughter about eight, but no one's come out of the house
since. They're both probably back asleep."

Socorro reached in his pocket and pulled out an old handkerchief. He wiped the chocolate from his hand. "Wish I
were."

Root wished he was, too. "What about Sankey?"

"I got her out of bed." Socorro took a second to smile at
the memory. "She doesn't look like much in her suits, but you
should see her in that little, silky green robe. Nice."

"What did she say?" Root asked.

"Yesterday she was at the radio station until five," Socorro
said, reading from his notes. "Then she went straight to Happy
Twosomes. She was there until a little after seven. Supposedly,
Greg Mayhew and the receptionist can confirm her story since
she talked to both of them. I'll catch up with them later."

"So where was she last night between eleven and eleven-
thirty?"

"At the same club as Delany. She sold the advertising to
them."

"But if Delany could have left without being missed, she
could have left without being missed."

"Bingo."

Root grunted. Great. Any one of them could have fired the bullets at Cassie Ferris, if someone really had shot at her. They hadn't found a gun and he didn't think they would.

"Sankey turned purple when she saw the papers from Weber's briefcase," Socorro went on. "Said somebody had been in her desk and her rights had been violated."

"You tell her it was Weber?"

"Yeah, finally. She calmed down some. Told me all about her 'opportunity' with Happy Twosomes. What a successful 'venture' it was, and how she hadn't told anyone at the station because they'd've been jealous."

"What about those accounting papers?"

Socorro frowned as he glanced at his notebook, then up at Root. "She claimed that was just one example of everyone's jealousy. The way she tells it, those write-offs are a black mark on her record. Black marks on everyone's record. And Roger wanted to show Walter Kraley how everyone was screwing up. She figured Kraley would forget that they'd had record sales lately and just remember the bad."

"I wonder if Bill Bankston will see it that way? Or Mandy McCormick?" Root said. "Did you tell Sankey that it was Cassie Ferris who found the briefcase, like Jacobs wanted us to?"

"Yeah. Did you tell Delany?"

"I think it was a mistake, but I did it. He was angry," Root said, as his phone rang.

"We've got her covered." Socorro shrugged. "If it'll make you feel any better, we can take a turn at watching her."

Root knew there wouldn't be time. He reached for the phone. "Homicide, Sergeant Root. Yeah? Now? Be right there." He put down the receiver. "McCormick is here."

"I'll go," Socorro said.

Root sat back down. "I'll try to reach Mayhew again."

"IT'S A COP," Jenny said, still staring out the window.

"How can you tell?" It wasn't someone Cassie knew; the car wasn't familiar either. He had to be a professional of some kind.

"From the Street Crimes course I took. We saw some of the police 'cool cars' and I remember that one because it wasn't very cool. A maroon Lincoln. Gross."

"It doesn't seem very smart to show you cars that are used undercover."

"They aren't really. The cool cars are the ones that have been spotted by the criminals, or gangs or whatever. Their cover is blown so they use the cars in places where it doesn't matter. To spy on innocent citizens like us."

Cassie felt her skin crawl with the knowledge that they were being watched.

She wanted to believe that Root and Socorro had put the man in front of their house as some sort of bodyguard, but what if Jacobs had sent him to gather evidence? That was intolerable. Cassie had spent more than enough time with some stranger peering at her, recording her every move.

"What are we going to do?" Jenny asked.

Cassie thought about it. They had to do something quickly. Jenny had to leave on her field trip and Cassie didn't want Jenny tromping through the wilds with just other college kids for protection.

Cassie ran a hand through her hair and realized she was sweating. "I just don't know."

"Maybe he's only watching one of us," Jenny said.

"That would be me."

"Then why don't we find out? I'll go to the store alone, and we'll see if he follows me—"

"Absolutely not! We don't know for sure that he's with the police. There's got to be more than one maroon Lincoln in the world."

"But, Mom—"

"Look, let me take a quick shower," Cassie said. "We'll decide when I'm finished."

Jenny frowned, but Cassie didn't give her time to argue. She grabbed some clean underwear and headed straight for the bathroom, peeling off her clothes as she went.

The spray of cool water felt good on Cassie's overheated skin. She soaped herself quickly and decided she would call Root and ask him if that was indeed a cop out front. If it wasn't, then he could deal with the man. If it was a cop, great. He could escort Jenny on her field trip.

She rinsed and stepped out the shower, rubbing herself with a towel. Jenny would complain about having the police following her, especially on a school outing, but with luck the man would be discreet. Maybe Jenny would never know he was there.

As soon as she was dressed, Cassie went to give Jenny her decision.

"Jen?" There was no answer. "Jenny?"

Cassie went through the house, picking up speed at each empty room. Sly stopped washing long enough to watch her. She ended her search by running to the kitchen window. Their car was not in the driveway. A note lay on the counter: *"Went to the store, be back in ten minutes. You can time me. Love, Jen."*

Cassie felt her heart begin to pound. She switched her attention to the street outside the window. The maroon car was there. Jenny didn't have police protection.

"So, WHAT ABOUT the station manager?" Jacobs asked.

"He's coming in this afternoon," Root said.

Jacobs nodded, then said, "Martinez is calling back people who were at that Happy Twosomes' party." Root knew it was as close as Jacobs would come to admitting that he'd gone too far the night before. It was enough for Root.

Jacobs rearranged his large body in Socorro's chair and went on. "She's got some kind of coding system; anyway, she's calling back the ones who seemed to be most observant."

"Good idea," Root said, carefully keeping the satisfaction out of his voice.

Socorro appeared. "Wilson just called in."

"And?" Jacobs asked.

Socorro pulled a chair from around the corner and sat down. Root noticed that Jacob's hadn't offered Socorro his desk back. "Jenny Ferris just left in the car," Socorro said, "but she left alone. I told Wilson to stay at the house and watch Cassie Ferris."

Jacobs nodded. "What about the sales manager? McCormick. Did you talk with her? What did she have to say?"

"She went over all the accounts and said that most of the ones that had been written off went out of business. Said that usually three people tried to collect the money before it was written off."

"Which three people?" Jacobs asked.

"The salesperson, the station manager, you know, Bankston, and her. Said they were all legitimate write-offs and she didn't know why Weber would be interested in them. I asked her about last night and she said that she was at her mom's house all night. They didn't leave except to walk down by the lake around 7:30. We'll have to check with the neighbors to see if anyone can verify it."

"How'd she seem? Nervous?" Jacobs asked.

"She didn't look too good. Pale, and she never could make eye contact."

Jacobs's eyebrows went together for a minute, then he asked, "And the owner of that dating club? You guys bringing him in?"

"We called Greg Mayhew, but we didn't catch him. He's calling back," Socorro said.

Root was curious to see what Mayhew had to say about the whole shooting incident. The timing was pretty quick, but he could have heard or seen something that would help. The other possibility was that Mayhew had driven around the corner and then come back on foot and done the shooting himself. Cassie Ferris wouldn't have seen him because of the hedge.

"This thing is ripe to break wide open," Jacobs said.

Root agreed and he wasn't sure he was happy about it.

"HE DIDN'T FOLLOW ME, did he?" Jenny said, as she raced in the door carrying a bag of groceries. She stopped when she saw Cassie's face. "Oh, Mom, you got worried."

Cassie could feel the lump of fear in her throat dissolving into anger. "Damnit, Jenny, don't you ever do anything like that again!"

"I'm sorry, I guess I just wasn't thinking. I didn't mean to scare you." She put her arms around Cassie.

"You could have been hurt."

"But I wasn't. I'm okay, really. I'm sorry."

"Just don't ever—"

"I won't, Mom; I promise. I'm really sorry," she said. "But see, even the police don't think I'm in any danger. That cop is out there because of you, not me. He's watching you."

So I've got the police following me, and maybe a man with a gun, Cassie thought.

Jenny carried the groceries into the kitchen and Cassie followed. "So, now what are we going to do?" Jenny asked.

Cassie looked out the window. The maroon car was still there, perched at the curb like a steel vulture. "Let me think a minute."

While Jenny put the milk and bread away, Cassie allowed her brain to whir. The shooting had stopped last night when Jenny opened the door. Those bullets hadn't been meant for anyone but Cassie. Which meant that Jenny just might be safer away from her.

"Is Brandi going on the field trip?" Cassie asked. "Could you ride with her?"

"Yeah. Do you want the car?"

"Yes," Cassie said, an idea forming.

"You're not thinking of following me are you?"

"No, of course not," Cassie said.

"Then what are you going to do?"

"I think I'll go to the station and see what I can dig up there."

"And how do we know the station is safe?" Jenny demanded. "What if the murderer is lurking around there just waiting to kill you?"

"We don't know that. We don't know anything." She put her hands on Jenny's shoulders. "Look, go get your stuff."

"But, Mom, what about the nut with the gun? What about him?"

"I've got an idea," Cassie said. "I'm going to sneak out and avoid that cop out front. If anyone else is watching the house I'll lose them, too. I'll be perfectly safe." Cassie used her best no-nonsense mother voice. "Now, get moving or you'll be late."

As soon as Jenny was in the other room, Cassie grabbed up the phone and called the police department. She ended up talking with Root.

"There's a man parked near my house," Cassie began. "It appears that he's watching us. Is he one of your people?"

There was just a moment's hesitation. It told Cassie all she needed to know.

"I don't think there's any reason for you to be worried." Root said.

"Fine, but Jenny is going on a field trip today and I want to make sure she's safe."

"Perhaps Jenny should stay home with you."

Right. "Sergeant Root, this trip is a big part of Jenny's grade and she needs to go, but I'm more concerned for her safety." Cassie stopped. "Maybe you don't have a daughter, but there is nothing more precious in the world."

There was the briefest of pauses.

"What exactly can I do for you, Mrs. Ferris?" came his almost curt reply.

"Jenny will be at Brandi McCullogh's house in fifteen minutes; they're leaving from there." She gave him the address. "Could you have someone follow her to protect her? In plain clothes, so she won't know about it?"

"What will she be wearing?"

TWENTY-FOUR

As soon as he arranged for someone to cover Jenny Ferris, Root went to an interrogation room. Bill Bankston was waiting for him. Bankston's face looked more pinched than usual and Root noticed a pimple forming just above the station manager's lip.

They shook hands, then Root sat down across the table from Bankston, not wasting any more time on the amenities. "Mr. Bankston, could you tell me where you were last night between ten-thirty and eleven?" Root asked.

Bankston tilted his head and watched Root for a moment as if deciphering the question, looking for the hidden meaning. He said, "I was at home."

"Alone?"

"Yes. I live alone."

"Did you talk to anyone on the phone during that time?"

"No."

"Could one of the neighbors verify that you were home?"

Bankston thought about the question, fingered the blossoming pimple, then moved his hand away and shook his head. "I don't think so. I live in a complex of townhomes and none of us associate much with each other."

Root nodded. That made three who could have shot at Cassie Ferris. Four if Mandy McCormick had been away from her mother's house for an hour or so. Five if you counted Mayhew, and in Root's mind, Mayhew still wasn't out of the running.

"Can you tell me about these papers?" Root asked, sliding the copies from the briefcase closer to Bankston.

"Where did you get these?" Suddenly Bankston was angry. "Did you have a warrant to take these out of the station?"

"SEE YOU LATER!" Cassie waved as Jenny got in the car and drove off. Then Cass moved nonchalantly to the mailbox, retrieved the mail and went back into the house.

Quickly she tossed the mail on the kitchen counter and picked up her purse with all of Roger's papers stuffed inside it. She reached down and rubbed her hand along Sly's silken back, as if for luck.

"Here goes nothing," she told the cat.

In a flash she was out the back door, locking it behind her. She almost ran across the lawn, straight to the small storage shed where she grabbed their aluminum ladder and pulled it out. It only took a second to lay it up against the six-foot wooden fence. She tested it once, then climbed quickly until she could slide her leg over the fence. It began to wobble, but Cassie hung tight, surveying the yard behind hers.

It was empty. She didn't see anyone moving behind the screened windows of the house, either.

With a quick breath before she could lose her nerve, Cassie shoved off. She landed hard and fell forward on her knees, then jumped up and brushed the grass from her pants. Then she swung around and took two quick running steps toward the fence, leaped up and pushed the ladder. It seemed to hang indecisively in the air, before slowly, painstakingly slowly, falling out of view, back into her own yard.

By now her breath was coming in spurts. She was past her prime for surreptitious escapes, and judicious fence jumping. Still, it seemed to have worked. She grabbed up her purse and started toward the side of the yard. Jenny would be waiting for her on the street. Cassie began to run across the grass, then up the walkway beside the house.

Just as she reached the front yard she heard a door open behind her.

"Hey, what are you doing?" a male voice called out.

She turned around. A man in cut-offs had stepped outside. On the street Cassie could see the Datsun moving toward her.

"I…I…" She couldn't think of a thing to say. "I…sorry." She ran toward the car.

"You come back here!" The man called.

Cassie reached the car, flung open the door, and said, "Go!" as she jumped inside.

Jenny hit the gas and they sped off. The man still stood in his yard, watching like a pit bull whose dinner had been snatched away.

"Are you okay?" Jenny asked.

"I will be if I ever catch my breath," Cassie said. "Go straight to Brandi's house, then I'll take the car."

THE SMELL OF ONIONS and greasy hamburgers filled Jacobs' office. Jacobs was talking with a big bite in his mouth, giving Root a disgusting view of masticated food. "We've stirred them up, that's for sure. Would you say that Bankston and Delany are angry? And McCormick is scared?"

Root kept his eyes on his notes so he wouldn't have to look

at Jacobs. "Yeah, that's fair." He swiveled to glance at his partner. "How would you say Rachel Sankey is feeling?"

Socorro squeezed more ketchup from the small foil packet onto his french fries. "She was pissed. Even when she tried the old buddy-buddy routine on me I could tell she was mad." He put the empty ketchup container on the lid of the Styrofoam box.

"We're narrowing it down, at least," Jacobs said. He shot Root a look. "If it's not Cassie Ferris."

"I think it's even money between Bankston and McCormick," Socorro said as he licked his fingers and started on the fries.

Jacobs snorted. "And they all know that it was Cassie Ferris who found the briefcase." Another bite, a few more chews and he went on without swallowing. "As long as we keep a tail on her ass, she's safe."

Root didn't agree with Jacobs' tactics or his conclusions, but he felt a little better knowing that both of the Ferris women were being watched. "We're running everyone's name through the computer to see who owns a gun," he said.

"Besides Cassie Ferris you mean," Jacobs said.

Socorro asked, "Martinez find anything new?"

"She's still calling people who were at the party; she says they've called all the numbers, but haven't actually talked to all of the people. She's supposed to report in a little bit," Jacobs said, putting french fries in his mouth. "What time is that Mayhew guy coming in?"

"Any minute," Root said. He put his lunch back in its container. "I'll let you two eat in peace while I handle him."

They'd already gone over everything new from their morning's work. They didn't need him.

"Fine with me," Jacobs said.

"Hey," Socorro said, "If you're not going to eat, how about leaving me your hamburger?"

Root handed it over and left.

JENNY WAS SAFELY OFF with fifteen college students, two professors and a cop, who was hopefully following at a discreet distance. Wild Basin was also a tourist attraction of sorts, so one man wandering in their vicinity wouldn't be conspicuous. It left Cassie with a lot of time and a lot to accomplish. She just hadn't accomplished much so far and she had to hurry before Mandy arrived.

Every door Cassie had tried was locked. Mandy's office, Bill's and the accounting office were sealed tight, and she had no idea where the keys were kept.

She glanced at Irma's desk. Irma sat in on the collection meetings. She had to because Bill's handwriting was atrocious, and someone had to take legible notes.

Cassie moved around Irma's desk and tried the metal filing cabinets. All locked. She pulled at the center drawer and discovered that it was locked, too. So was every other drawer. Cassie had expected as much after her other disappointments.

There was one more office to check and she'd saved it for last, knowing she couldn't miss with this one. She slung her purse over her shoulder and started down the hall.

The sales cubicles were open to the hallway, without any doors at all. Even the walls stopped short of touching the ceiling. Cassie couldn't be locked out of Rachel's office.

She halted just inside it, glanced around the empty hall again, then slid over to the desk and sat down. Where to start? She decided on the filing cabinet and swung around to face it. It was low and sleek and made of wood. It was also locked.

She turned back around and tried the desk. Every drawer was tightly closed and locked against prying eyes and hands. Great. So how the hell had Roger gotten all his information?

Cassie thought about it for a minute. Roger was Walter's little pet, and as such, he probably had a master key to the offices. No doubt Bill and Mandy didn't lock their desks; they had no need to. Under usual circumstances their office doors protected them.

But Roger had gotten things out of Rachel's desk, too. Where else would he have gotten the Happy Twosomes' agreement? Cassie looked around and noticed a letter opener, slim and elegant. She picked it up and wondered if this was the tool Roger had used to break into Rachel's desk. She felt around underneath the desk until she found the lock on a side panel. Then she got off the chair, squatted down to see more clearly, and started to work.

The letter opener slid easily into the lock and with great care, Cassie turned it right, then left. None of the drawers opened. She jiggled the opener, pulled it part way out and wriggled it some more.

The churning sound of the elevator interrupted her. She started, knocking against the chair so hard it fell backward. Who would come here on a Saturday?

Hastily, Cassie crawled out from under the desk, set the chair upright, put the letter opener back where she'd found it, then picked it up again and wiped it with a tissue. The elevator was grinding to a halt, just as she dropped the letter opener on the desk and scooted into the hall.

Cassie was barely out of Rachel's office when the elevator doors opened and Mandy came storming down the hallway.

"Hi. I wasn't expecting you so soon." Cassie asked.

Mandy marched up to her and grabbed both of Cassie's arms. "I could say the same for you, except I can guess what you've been up to! You just don't listen, do you?"

Cassie stumbled backward. "What? What's the matter?"

"I warned you didn't I? Damn it, Cassie, I told you to leave it alone!"

"I don't know what you're so upset about. I didn't do anything."

"Bullshit! I was at the police station less than an hour ago, so don't tell me what you've done and what you haven't done." Mandy practically dragged Cassie down the hall. "We've got to talk. Now."

Mandy's hand was clamped firmly on Cassie's arm as she pulled her toward her office. Cassie shook herself free of Mandy's grip. "Let go, Mandy. You're overdoing this."

"Hardly," Mandy snapped, digging into her huge purse.

"WAIT A MINUTE," Greg Mayhew said. "What happened last night?"

Every one of Root's nerves began to tingle. "No one said anything happened."

"You asked where I was after I dropped Cassie off," Mayhew said. "Obviously something happened last night. Is Cassie all right? Is Jenny?"

So, that's the way things were going, Root thought. For the laid-back type, Mayhew was certainly getting worked up. "We're merely trying to establish where everyone was between ten-thirty and eleven-thirty."

"I dropped Cassie off at her house shortly before eleven." His face looked tight and his shoulders muscles were twitching.

"Did you hear or see anyone near the yard?"

"I heard something in the bushes while we were saying good-night, but I didn't see anyone. If I had, do you think I would have driven off? What happened last night? Is she all right?"

"She's fine, so is Jenny," Root said. "So, you left Cassie Ferris on the porch? You didn't go in the house at all?"

Through clenched teeth Mayhew said, "I don't see how that's any of your business."

Root didn't either really, but he said, "Everything about this case and the people in it are my business."

"I wasn't in the house after we went to dinner."

"Okay." Root glanced up at the viewing window. There wasn't supposed to be anyone watching, but he could never be sure about Jacobs. "Mr. Mayhew, what time did you get home last night?"

"Eleven twenty-two."

"Very precise."

"There's a digital clock in my car. I noticed it when I drove into the garage."

"Anyone see you come in?"

"Not that I know of," Mayhew said.

"Do you own a gun?"

Mayhew turned pale and Root went on, "We're checking the computer, of course. If it's registered we'll find out anyway." He leaned closer. "Now, do you own a gun?"

Mayhew stared at him. Then he said, "Yes. A .22 pistol."

Root wanted to smile. "Thank you."

MANDY UNLOCKED her office and practically ordered Cassie inside. Cassie sat down in one of the side chairs while Mandy took the other, the one between Cassie and the door. Then Mandy flipped the lock barring them both inside.

"Why the hell did you have to go out and find Roger's briefcase?" Mandy demanded.

Cassie had never seen Mandy so angry. "Because the police needed it if they were every going to solve Roger's murder."

"Bullshit! The only thing you did was keep the investigation alive. It was almost dead. Didn't you realize that? It would have been over if you hadn't butted in!"

"That's not true."

"It would have gone down as one of those unsolved crimes, there are hundreds of them, but oh, no, Cassandra Ferris, girl detective had to butt in. I told you to leave it alone!"

"I want it over and done with."

"Oh, really? And do you want cops watching you all the time, too?"

"What?" Cassie said. "No, of course not. How did you know?"

"I went to your house a few minutes ago. I thought I could catch you before you left, but you weren't there. Instead I saw some man watching your house."

Cass tried to shrug it off. "It's not—"

"After I drove off I decided to go back and get his license number, but guess what? By that time he was peeking in your windows! Damn it, Cassie, I'd bet you money that he's a cop."

This is ridiculous, Cassie thought. "He'll go away when they get Roger's killer."

Mandy looked at the ceiling. "Give me patience!"

"I don't get any of this. Why do you want the case closed?"

"You really don't know?"

"Know what?"

Mandy leaned forward. "You really haven't figured it out?"

"Who killed Roger? No, of course not. Have you?"

"Oh, Cassie." Mandy shook her head sadly, her voice soft. "I'm so sorry. I didn't realize…"

"What?"

"We all know who killed Roger."

"So who is it? What do you know that I don't? And who is this 'we'?"

Mandy closed her eyes, as if summoning the courage to talk. Finally she sat up and opened her eyes. "All of us. We figured it out this week. It's so obvious. I can't believe you don't know."

"Then who was it?" Cassie asked.

"Oh, God, Cassie." It came out like a prayer.

"Just tell me who killed Roger."

TWENTY-FIVE

ROOT CHARGED INTO his office, swearing. "Damn it!"

Socorro looked up. "What?"

"Cassie Ferris is gone!

"What!" Socorro blinked. "How? Wilson followed her when she picked up her kid this morning and watched her come back. Balchek was in place before Wilson left. How did it happen?"

"How the hell should I know?" Root asked. "Balchek just called in. It seems Mandy McCormick went over to Cassie Ferris's house after she left here and guess what? No one answered the door."

"Not possible. Cassie Ferris is there; she's got to be. She's just holed up. Maybe taking a nap."

"Balchek decided to find out for himself. He rang the bell; he looked in the windows. She's gone."

Socorro groaned, his heavy body seeming to shrink. "Jacobs is going to have our asses."

"Among other things." Root preferred anger to defeat, since it kept him moving, thinking.

"I guess we'd better do something," Socorro said, but he didn't stir.

"Yeah. Tell Jacobs. We might as well get it over with," Root said. He started down the hall, but Jacobs was already coming toward them. Now the shit was really going to hit the fan.

"I've got some news," Jacobs said.

Root stopped and realized that Socorro was beside him like a huge seal puppy.

"You've heard?" Socorro asked.

"What?" Jacobs said. "You've got something, too?"

"Cassie Ferris is gone," Root said.

"Son of bitch! How the hell did she get away?"

"We don't know, but she's not at home."

"Damn it! Now is not the time to be telling me this."

"We've still got a tail on the daughter," Root said. "We know where she is."

"We'll find Mrs. Ferris, sir," Socorro said.

Root started to move, but Jacobs stopped him. "Wait a minute, maybe it doesn't matter. Not in the long run. Forget it for now—one of you needs to go see this guy." He thrust out a hairy hand and gave Root a slip of paper. "Martinez just got off the phone with him."

"He was at the party? He saw something?"

"Between six-thirty and seven he saw a girl going in that private lounge. She was carrying a plate of food."

"A girl?" Root asked. His heart pounded a little harder. Did that mean someone young? Or was it just the man's way of describing a woman of any age. "Did he describe her?"

"Yeah. Said she was pretty, slender, between five-three and five-seven. Just get the pictures of your suspects and take them over there."

"Right away," Root said, moving off.

MANDY CLEARED HER THROAT and said softly, "Jenny killed Roger."

"Jenny!" Cassie was stunned into speechlessness. Jenny?

Her daughter Jenny? And this was her friend Mandy saying a thing like that? "You think it was Jenny?"

Mandy leaned forward, her face as pale as it had been the morning after Roger's death. "Everyone's figured it out but you, Cassie. That's why you've got to stop this. Let this whole thing just die and fade away."

Cassie's fury rose, lava-like. "Jenny didn't kill anyone!"

"I'm sure she didn't mean to. It was a horrible mistake. She probably just wanted to make Roger sick. To teach him a lesson, but it was too much and…" She stopped.

"I don't believe it!" Is this what her friends thought? Were these the kind of people she called friends? All of them talking about Jenny behind her back … accusing Jenny! "Why would you think a thing like that? Why would anyone think that?"

Mandy sat back; for once she wasn't selling Cassie. "At first no one suspected, but then when the police kept talking about plants—"

"Jenny told half the people on this staff about poisonous plants. She told you!" Cassie's head began to throb. "Jenny stood right outside at Irma's desk and lectured about poisonous plants, for God's sake. She talked about them on the patio that night at Happy Twosomes."

"Yes, but we couldn't identify them. We just knew names."

"She pointed half of them out!"

"And then she went and had a fight with Roger." Mandy's voice softened. "It's just so obvious to everyone but you. I'm so sorry, Cassie."

"No. Wait. You think she killed him because of that stupid fight? Everyone on the staff hated Roger." The pain in her head was getting worse.

"Listen, Cassie, there's more." Mandy let out a sad sigh. "That night at the party, right after Jenny's fight with Roger, Scott went in the staff lounge. Roger was sick and he asked Scott to bring him some more food since the trays were empty, but Scott wouldn't do it."

"So what?"

"Scott went downstairs and saw Jenny getting a drink in the ballroom. He told Jenny that Roger needed something to eat. Then Rachel saw Jenny going into the staff lounge. Jenny was carrying a plate of food—it had to have been for Roger. And that must have been the way Roger got the poisonous plant."

Cassie stood up; she couldn't listen to any more of this. "You're wrong, all of you. Jenny wasn't anywhere near Roger after the fight. And she didn't go in the ballroom, either." She was contradicted by a sudden of vision of Jenny in the flickering light of the Happy Twosomes' pool, lifting a glass and saying, *"I stopped off and got this."* Cassie still didn't believe it.

Mandy stood and touched Cassie's arm. "I tried to make you stop."

With an angry gesture Cassie jerked away from Mandy's hand. "It doesn't matter what I did, because Jenny didn't kill Roger. That briefcase will only lead the police to the real murderer."

Mandy shook her head.

"You're all crazy," Cassie went on. "I don't care what anyone saw or what anyone told you. You're wrong!" She reached for the doorknob and yanked on it, but it didn't budge. "Open this damn thing!"

Mandy reached past Cassie and flicked a button. "It's open."

"Thank you." Cassie flew along the hall and down the stairs.

How could they believe such a thing? How could Mandy, someone she'd known for twenty years, believe such a thing? This was the real definition of insanity!

Cassie whipped past her office, and out the back door. It was sticky hot, but she hardly noticed as she ran over to her car and yanked open the door. *Damn them anyway.*

She jumped inside the Datsun and jammed the keys into the ignition. Maybe she couldn't stop them from talking, but she could, and would, figure out who really murdered Roger. That would shut them up.

She turned the key and heard only a slow clicking sound, then a faint whir as the motor tried to catch. The sound faded. It was the battery, again.

"Damn!" She slammed her hand into the steering wheel. *Why now? Why me?*

Without thinking she turned on the dash lights to confirm her suspicions. There was only the dimmest glow that disappeared as quickly as it had begun.

She turned off the lights and tried the key again. Only clicking this time, then nothing.

"It isn't fair!" she said, her voice rising. Out of the corner of her eye she saw Mandy coming out of the building.

Cassie grabbed her purse and keys and threw herself out of the car.

"Cassie?" Mandy asked, coming toward her, "Can I help?"

"No, thank you." Cassie went straight past her toward the building.

"Please don't be angry, Cassie. We're friends. I didn't want to have to tell you."

Cassie spun around and looked at Mandy. "That's the

worst part, Mandy. We are friends and yet you really believe that crap about Jenny."

Cassie didn't wait to hear more. She let herself into the station and allowed the heavy door to slam shut.

ROOT WAS SITTING on a black leather couch in a living room with futuristic looking sound equipment that covered one wall. He was trying not to think about Cassie Ferris and where she might be. Who might be with her.

At least Jenny Ferris was safe; that was Root's one consolation as he tried to keep himself focused on the man in front of him, a man named Kevin Traeger. A guest at the Happy Twosomes' party.

"So you spent most of the evening upstairs at Happy Twosomes?" Root asked.

Traeger, in a knit shirt and khaki shorts, pulled his modern leather armchair closer and leaned forward. "That's right. I don't dance and you can't make conversation with a band playing anyway, so I stayed in the lounge."

"The big room with the biography books and tapes?"

"Right. Or across the hall in the little taping room." He smiled and expensive white teeth flashed. "Watching people make their tapes was a real kick. I enjoy watching people."

"And between six and seven where were you?"

"Right there. Sometimes I'd be standing in the hall, you know, talking to someone."

"How can you be sure of the time?"

"Oh, I had a date at seven-thirty," he said. "I checked my watch pretty often. I'm a very punctual person."

Root looked at his own watch. *Where was Socorro right now?* Root hoped he had already found Cassie Ferris.

"Do you remember the door next to the taping room?" Root asked.

"Yeah. They were keeping that room private, weren't they? Just for staff or something? They make tapes in there, now."

"That's the room. Tell me about everyone you saw go into, or come out of that room between six and seven o'clock."

Traeger scooted back in the chair and casually pulled one foot up so that his deck shoe rested on the leather. His fingers locked around his knee, and then he closed his eyes. He looked like a stork meditating. Root wanted to hurry him, but he knew better.

Eventually, Traeger opened his eyes. "Okay," he said. "First there was Roger Weber. I saw him at another Y-96 party, so I knew who he was. He left the room a little before six-thirty. Give or take a few."

"He was the first person you noticed going in or out?"

"Right. I don't know what time he went in," Traeger said. Root nodded and Traeger continued, "Then I heard some noise downstairs—"

"What kind of noise?"

"Loud voices. Like an argument."

"Okay. And what did you see?"

"I looked down there, but I only saw Weber. He was coming up the stairs and he bumped right into me. Didn't even stop, just went back in that room. A few minutes later one of the other disk jockeys went in. Scott Delany."

"You recognized him, too?"

"Oh, yeah. I know most of them." He put his leg down. "Scott Delany left around five minutes later."

"Who went in next?"

"Then there was this girl. I don't know who she was, but when I first got to the party she was at the front door. She went in the room about six-forty-five or so."

"Was she the one you told Officer Martinez about? The one who was carrying a plate of food?"

"Yeah, that's the one."

"Did you see the food?"

"Not really. Just hors d'eouvres, I think. I was sitting in the lounge then, so she was about twenty feet away from me."

"But you did see her clearly when you arrived at the party?"

"Oh, yeah. " He grinned. "Pretty girl. And she had her hair pulled up—kind of wild looking."

"How long was she in the room?"

"About three minutes. That's all."

"After that who went into the room?"

"No one, but the Cass Woman opened the door a few minutes later; she didn't go in. She was the last one I saw until I left."

"And what time did you leave?"

"About ten after seven."

Root's innards were tingling. "Mr. Traeger, I'm going to show you some pictures of women who were at the party. They won't be dressed the same as they were then, and their hair may be different, but I want you to look closely and see if you can identify the woman you saw carrying the plate of food."

He reached into his notebook and pulled out pictures taken when the witnesses made their formal statements. Added to them were similar Polaroids of three policewomen in civilian clothing, just to keep Traeger honest.

Root laid all seven pictures on the table in front of Traeger. "Are any of these the woman you saw carrying the plate of food?"

Traeger leaned over the table, studying each one. He took his time, looking at one carefully before moving on to the next. Then he smiled and picked up a picture. "This is her."

He handed the photo to Root.

TWENTY-SIX

CASSIE CALLED GREG FIRST, and as luck would have it, he was out. She left a message at his house as well as at Happy Twosomes, explaining her dilemma and asking him to call. He would give her a jump, or a lift, but for now she had to wait and while she waited she paced her tiny office.

Mandy's words had formed a ball of fury that was scorching Cassie's insides. She wanted to start hitting out to release the pressure. Luckily there was no one at the station except for the part-time jock who was on the air. If there had been anyone else—her dear friends—she might have been a real danger.

Cassie forced her body to stop moving and made herself sit at her desk. She had to think.

She pulled Roger's papers out of her purse. One more time she read through them trying to comprehend their meaning.

In a few minutes she was up and walking again. She kept going back to the Friday Roger had died. She tried to piece together everyone's day. What they'd said, where they'd been. An idea came to her and she hurried into the control room.

"Excuse me," Cassie said, shouting. Frankie Valle's, "Big Girls Don't Cry", was almost deafening.

The jock spun around, his eyes wide. "Oh, hi." He sucked in a breath. "I didn't know anyone was in the station."

"Sorry. I didn't mean to startle you. I have a quick question."

He cranked down the monitor and pulled off his headphones. "Sure. Yeah. What'd you want to know?"

"Didn't you fill in for Scott Delany the night of the Happy Twosomes' party?"

"Yeah. I did the last couple of hours of his air shift."

"When did Scott ask you to do that? When did he work that out with you?"

The jock looked puzzled, but said, "I don't know, the week before, I think."

"So it wasn't a last minute thing?"

"No."

"Thanks." Cassie nodded and left the control room, going back down the hall to her office. Did it matter when Scott had made his plans to attend the party? She wasn't sure. She could still hear the words to the song, "Shame on you, you told a lie—" She closed her mind to them and other words rushed in to take their place.

Greed not need.

They formed a new rhythm, one that she moved to, back and forth across her office. *Greed not need.* She picked up the papers again, staring at them as she walked.

Greed not need.

Her eyes widened. Of course! Those papers that Roger had so carefully gathered were indications of embezzlement all right, but Roger had made a mistake. A tactical error. Instead of going straight to Walter with his suspicions, or getting proof by tracking down the clients, he decided to make the embezzler suffer. At the Driskill.

That mistake had cost Roger Weber his life.

Cassie grabbed her purse and started for the door. She'd only taken three steps when she remembered her battery was dead.

"Shit!"

She tossed her purse on the floor, snatched up the telephone and began punching numbers.

"Austin Police Department, Homicide. Sergeant Pruitt."

"I need to speak with Sergeant Socorro, please," Cassie said, slurring the words in her hurry.

"Socorro? I'm sorry, Ma'am, he's not here."

"What about Root?"

"He's out, too. Could someone else help you?"

"Is there anyone else working on the Weber case?" Cassie asked.

The male voiced paused, then said, "Senior Sergeant Jacobs is in charge of that. Do you want to talk to him?"

"No!" She was positive of that. "I need to leave a message for either Root or Socorro. Tell them that Cassie Ferris called. I'm at the radio station and I know who killed Roger Weber. It's urgent that they call me back."

"Let me have you to talk to Jacobs."

"No! Just have Root or Socorro call me." Cassie gave him the station number and hung up.

She looked at her watch and began to pace again, faster now, charging like an atom around the tiny office.

She went out into the hall, then up the stairs.

Greed not need; it kept coming back to her. Just like Mandy had said, it was so obvious when you thought about it.

She moved by the receptionist's desk, then Irma's, glancing behind it to Bill's locked office. Then she passed Mandy's office. Cassie was still furious with her for thinking Jenny could kill someone, but that could be worked out later.

Damn. She remained on the move, past the sales cubicles, almost to the elevator. Then she turned around and began the march back. She desperately needed to talk to someone!

Moving mindlessly she spun around and started up the hall one more time.

"Cassie." The voice was quiet, yet frightening in its unexpectedness. "Stop walking, please."

Cassie stopped, terrified because now she knew she was right.

"Don't turn around," the voice continued.

Her body tingled. She could hear soft footfalls on the carpet. They came to within a few feet of her back.

"Now, start toward the elevator. Slowly."

How stupid of me. Cassie thought. I called and told Roger's murderer exactly where to find me.

Cassie's voice sounded like rusted metal. "Why should I do what you want?"

"Because I have a gun and I will shoot you."

Cassie seemed to lose contact with her body. "Okay. I'll do what you say."

Slowly Cassie began to walk down the long deserted hallway, her mind a void, her body rigid, her whole awareness focused on the unseen gun behind her.

"I'm sorry about this, Cassie." The tone was almost apologetic. "I didn't want to kill you. I really didn't."

Then Cassie remembered. "You shot at me last night."

"But I didn't hit you." There was an agitated jangle of bracelets. "I could have if I'd wanted to; I'm a very good shot, my brother taught me. It's his gun."

"Does your brother know what you did?"

"He died in Vietnam," Rachel said.

"I'm sorry." The numbness in her arms and legs was replaced with a seeping cold. "You know, killing me won't help. The police already have the briefcase."

"I know, but it doesn't prove anything. Move faster," Rachel said. Something brushed lightly against the back of Cassie's shirt. She shivered and began walking again. Rachel added, "Eventually the police will give up. They would have already if it hadn't been for you."

"Rachel," Cassie said. "The police could make a mistake. They might arrest Jenny. I know you don't want to hurt Jenny."

"I don't want to talk about it." They reached the elevator. "Don't turn around, just move out of the way," Rachel said. "No, not so much. Just a step." Cassie heard the jingle of Rachel's bracelets as she pushed the down button. The elevator began its slow ascent to reach them.

Cassie suddenly understood why Rachel wasn't worried about Jenny. "You framed Jenny. You hoped the police would arrest her!"

"That's not true. I didn't mean to. It was just an accident. She just gave me the idea."

"You heard her talking about poisonous plants at Irma's desk. And then you went out and got one of those plants."

"No, you're wrong. We'd already decided to put Meadow Saffron in the planters at the club. That's why I listened, because I knew the name. When Jenny said they were poisonous, I looked them up."

The elevator was grinding slowly toward them. "And then you decided to kill Roger?"

"No! Of course not. God, Cassie, I'm not really a murderer." Rachel sounded like she believed her own words. "But Roger found out…something. It wasn't so terrible, but he was hateful about it."

Cassie knew what it was. "You embezzled money to buy into Happy Twosomes." The elevator doors opened. Then the office phone rang, a chiming sound that came from a dozen phones at once. It's Greg, Cassie thought. Or maybe the police. Would they come to her rescue if she didn't answer the phone?

"Get inside the elevator," Rachel said. "And get in the corner. Don't look at me, either!"

Cassie wondered if there really was a gun. She might have balked except for the very real bullets that Rachel had fired the night before. She moved into the corner of the airless elevator; Rachel's perfume invaded the enclosed space. Obsession.

The doors closed and the elevator rumbled its way downward.

"You went to the Driskill for ascertainments that Friday afternoon," Cassie said. "That's when Roger told you he knew about the money."

"He wanted me to go with him on Saturday and explain to Walter what I'd done. Can you believe that? Oh, and offer to make restitution. Like Walter was really going to forgive me and let the whole thing go! Roger just wanted me to grovel. And to worry about it all day. To suffer. He was a pig!"

"And you went straight to Happy Twosomes and got some of that plant."

"Yes, I did! I chopped it up in the kitchen at the club and then kept it in my purse. I even mixed it up with some paté so he wouldn't notice the taste."

"And you lied to Mandy. You told her Jenny had taken Roger some food."

"I didn't plan to; really I didn't. Scott said he'd told Jenny that Roger wanted something to eat and it just slipped out. I'm not a bad person. They might not have convicted Jenny."

"Damnit, Rachel—"

"No more talking, Cassie, it's just upsetting me. Go straight into the women's bathroom. And don't look at me! Turn the other way."

Cassie turned away from Rachel's voice and decided that this was her chance. If she moved compliantly, slowly, just until they came to the corner of the hall, she could make a run for it.

With great care she began shuffling her feet. She even lowered her head.

Then she felt something hard against her spine. A hand grabbed the top of her arm.

"If you try to get away from me," Rachel said, "I'll shoot you right here and I'm very good with a gun."

Cassie nodded, but she had no intention of complying. She tensed her body to run and just that tiny movement caused Rachel's nails to dig into her arm.

"I mean it, Cassie; this is aimed right at your heart. You'll die before you even know I pulled the trigger."

There was no reason to doubt it.

Cassie took a breath and walked straight into the bathroom. Rachel turned on the light.

"Can I look at you now?" Cassie asked.

"No. And don't look at the mirror. I don't want to see your face. It would be too hard."

Rachel was trying to keep this so neat, so ladylike. Trying

to keep her distance from Cassie, just like she'd done with Roger. Cassie couldn't stand it. She swung around. And there was Rachel in one of her expensive sweaters. She was all dressed up to kill.

"Damn it, Cassie! Why did you have to do that? This could have been so easy!"

"Who would it have been easy for, Rachel? Not me," Cassie snapped. "And haven't you figured out that if I die the police are going to work that much harder? They'll catch you."

"You may be smart, but you don't know everything." She held her purse out and dropped it on the sink farthest from her. "Open that. There's something in it for you."

Cassie picked up the purse. Inside was a baggie with half a sandwich. Cassie pulled it out and held it up. "This?"

"Your lunch. Now eat it."

"What's in it?"

"A plant. Nothing but a plant. It won't make you sick, you'll just die."

Cassie almost laughed at the absurdity. "A poisonous plant."

"So?" Rachel tossed her head back, her red hair catching the light. "It's yellow jasmine. You'll be dead in less than ten minutes, with no evidence. I'll walk you to your office. You can die there." Her face grew hard. *"Bon apetite."*

It was that remark, said with the same sarcastic twist that Brad had always used, that caused something in Cassie to snap. She dropped the sandwich back in the purse. "Fuck you."

"Damn it, Cassie! Eat it! Eat it or I'll shoot you."

"Then shoot me!" Cassie flung the purse at Rachel. Then she threw herself forward to get the gun. There was a flash of light and an explosion. The bullet hit the ceiling and Rachel screamed. Cassie grabbed one of Rachel's arms. The other was waving wildly, the gun uselessly at the end of it.

Rachel shoved hard and Cassie fell back against the towel rack but she didn't release her hold. Rachel leaned forward, her teeth barred, trying to bite Cassie's hand. Cassie kicked out and caught Rachel in the knee. Rachel shrieked as she fell to the tile floor. Cassie stayed with her, grabbing a fistful of hair.

"I'll shoot you!" Rachel said.

They were both on the floor now. Cassie twisted as she tried to get the gun. Rachel bucked, her whole body convulsing. Cassie's head hit the porcelain sink. For a moment she was stunned and her eyes closed with pain. When she opened them the gun was in her face.

"Get off me," Rachel commanded. "Now!"

"I can't—"

"Get up!"

The gun was inches from Cassie's eyes. It was black and ugly, and it stared at her.

Through clenched teeth Rachel said, "Get off."

It would be easy to obey Rachel, but that would mean death, and Cassie refused to die easily.

In a quick move, she flung herself to the right, grabbing for Rachel's hands at the same time. Another shot and Cassie felt something hit her shoulder.

She turned her head and saw that her shirt was charred from the bullet. Blood oozed from thread to thread across the material.

"Get up!" Rachel was hysterical now. She pounded on Cassie. Cassie started to fall backward, hit the sink instead, and landed full on Rachel.

As Cassie's blood touched her, Rachel twisted, jerking and flailing. "Stop it! Get off me."

Cassie rose halfway, then jammed her knee into Rachel's stomach. She put all her weight behind it. Rachel screamed. Cassie snatched the gun with her right hand. She pointed it in Rachel's face.

"Don't hurt me," Rachel cried. "I didn't want to hurt you. I really didn't."

The door flew open from the outside, grazing Rachel's prone body. Suddenly there was another gun pointed at Cassie, this one in a man's hand.

Cassie's eyes slowly traveled along the gun to an arm, a sleeve, a neck; then she saw Root in the doorway. He said something. She couldn't make out the words. She looked at her shoulder, red with blood. Inside her shirt the blood was rolling down her skin to her stomach. It was warm and sticky. Below her Rachel was sobbing.

Cassie stared at Root, then held Rachel's gun out to him.

"I think you should have this," she said, as her bones melted and she sank to the floor.

TWENTY-SEVEN

A SMALL CANDLE FLICKERED beside the bud vase of pink carnations, casting a soft glow on the lace tablecloth. Cassie looked around at the other diners, then across the table to Greg. She couldn't help but smile. Life seemed to be going her way.

"This was a wonderful idea," Cassie said. It was her first outing since she'd left the hospital four days before.

Greg smiled back at her. "Thank you. I thought you deserved a celebration, but I did promise Jenny that I'd have you home by ten. And that I wouldn't tire you out. How are you feeling?" He glanced at her shoulder.

Her dress covered the bandage that became smaller with every doctor visit. "I'm fine." The bullet had missed everything vital according to her doctor, although Cassie had disagreed with him. The bullet had hit her, and she was vital. Still, there would be no permanent damage except a scar. She was told she could it have removed later with cosmetic surgery. Cassie wasn't going to bother; she just wouldn't be wearing any strapless dresses in the future. Or maybe she would.

Greg lifted his wineglass. "I'd like to propose a toast."

"To?" Cassie asked lifting her glass. Hers was filled with sparkling water.

"To you. And your many successes. Past, present and future."

They touched glasses. "Thank you. I'll try to live up to that." She sipped her drink.

"You already have," Greg said.

"Thanks." Cassie smiled, placing her glass carefully on the table. "I didn't tell you, I called a lawyer today who specializes in family law."

"And?"

"She said she'd take me on as a client, and she said there might be other ways of getting Beth back without the expense of a full hearing."

"Such as?"

"Well first, we're just going to ask Brad. Officially, of course. You see, with Linda pregnant he might be more willing to let Beth go. You know, to have some private time with Linda. They've never had that together," she said. "But if he says no, then we'll go to court."

"What does the lawyer think of your chances of winning?"

"I told her everything," Cassie said. "Everything. And she still thinks we have a ninety percent chance of getting Beth back." She laughed. "Then I called Walter's office in Chicago and asked when I could get the reward money. He wants to do a special presentation at the station; you know, make it very public with speeches and everything. I convinced him that it had to be soon."

"Not to be nosey, but I guess I am," Greg said with a grin. "Are you getting the full reward?"

"Oh, yes, although actually, Walter has decided to give two rewards. I get twenty-five thousand dollars and another ten thousand will go to the police department, or Root and Socorro. Walter doesn't know if that's permissable yet, but he wants them to have something too, since we all came to the right conclusion about the same time. Besides, the police have a witness who will testify in court."

The evidence Cassie had found in the briefcase pointed clearly to embezzlement, a motive for Rachel, and the reason Roger had been so urgently trying to meet with Walter. The picture the police had, and the witness, sewed things up nicely.

Greg shook his head. "It's still hard for me to believe Rachel stole the money to buy into the club."

Cassie believed it, but she wasn't sure she'd ever understand it. "I don't think she stole all of it." Cassie said. "She was very good with money and she already had investments. Walter thinks she'd been taking money for years, long before he bought the station."

"It seems so unnecessary."

"Greed not need," Cassie said. Walter's theory was that Rachel had taken her belief in money too far. She had begun to think it could buy self-esteem and self worth.

To Cassie, Rachel had always seemed to have those things in abundance.

"You look deep in thought," Greg said.

"Mildly deep. Not to be nosey or anything…" Cassie said and Greg smiled. "How did you meet Rachel? How did she get involved in Happy Twosomes in the first place?"

"Ah, that," he said. "It was just one of those chance things. My real estate broker was a client of hers. His office was right next to the building we leased for Twosomes and one day he brought her over to meet me. He said that when I got ready to do some advertising, Rachel was the person to talk to. After that she stopped by almost once a week. She was very good at her job."

Cassie noticed a couple being seated on the other side of the restaurant. The man had his back to her, but for a moment Cassie thought it was Root. Then she glanced at the woman with him. She was just a girl really. Blond hair and a little too much make-up. Somehow she reminded Cassie of Beth. Obviously not someone Root would be out with. She looked back at Greg. "And then Rachel asked to buy into the club?"

"No. It was after that. You see, she was there when I got the phone call about the financing. Sam, my banker, couldn't lend the full amount I needed which left me without enough for remodeling the building and fixtures. That's when she said she had some money. That was the start." Greg picked up a spoon, studied it a moment, then laid it back on the table. "The crazy thing is that she was a good business partner for me. She helped with the decorating of the club and she really worked hard at it." He shook his head. "She's so talented. She would have been a success at almost anything."

Greed, not need, Cassie thought again.

"By the way," Greg said, "the club is sold."

"You're kidding? So fast?"

"My partner in Dallas saw the initial membership figures and agreed to buy me out."

"That's wonderful!"

"I think so," he said. "And Rachel will get her money out of the club, too. She'll need it for a good defense attorney."

Cassie shuddered, causing a twinge of pain under the bandage.

"Your shoulder?" Greg asked.

"I'm fine," Cassie said. "So, what does selling the club mean? Will you be leaving Austin?"

Greg hesitated. "I don't know yet. I think I'm going to set up practice here. At least for a while, and see how it goes." He looked at Cassie. "I'd like to keep seeing you, if that's all right."

"Of course." Cassie smiled and lifted her glass. "I'm officially dating men for the first time since my divorce."

"I hear a plural in there."

"You don't like plurals?"

"No, no." He studied the tablecloth for a moment, then looked back at Cassie. "Actually, I don't know if I like them or not."

Cassie laughed. "I think I need plurals right now."

"Oh, I agree. Professionally. Don't ask me how I feel personally or I'm liable to tell you the truth." Then he smiled. "You look beautiful tonight, in case I haven't mentioned it."

"Thanks. You, too." Cassie smiled, and noticed that his hair needed a trim. There was just the hint of a curl under his left ear. It made him look very boyish and endearing. He was endearing.

The waiter appeared to take their order.

"Cassie?" Greg asked. "What are you having tonight?"

"The beef brochette."

"Excellent choice," the waiter said.

While Greg told the waiter what he wanted, Cassie glanced across the room again. The man she'd noticed before was looking at the board listing the evening's entrees. It was Root.

"Isn't that Sergeant Root?" she asked Greg.

He followed her gesture, then nodded. "That's him."

"That can't be his wife," Cassie said.

"He's divorced."

"How do you know?"

"We talked while you were in surgery."

"Ah. Sounds like I missed all the good stuff."

Root had visited her twice in the hospital. The first had been an official visit and Socorro had been with him. They'd asked a million questions and finally, Cassie had fallen asleep in the middle of one of her answers. The second time Root had stopped by, he'd been alone and he'd brought her flowers. He'd only stayed a few minutes and then his beeper had gone off. He'd apologized as he'd flown out the door.

"Would you excuse me for a moment?" Cassie said. "I never got a chance to thank him for showing up at the station when he did. It was a timely appearance."

"Is that my competition?" Greg asked.

Cassie smiled. "I don't think so. Does it matter?"

"We'll talk about that later."

Cassie got up and moved carefully among the tables. Root must have sensed the movement, because he turned and saw her.

"Hello," he said, sounding surprised, as she reached his table. "Here, sit down." He stood up, and held out an empty chair for her. He was in a dark suit that looked new, and he seemed charged with energy. "Should you be out?" he asked.

"Of course," Cassie said as she sat down. "I'm fine."

"That's good to hear." He sat beside her and gestured to the young woman across the table. "I'd like you to meet Angela Root, my daughter. Angela, this is, Mrs. Ferris. Also known as the Cass Woman."

"Really?" Angela said. The pose of teenage sophisticate disappeared as her eyes flew open and she smiled. "Dad said he knew you, but I didn't believe him!"

The innocence in the smile made Cassie want to hug her.

"It's nice to meet you, Angela. I hope I'm not interrupting?"

"It's my birthday." Angela looked at her dad, then back at Cassie. "Could I have your autograph?"

"Of course."

"Here," Root pulled a business card from the pocket of his suit, then a pen. "This will have to do."

Cassie took the card and wrote on the back, "To Angela. Here's hoping that this birthday is the start of a wonderful year. Best Wishes, Cassie Ferris." She slid the card across the table. "There you go."

"Thanks." Angela said. "I listen to you sometimes. Is Tracker Forman as awful as he sounds?"

"Yes," Cassie said. "But he promises that he'll reform and stop the sexist comments."

"That's good. He can be kind of funny. I mean, maybe he's more for older people. Well, that's not the station I listen to all the time—just when Mom has it on. I'm sorry—"

"I have a daughter about your age and it's not her station, either." Cassie smiled, then glanced at Root, intending to draw him into the lightness of the conversation. The look on his face made her suddenly serious. It brought up the reason she knew him and how he'd probably saved her life. "I really didn't mean to interrupt your dinner," she said, "but I wanted to thank you. For showing up at the station when you did."

"Just doing my job." But his mustache twitched and then he smiled. It was like lightning on a hot summer night. Cassie felt the charge from it all through her body.

"Excuse me," Angela said, jumping to her feet. "I think I'll go to the restroom."

"Of course," Root said, and Angela winked at Cassie before she scooted off on her high heels.

Cassie smiled. "She's beautiful."

"And she's very intuitive," Root said. He watched Cassie. "I've been wanting to call you, but I didn't know how you'd feel about that."

She paused. "I'm not sure I know, either."

"My divorce isn't quite final yet. In a few months, it will be."

Cassie tipped her head up at him. "Sometimes people go a little crazy right after a divorce…"

"I've heard that."

"But maybe, Root, you could call in a few months."

"Wayne," he said. "You could call me Wayne."

"All right. And you can call me Cassie."

His eyes, that funny hazel color, were dancing in the candlelight. "I will. In a few months."

"Okay." She felt as if she'd been drinking champagne. "I'd better get back to my table."

He stood up as she rose to leave and briefly touched her hand. "It was nice seeing you," he said. He was smiling again.

"Thank you. You, too." She turned away and started back across the restaurant, listening to the sounds of people talking and the soft laughter.

The highlights of life.

It seemed to her that she had been missing out on them in the past several years, but it wouldn't be happening again.

Never again, Cassie thought. *Never again.*

HARLEQUIN®
INTRIGUE®

WE'LL LEAVE YOU BREATHLESS!

If you've been looking for thrilling tales of
contemporary passion and sensuous love stories
with taut, edge-of-the-seat suspense—then
you'll love Harlequin Intrigue!

Every month, you'll meet six new heroes
who are guaranteed to make your spine tingle
and your pulse pound. With them you'll enter
into the exciting world of Harlequin Intrigue—
where your life is on the line
and so is your heart!

THAT'S INTRIGUE—
ROMANTIC SUSPENSE
AT ITS BEST!

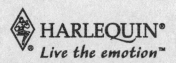

HARLEQUIN®
Live the emotion™